I0653815

OTHER BOOKS by KASSANDRA LAMB

The Kate Huntington Mysteries
Psychotherapist Kate Huntington helps others cope with trauma, but she has led a charmed life...until a killer rips it apart. (10 novels)

~

The Kate on Vacation Mysteries
Even on vacation, Kate Huntington can't stay out of trouble. (4 novellas)

~

The Marcia Banks and Buddy Cozy Mysteries
Marcia Banks trains service dogs for veterans, and solves crimes on the side, with the help of her Black Lab, Buddy. (13 novels/novellas)

~

The C.o.P. on the Scene Mysteries
Eight days into her new job as Chief of Police in a small Florida city, Judith Anderson finds herself one step behind a serial killer. (spinoff from the Kate Huntington series; 4 stories–more to come)

~

Romantic Suspense
written under the pen name of Jessica Dale

FELONY MURDER

a C.o.P. on the Scene Mystery
Kassandra Lamb

a misterio press publication

Published by **misterio press LLC**

Cover design by Melinda VanLone, Book Cover Corner; Photo credit: © Charles Morra | purchased right to use from Dreamstime.com

Copyright © 2024 by Kassandra Lamb

All Rights Reserved. No part of this book may be used, transmitted, stored, distributed or reproduced in any manner whatsoever without the writer's written permission, except very short excerpts for reviews. The scanning, uploading, and distribution of this book via the Internet or by any other means without the publisher's/author's express permission is illegal and punishable by law.

Felony Murder is a work of fiction. All names, characters, events and most places are products of the author's imagination. Any resemblance to actual events or people, living or dead, is entirely coincidental. Some real places may be used fictitiously. The City of Starling, Florida, and Clover County, Florida, are fictitious.

NO AI TRAINING: Without in any way limiting the author's and [publisher's] exclusive rights under copyright, any use of this publication to "train" generative artificial intelligence (AI) technologies to generate text is expressly prohibited. The author reserves all rights to license uses of this work for generative AI training and development of machine learning language models.

The publisher does not have control over and does not assume any responsibility for author or third-party websites and their content.

CHAPTER ONE

My private line rang, interrupting my train of thought. I grabbed the receiver and barked out a hello.

And realized too late that I should've restrained my annoyance. Only a few key people had my private number—like the mayor and the chair of the city council.

Silence on the line.

Yup, I'd pissed somebody off. Not the first time, probably wouldn't be the last.

"Chief Anderson?" A tentative voice, male...and young.

"Yes." I tried for neutral but my voice was still a bit brusque.

"I'm sorry to bother you, ma'am, but I've run out of options. My trial is coming up in three weeks and I'm innocent. But I could end up in the electric ch–"

"Who the hell is this?" I yelled into the phone. "And how did you get this number?"

My assistant, Officer Gloria Barnes, appeared in my doorway. As usual, her uniform was impeccable, her dark hair tucked into a neat bun. But her forehead was creased, her lips a thin line.

"If I answer the second question," the young man said, "will you hear me out?"

I ground my teeth but forced myself to stop and think. Yes, finding out how he'd gotten my private line number merited a little of my time.

"You've got two minutes."

"My name is Juan Alvarez."

He had no accent, so not a first-generation immigrant. In Florida, odds were high that he was Cuban-American.

"I'm going to trial soon on a felony murder charge." His voice was now moving toward frantic. "A supposed drug deal that ended badly. But I wasn't there. I had nothing to do with it."

"What's the case number?"

I was surprised when he rattled it off.

Most accused who were awaiting trial had no idea what their case number was. They didn't realize it was a useful piece of information when dealing with law enforcement and/or the legal system.

I no longer thought of it as the justice system, because justice did not always prevail. Instead, it enforced the law—most of the time—for better or worse.

"Will you look into my case? I tell you, I'm being set up."

"I'll take a look at the file." I paused. "Beyond that, no promises. But only if you tell me how you got my private number."

"It's on the bathroom wall on the men's side of the county jail."

A voice yelling in the background.

"Gotta go." Juan disconnected.

I cussed a blue streak.

Barnes took a step into my office, her dark eyes wide. "Chief?"

"Get me the jail superintendent, asap! Then get the number changed for my private line."

After chewing out the jail super, I brought up Alvarez's case file on my computer.

Juan Alvarez was indeed about to go to trial for felony murder, in a drug deal that had apparently gone sideways. According to the file, he was a member of a gang who'd met up with one Miguel Navarro to sell the latter cocaine.

But somehow Navarro had ended up dead, and Alvarez's compadres had both cut deals to lower their sentences, fingering Alvarez.

No one, however, had admitted to actually wielding the knife that killed Navarro—a knife that was still missing. And there were no weapons in Alvarez's home when he was picked up.

I sat back in my chair and sighed.

My private line rang. My heart rate jacked up a notch. I glanced at the caller ID and breathed out another sigh, this one relieved. I knew this caller. "Hello."

"Hey there." Sheriff Sam's lovely baritone. "How's your day going?"

Should I pretend everything's hunky-dory or 'fess up that I'm having a lousy morning?

"That bad, huh?" There was no fooling Sam. He knew me too well.

"Some guy with a felony murder charge hanging over his head got ahold of my private line number."

A beat of silence. "Not good." His voice was grim.

"It gets worse. He got it off the men's room wall in the jail."

Sam's turn to cuss a blue streak.

"I took the liberty," I said, "of chewing the jail super's ass personally. Hope you don't mind." The jail was under Sam's purview as Clover County's sheriff, but the City of Starling shared in its expenses, since it often temporarily housed many of our less-desirable residents.

"No problem," Sam said. "The question is how did someone *in jail* get that number in the first place?"

"I can make an educated guess or two." Unfortunately, a couple members of my police department had passed through the jail recently, facing charges for corruption, or worse.

"Who's the prisoner?" Sam asked. "I'll yank his phone privileges."

"No, don't do that. I'm going to look into the case."

"Why?"

"Because the guy was arrested in early July."

The sound of air being blown out. "Two months before you took over," he said.

"Yeah. While Chief Black was still here, and guess who the lead detective was?"

"Patterson."

"Yup. Patterson." One of those corrupt cops now in jail.

Another sigh on his end. "I'll get that wall scrubbed down right away."

"No need, I'm sure someone is already working on it. I hope you don't mind, but I really needed to chew *someone's* ass."

Sam chuckled. "See you tonight?"

"Hope so."

Another soft chuckle. "God willing and the bad guys behave."

I disconnected, grabbed my Glock from my desk drawer and my black wool jacket from the back of my chair, and headed out.

Barnes started to rise from the chair behind her desk, just outside my office.

I held up a hand. "I have an errand to run. Shouldn't take more than an hour or two."

I usually took Barnes with me when I went out into the field. It was part of our deal. She handled a lot of tedious details for me, while learning to be a detective at my elbow.

It was an unorthodox arrangement, but one I'd made out of necessity, after Chief Black had cut the department's budget to the bone, right before he'd retired. A not very discreet attempt to sabotage me as the new chief.

I'd pulled Barnes out of the rookie pool. And now I was damned glad the circumstances had made that happen. The young woman had quickly made herself indispensable.

I would fill her in later, if Alvarez's story seemed to have merit.

———◆———

Twenty minutes later, I arrived at the Clover County jail, a short distance past the city/county line. When Starling had incorporated back in the 1960s, the deal had been struck with the county regarding the shared expenses and use of the facilities.

Within a few minutes, I was sitting at a large metal table in a stark interview room, waiting for the prisoner to be brought to me. The walls were the color that my college roommate used to call baby-shit green. And their dinginess said the paint—most likely purchased at an Army surplus store—had been applied many years ago.

Maybe I'd have a chat with Mark Hayes, the chair of the city council, about forking over some funds to give the jail a facelift. Not for the prisoners, but for the members of the public and law enforcement who had to come here. The place was depressing enough.

Councilman Hayes had been generous with me so far—pushing through a supplemental budget—and even more so since he'd declared he was running for mayor against the incumbent.

I had to walk a fine line, though. I couldn't be seen as taking sides with either candidate, or I might be out of a job after the election.

Holy hell, how I hated politics.

The door opened, saving me from further thoughts along those lines.

The bright orange in Juan Alvarez's striped jumpsuit did nothing good for his complexion. His skin was an ashen beige color, his brown eyes big in his face. Tall and slender, he was probably a handsome kid, when he didn't look like a deer in headlights.

He shuffled over to the other chair, where the guard attached his handcuffs to a large metal ring welded to the table's surface. Both the table and the chairs were bolted down. I'd double checked when I'd entered the room.

As the door swung shut, Alvarez said, "Thank you for coming, Chief Anderson."

I frowned. "I read the case file, now tell me your story."

And make it good, I thought. If this was a waste of time, I would not be a happy camper.

"Last year, when I was sixteen, I was approached by a gang and invited to join them. I declined. They didn't take it well, but at that point I was more afraid of my *abuela* than of them. She would've killed me if I'd joined a gang."

He paused for breath. His diction was good, and he had no accent. Definitely not a first-generation immigrant.

"Besides, I had no interest in that life. I'd planned to go to college...." He trailed off, dropped his gaze.

Then he cleared his throat. "They harassed me for a while, but eventually left me alone. I was surprised. Most gangs don't ever take no for an answer. Well, apparently these guys had other plans."

He paused again, sucked in a big breath. "Seven months ago, out of the blue, I was arrested for selling drugs and for felony murder."

He leaned forward. "I had no idea what the police were talking about. But I had no alibi for the Friday night in question, which was back in May. My family had gone to my cousin's birthday party, but I'd stayed home to study for the SATs. The test was the next morning." He swallowed hard. "I was alone all evening."

The kid was well-spoken, maybe a little too much so. His story sounded a bit rehearsed. Was he coached, maybe by his lawyer?

"I was told that my, quote, *cohorts* had turned me in, to get lighter sentences for themselves." He grimaced. "The cops named two guys I'd never heard of before."

He scrubbed a long thin hand over his face. "The state attorney's office offered a deal, but I don't want to go to prison for something I didn't do. That's not how I'd planned..." he choked up some, "...for my life to go."

Stalling while I processed what he'd said, I asked, "How come you're here in the county jail, and not at Raiford state prison?" That's where prisoners usually awaited trial.

"My lawyer arranged that. My *abuela* was sick, couldn't drive all that way to visit me." He looked away, blinked twice. "She's the only one who visits. My parents have disowned me."

He stopped again to suck in air. "Or she *was* the only one. She died last month. I'm praying they don't move me now. Those two guys who said I was their accomplice..."

He turned his head back toward me. His eyes locked on mine. "They're in Raiford, and I'm scared they'll kill me if I go there."

I nodded. They just might. A prison shanking, if they got away with it, would close the case. And they wouldn't have to testify, and perhaps get caught in a lie. But that wouldn't mean this kid was innocent, although it would be a moot issue then.

"So, why should I believe you?" I asked.

He shrugged. "I have no record, never been in any trouble. And I get all As... I mean, I *got* all As and Bs in school." He stopped, swallowed hard again. "But I don't know how you prove you weren't somewhere, when you have no witnesses to where you really were."

He had a good point. It was hard to prove a negative.

"Your trial begins next month?"

"Three weeks and two days."

"Okay." I started to push myself to a stand. "I'll talk to these two guys, see–"

No," he interrupted. "Please don't let them know I'm saying they're lying. Then they'll come after me for sure."

I pursed my lips. "Okay. I have another angle I can use as my excuse for talking to them. I'll keep you out of it."

I headed for the door, but once there, I turned. "What was the deal the ASA offered?"

"Life without parole."

My jaw dropped before I could catch it. "For felony murder?"

He shrugged. "She said that or the death penalty were the only options under Florida law for felony murder." His eyes grew shiny. "But honestly, I'd rather be dead than be in prison all my life...and have my family believing I'm a killer and a gang member."

I tried to ignore the ache in my chest as I reclaimed my gun and phone from the guard. I'd always had mixed emotions about felony murder statutes, which allowed anyone who participated in a felony to be charged with first degree murder if someone died during the commission of that felony. Even if the person being charged wasn't the one who killed the victim.

It was meant to be a deterrent—you commit a felony, someone dies, you pay for that death. But that's assuming criminals were smart enough to think such things through ahead of time.

Ha!

And I'd seen the law applied rather harshly, as may well be the case this time, if Alvarez was telling the truth.

I exited the jail, then took a deep breath. Mid-February and already northern Florida was showing signs of spring. Azaleas bloomed along one side of the parking lot. And despite the cold front that had blown through last night, dropping us from yesterday's high of seventy-three to the low sixties today, a whiff of a warm breeze stirred my short hair.

I shoved a stray dark strand out of my eyes as I stood by my car, thinking. My phone rang, pulling me out of my reverie.

I climbed into my car and started the engine. *Bradley* flashed up on my Bluetooth screen.

Smiling, I accepted the call from my second in command. "Hey, *Lieutenant*," I said in a cheerful voice, acknowledging his recent promotion.

"Chief, where are you?" His tone was frantic.

My heart rate kicked up. Bradley was rarely anything but laid back. "Near the county line. Why?"

"Someone just shot at the mayor. His driver's down."

CHAPTER TWO

I popped the portable light bubble onto the roof of my compact and hit the button for the jury-rigged siren. Since my predecessor had preferred having detectives submit mileage for the use of their personal vehicles, I had only two unmarked sedans in my motor pool at this point. One was driven by Bradley and the other was shared among the other detectives.

I hoped to add two more unmarked vehicles with my next budget. Although personally I didn't require anything fancy, it was undignified for the Starling CoP to be driving an eight-year-old beige compact while on duty.

But one thing I had to give my little car, it had great acceleration. I floored it and made it to the municipal building—home of the police department as well as the city government—in thirteen minutes flat.

Only to be stymied several blocks out by a cordoned-off road and a significant crowd of bystanders, gawking at the front of the building. I jumped out of my car and hoofed it the rest of the way.

Paramedics were loading a man into an ambulance. He had blond hair.

Thank God it's not the mayor.

Then a small spurt of guilt. This man, no doubt the mayor's driver, was somebody's son, husband, father.

I stifled the feeling—no time for that now—and shoved through the crowd. "Make way. Chief of Police." Most quickly stepped aside, opening a path. A few were a tad slower.

I thought I saw Sam's khaki-clad shoulders. I did a double-take. He was talking to a woman beside him, head bent down.

What the hell...why's he here? And why was he standing passively in the crowd of looky-loos?

I shook my head. No time for that now, either. I broke through the crowd, only to realize that the official scene entrance was thirty feet to my left.

Damn! I didn't want to take the time to wade through more onlookers, some now pushing the limits by leaning forward over the crime scene tape that established the scene's perimeter.

And I was definitely in no mood to do so with any degree of politeness. Better to break protocol.

After all, I am the chief.

I ducked under the tape and turned back toward the crowd, holding up my badge. "Stay back, folks."

"Hey," the uniform with the scene log yelled from the official entrance.

I swiveled, pointing my badge in his direction, then jogged over.

Recognition bloomed on his face as I got closer. "Sorry, didn't recognize you at first, Chief." He scribbled in the log.

"Where's the mayor?" I asked.

"Inside the building."

I nodded and took off for the front door, noting that my CSI team was already examining the sidewalk and front wall of the building.

I'd expected more chaos inside. But the lobby was eerily quiet, except for the tap of my low-heeled pumps on the white marble floor as I moved toward the elevator.

Wait. Soft echoes off to the right—voices. I headed that way.

Lieutenant Bradley, Mayor Daniels, and three others in business attire, one woman and two men, were crammed into a small room off the lobby. They were all talking at once.

"What happened?" I called out.

Nobody paid me any attention.

The mayor, a wiry man only slightly taller than my five-seven, was talking the loudest, and gesturing wildly.

I cleared my throat, twice.

No response.

I put my fingers in the corners of my mouth and whistled. Everyone froze.

"What the hell happened?" I demanded.

The cacophony of voices erupted again.

Bradley held up a hand and stepped forward. The others fell silent, finally.

"I was in an interview room upstairs, with a burglary suspect," Bradley said, "when I heard two shots. I ran down the fire stairs and found Mayor Daniels in the lobby, calling 911, and his driver was out on the sidewalk. Shoulder wound. The other bullet must have gone astray."

"Canvassing?" I said.

"Sarge and the uniforms are on it, and they're looking for the stray bullet."

"Hopefully, it didn't go through somebody's window," I muttered for only Bradley's ears.

He nodded grimly. Stray bullets in a city were not a good thing.

"Any info on the shooter?"

"Not yet. Collins and Cruthers are wading through the bystanders, trying to find anyone who saw anything."

Wading *is the word for it.*

"The mayor see anything?" I said in a low voice.

Bradley made a face and shook his head. "He'd dropped his phone and leaned down to get it, then heard the shots and old instincts kicked in. He hit the ground."

"'Old instincts?'"

"Yeah." He lowered his own voice. "Believe it or not, he was in the Army. Desert Storm."

"Okay, thanks." I stepped around Bradley and scanned the others, huddled together a few feet away. "Mr. Mayor, I'm assigning a uniformed officer as your driver, *for the time being.*" I emphasized the last part, so he wouldn't get any ideas about keeping his police detail indefinitely. I was already short-staffed. "And a detective will also go with you wherever you go. You'll introduce her as an intern who's shadowing you."

"Wellbourne?" Bradley asked in a low voice.

I nodded, without breaking eye contact with the mayor. "And you are to wear a Kelvar vest whenever you leave your office, sir, even inside the building."

The mayor opened his mouth, and I held up a hand. "No arguments, please. It's for your own protection."

He blinked and closed his mouth again.

"I'm also looking into the driver's background," Bradley whispered in my ear, "to see if he might be the actual target."

I nodded again, a little absentmindedly. I was trying to figure out who the third man was. The tall, husky guy was the city manager, and the woman was the mayor's admin assistant.

I closed the gap between me and the third guy in two strides. He was medium build, medium height and nattily dressed, his brown hair cut short in a buzz cut. A bit older than me—late forties to early fifties.

I extended my hand. "I don't think we've met. I'm Judith Anderson, Chief of Police."

A smile lit up his tanned face. Blue eyes sparkled with amusement, which seemed rather inappropriate under the circumstances. "I figured that's who you were."

He took my hand and gave it a firm shake. "I'm Peter McAllister, the new special assistant to the mayor."

His hand was warm and a slight frisson of energy passed between us.

My eyebrows went up as I pulled my hand loose. I didn't query further why the mayor needed another assistant, nor did I ask what made him so special.

Instead, I turned slightly to include everyone in the room. "We're going to need to know where all of you were during the last hour."

"I was at the doctor's," Mr. Special Assistant immediately piped up. "Dermatologist. Annual checkup."

Barnes had pointed out that skin cancer was all too prevalent in Florida and one should get an annual going-over by a dermatologist. Looking out for my health wasn't in her job description, but she seemed to think it was part of her role.

McAllister raised a hand halfway to his face, then glanced at it and let it drop back to his side. Was he about to touch some spot the dermatologist had worked on? Or was it only a nervous gesture?

"When I got back," he said, "the roads were already closed around the building. Had to park a few blocks away."

"Thank you." I turned to the others.

All of them looked a little nervous. Understandable, since their boss had just been shot at.

Indeed, Mr. Mayor was the only one who didn't seem anxious. He wore his usual red-faced expression of anger, his response to anything he didn't like.

"Lieutenant Bradley will take your statements," I said and quickly left the room before Mr. Mayor could explode in my direction.

On the elevator to the third floor, home of the Starling PD, I texted Sam.

Where are you?

A pause before he responded. *At my desk.*

Oh, I thought I saw you in the crowd.

What crowd?

The elevator door opened and I stepped off. I called Sam instead of texting.

"What crowd?" he asked again when he answered.

"In front of my building." I filled him in on the attempt on the mayor as I walked to my office.

He whistled softly. "That was pretty brazen."

"Yup, and we've got nada so far on the vehicle or the shooter."

"Anything I can do to help?"

"Not yet. Maybe later, when we know more."

"Why'd you think I was in the crowd?" he asked.

"I saw a guy with your build, sandy hair, khaki shirt, and thought it was you. He even moved like you. But he was turned to the side, so I didn't see the face."

Sam chuckled. "Well, they say everyone has a doppelganger."

I snorted. "I'm not sure I can handle two Sam Piersons."

"Well, then just stick with this one."

I smiled. "That's the plan."

We signed off, and I sighed. Chatting with Sam had been a short reprieve.

Now I had to buckle down and find a would-be assassin, before he struck again.

Barnes was at her desk. She had caught most of what I'd told Sam. Her eyes were round in her face. "Sheriff Pierson has a double?"

"Apparently." I gestured for her to come into my office. She did so, closed the door and sank into the one comfortable visitor's chair.

I went behind my desk. "You know this town better than I do." I'd been the chief of police for not quite six months. "Any thoughts on motive regarding the mayor?"

She stared at the ceiling for a beat. "The mayor's made some enemies, that's for sure. But I can't imagine anyone hates him enough to kill him." She stopped, her gaze now on me. "But the mayoral race *is* starting to heat up."

"Already? The election isn't until November."

Barnes shook her head. "Nope, the city has its own local elections, in August, every two years."

"That doesn't sound very efficient." Elections couldn't be cheap, and the mayor was a bit of a miser.

"Which is the excuse," Barnes continued, "that Mayor Daniels used when he tried to get it changed to the same day as the federal elections. But the city council wouldn't do it. The mayor and the council have been mostly at odds ever since Mark Hayes took over as council chair, right after the last election."

I tilted my head to one side. "Why would the mayor work that hard to change the election date? It would only gain him a few extra months in office."

"Turnout would be better. Not many people bother to vote when it's only the local positions on the ballot. Only those who are disgruntled with the city government tend to come out."

"Ah, and that's hard on incumbents."

"Exactly," Barnes said, with a slight smirk.

Something told me she would be in line on election day to vote against Mr. Mayor.

"Anyone else running for mayor this time around besides him and Hayes?"

Barnes shook her head.

Dang, I'd been hoping for another candidate/suspect. I couldn't imagine Hayes—who was a gentle, soft-spoken man—literally gunning for his opposition. Now, if his wife were still alive, that would be another matter. She had been highly ambitious, far more invested in his political career than he was.

Which, in a roundabout way, is what got her killed last fall. My chest ached a little at the memory. Not so much for her—she wasn't a particularly pleasant woman, although she didn't deserve to die—but for Hayes and his kids. They all still looked kind of shell-shocked.

"Okay," I said, "do a background check on Mr. Mayor. Let's make sure we're not overlooking any old enemies."

My detectives gathered in my office at the end of the day—all except the newest one, Wellbourne, who was guarding the mayor.

She was actually on loan from the Florida Department of Law Enforcement. And even with her aboard, we were still short a detective.

Collins gestured to his partner Cruthers, the oldest of the detectives, and the latter took the one comfy chair. The fifty-plus Cruthers always reminded me of a bear, big and shaggy.

While the recently promoted Sergeant Collins, thirty-something and boyish-faced, made me think of an eager twelve-year-old, trying to please his elders. I hoped the job wouldn't wipe away his eagerness too soon.

He and Bradley perched on the front edges of the other two chairs. And Barnes took up her usual position, her butt leaning against the doorjamb of my closed door, her pad in hand to take notes.

Cruthers led off. "We've got conflicting reports on the vehicle, but the most consistent description is a white van or SUV with heavily tinted windows. It was driving south, in the lane closest to the building, so unlikely that the driver was also the shooter."

I nodded. He would've had to lean over the passenger's seat, while keeping the vehicle in its lane. Not conducive to careful aiming.

"A uniform found the other bullet," Bradley said, "embedded in the building's wall, behind where the mayor had leaned down to grab his phone."

"Phew," Collins said, "today was definitely his lucky day."

I gave him a feeble smile. Being shot at wasn't exactly lucky, but yes, dropping his phone right at that moment had been.

Something niggled at the back of my brain.

Barnes was talking now. "Based on an initial background check, the mayor doesn't have any significant enemies from his past. Before he was elected, he was a junior partner in a local law firm." She named the company. It meant nothing to me.

"Junior partner?" I said. "At his age?" He was at least mid-fifties. Most good lawyers would have made full partner by that age.

"He was late becoming a lawyer," Barnes said. "After his stint in the Army, he went to college, then taught high school chemistry for almost a decade. Went to law school at night."

"So," I said, "we should talk to the folks at that law firm."

Bradley glanced sideways at Cruthers.

The latter said, "I'll see if I can get an appointment for first thing in the morning."

I was tempted to remind him to push hard if they resisted—this was an important case. But Cruthers was experienced. He knew what he was doing.

I asked, "Anything from Bert and Ernie yet on the bullet?"

Collins snickered.

Yes, our two crime scene investigators are named Bert and Ernie, and they even look the part. Bert is tall, lean, and serious, except when he's razzing his subordinate, the rather flaky, shorter and plumper Ernie.

"Nada," Bradley was saying. "It was a 'mooshed-up mess,'" he made air quotes, "as Ernie put it."

"What about the bullet that hit the driver?" I asked. "And is he okay?"

"Yes," Bradley said. "His shoulder was pretty torn up, but they were able to repair it. The hospital's sending the bullet to us."

"And nobody actually witnessed the gun going off?" I asked the group.

"Nope," Collins said, "everyone was going about their business until they heard the shots. Then they looked around and saw the SUV, or van depending on who you talk to, speeding away."

"No plate number?"

"Yes and no. The plate was stolen," Bradley said. "On my way home, I'm going to follow up with the owner of the red Fiat that plate is supposed to be adorning."

"So, a semi-solid ID of the vehicle is all we've got," I said, blowing out a frustrated sigh. "And maybe something from the bullet that hit the driver."

Bradley nodded. "That pretty much sums it up."

"Okay everybody, go home and get a good night's sleep. We hit the ground running tomorrow."

As they all trooped out of my office, I sat at my desk trying to snag the niggling thought flitting at the edge of my brain.

But I couldn't seem to get it to come out into the light.

CHAPTER THREE

The next morning offered no new leads.

The Fiat owner hadn't even noticed that his license plate had been switched out with another one, which was expired. Collins tracked the expired plate back to a car sitting on cement blocks in someone's backyard. Its owner swore he hadn't noticed anyone hanging around his old junker.

A dead end, for now at least.

As was the mayor's former life as a lawyer. The senior partner Cruthers had spoken to at his law firm swore he was well liked, had no enemies among the staff or the clients. He handled corporate and tax law cases, never the more adversarial civil or criminal litigation.

Since we weren't making any progress on the mayor's case, I decided to drive out to the state prison in Raiford and check out Juan Alvarez's accusers. Barnes was away from her desk, so I was able to sneak out without giving any explanations.

By mid-morning, I was sitting on one side of a glass panel. On the other side sat a man covered in tattoos, even on his shaved head. His skin was a pale white, underneath the mostly blue and black markings.

My stomach felt a little queasy at the sight.

Alfred Taft was thirty-six, a big guy. His orange jumpsuit stretched taut across broad shoulders and a sizable belly. He laid one hand on the counter in front of him. Its back was decorated with a swastika, and H-A-T-E was spelled out across the knuckles, a not uncommon prison tattoo. He used the other meaty paw, knuckles adorned with L-O-V-E, to pick up the phone receiver.

I picked up the one on my side and introduced myself. "Mr. Taft, I'm looking into the murder of Miguel Navarro."

"Call me Alfie." He gave me a big grin, which I suspected was meant to be friendly. But combined with the abundance of tats, it came across as menacing.

I noted that his teeth were straight and pearly white. What lifelong gang member went to the dentist regularly?

"I already copped to that," he added.

"Yes, I know. This is a routine audit of the case, before it goes to trial. Making sure we've got all the *t*'s crossed and *i*'s dotted." I wasn't about to tell him that the detective on the case was now in jail himself, for taking bribes.

Taft nodded, still trying to maintain the friendly smile, but it was sagging some.

"You and your partner never did reveal who wielded the knife," I said.

"Weren't me." He shook his big head, letting go of the smile completely.

"So which of the other two was it?"

"Don't know. It was dark. I saw a flash of light...musta been from the streetlight hittin' the knife. And the guy was on the ground, blood poolin' next to him."

He gave a fake shudder, and I almost laughed out loud. He was a lousy actor.

"And where was Alvarez?"

"Standin' right there next to me."

"Tell me more about him," I said conversationally. "Why was he there?"

"He was new to the..." he trailed off.

"To the gang?"

He shook his head again.

I scoffed internally, but kept my expression neutral. This guy's tats strongly suggested he was a member of a gang. But which one?

I deferred that question for now. "This was some kind of initiation then?"

"No. He, uh, had just started hangin' out with us. We didn't know him too good yet."

"Okay, so you have no idea if it was him or your other compadre who actually used the knife?"

Taft stiffened in his chair. His upper lip curled slightly. Then he seemed to catch himself, and he fake smiled again. "We weren't quite *compadres* yet." He seemed to spit out the Spanish word.

I asked a few more questions but got no new information. Finally, I sent him on his way, and a guard went to find his non-compadre.

Michael Thompson—lots of nice Anglo-Saxon names in this crew—had a full head of blond hair. He also had tattoos that crept up his neck and down his arms but ended at his chin and wrists. Except for some blue-gray blurs on his battered knuckles, faded tats perhaps, which had once covered those scars. This guy had been in a brawl or two. Or two thousand...

He wasn't quite as scary looking as Taft, but he also wasn't as friendly.

He gave me basically the same spiel. Alvarez was just some kid who'd started hanging out with them recently. He, Thompson, didn't know if it was Alvarez or Taft who knifed the guy, only that it wasn't him.

"Why were you meeting with Navarro to begin with?" This was a question I hadn't asked Taft. And I knew the answer from the case file, but I wanted to see what this guy would say.

"We was sellin' him drugs, and he tried to stiff us. Said he only had half of what he was supposed to pay us, that he'd get the rest to us the next day. Alfie was tellin' him, no way, that's not how it works, when he went down and started groanin'. I got the hell out of there."

That was a lot of words, but they told me nothing new. I asked more questions and got no additional info.

I thanked him for his time, as if we were winding down, then said, "Oh, by the way, who proposed the plea deal, you or the prosecutor?"

"We told him we'd give up the third guy for a lighter sentence."

I zeroed in on the *we*. So these two heavily tattooed thugs, both in their thirties, *offer* to give up the third member of their trio, a teenager with no police record, and the ASA goes for it? There was something seriously wrong with this picture.

"And what is that lighter sentence?" I asked. That info was not in the police case file.

"Ten years for drug possession and distribution."

Which meant he could be out in six to seven years. The file had said that a small amount of cocaine, slightly less than a gram, was found on Navarro's body.

Was that what these guys had been selling him, or did he already have that much on him?

"The drugs," I said, "what were they and how much?"

"Cocaine, and I don't remember how much."

"An eight ball or two?" That would be three and half to seven grams.

"I said I don't remember." His tone was even less friendly than before.

Because you've done so many deals, before and since. I opted to keep that thought to myself.

"Lemme see if I've got this right," I said instead. "You all meet up with Navarro and hand him the cocaine, and he hands over the money. Did you count it?"

"No, before we could, he told us it was only half. Then he wouldn't give the goods back."

"Did you take the drugs back after he was knifed?"

"I didn't. One of the others might've. I hadn't set up the deal. I was along as extra muscle."

Okay, it could've gone down that way, but a few things didn't completely add up. If the gram Navarro had on him was what he'd just bought, that hardly seemed worth the trouble and risk of setting up a buy, for him or these thugs. It would only be a couple hundred dollars for them. And if Navarro was a regular user, a gram wouldn't have lasted more than a day or two.

More likely the amount was at least an eightball, an eighth of an ounce or three and a half grams—a common way for cocaine to be packaged—which would be around five to seven hundred dollars. And when Navarro couldn't pay the whole amount, they sure as hell wouldn't have stood around dividing the eightball up into portions.

But if Navarro already had a gram of cocaine, would he have been buying more? Addicts were not great at planning ahead.

Plus Thompson was only along as extra muscle? Navarro wasn't a big man—five-eight and one-hundred-forty pounds. No doubt Alfie Taft could've taken him down with one arm tied behind him. Okay, maybe one other guy would go along, to watch Alfie's back. But two?

Thompson rustled in his chair. "Ya gonna sit there all day starin' into space?"

I bit back a snarky response. "Was there a fine, in addition, to the jail time?"

"Five grand each."

"That's a lot of money to come up with."

He shrugged but didn't say anything.

"And nothing for the murder?" I asked.

"No, 'cause *I* didn't murder nobody."

But he still could've been charged with felony murder. Could the ASA have added a manslaughter charge instead, as part of the plea deal? I wasn't sure how that worked here in Florida. Maybe it was felony murder or nothing if there was no evidence directly tying Thompson to the killing itself.

I swallowed a sigh. One of the many frustrations of this relatively new job—having to learn the laws and sentencing guidelines for this state.

I nodded. "Thanks for your time."

He shrugged again. "I got nothin' better to do." He hung up his phone receiver and rose from his chair. I watched as he swaggered over to the guard by the exit door. They exchanged a small nod, which I thought was interesting.

I pondered the disparity of sentences as I made my way out of the prison. The two guys, obviously gang members and no doubt with records longer than my arm, were offered sweet deals, with no jail time for the murder itself. But the ASA is going for felony murder—with a minimum sentence of life without parole—for Alvarez, who has no record and swears he wasn't even there.

I walked across the parking lot toward my car. Was the ASA convinced Alvarez was the killer, or was it all about whether she could win the case? She's got two guys who are willing to flip on the third one. Those both go in her win column. But the third guy isn't willing to confess, so she goes after him in court with the testimony of the first two, hoping to make that win number three. At worst, she gets two out of three.

Or... I stopped by my car, my hand on the door handle, *maybe she's a bigot?*

That would be a bit surprising, since she was African-American, but she might be prejudiced against Latinos.

I climbed into my car, and once again had a niggly feeling. And it wasn't the same one as before.

Was it something about the tattoos? Or something else, maybe something one of them had said?

Again, I couldn't get the feeling to reveal itself.

I started my car and pulled out of the lot, ordering my niggly feelings to get in a row and present themselves in an organized manner.

They did not comply.

⚬

Councilman Hayes was exiting his car as I pulled into the municipal parking lot. He held a white paper bag with a grease stain on its side. His lunch, I deduced.

He fell into step with me as we headed for the building's back door. "How are things going?" he asked.

"Slowly," I said.

I hadn't thought my tone was defensive, but he winced. "I meant that as a generic greeting, Chief, not as quizzing you about the mayor's case."

He paused. "I take it you have few leads?" His voice was sympathetic.

"None worth mentioning at the moment," I said. I was tempted to ask him about the mayoral race, and the rivalry between himself and the mayor. But I decided to wait on that. I doubted he'd appreciate being treated as a suspect, so best not to go there until I had to.

With any luck, my detectives had come up with some new leads while I was at Raiford.

On the third floor of the municipal building, I invited Barnes to join me in my glass-walled office. I paused to close the blinds against curious eyes before taking my desk chair. It was time to fill her in on the Navarro case.

She listened attentively from the comfy visitor's chair, the purchase of which had been one of her first tasks when she'd started with me. The other two chairs I'd inherited from my predecessor. They were chrome and black vinyl contraptions that had people squirming in less than five minutes.

I suspected Chief Black had picked them specifically *because* they were uncomfortable, to discourage visitors from lingering. I kept them for the same reason.

"For now," I concluded, "keep it to yourself that I'm looking into this."

Barnes sat up straighter. "Are you thinking that either Patterson or Chief Black took bribes to not investigate too thoroughly?"

"Maybe," I said. My predecessor was another former police officer awaiting trial for corruption, only he was out on bail. "But not necessarily. If there was anything like that going on, though, I want to find out before the case goes to trial. Afterwards, it could get Alvarez off on a technicality, even if he's guilty."

She nodded and rose from her chair. "What can I do?"

"A complete background check on all four of them. Dig as deep as you can."

"On Alvarez, Taft, and Thompson. Who's the fourth?"

"Navarro, the victim."

"Got it, Chief." She left my office.

My stomach growled a few minutes later. I should've stopped at the deli on my way in.

I stuck my head out my door. Barnes was hunched over her keyboard, working on those background checks. "Hey," I said, "I'm going to the deli. Want something?"

"Sure," she said without looking up. "I'll take my usual."

"What's your usual?"

She glanced up with a small grin. "Just tell them it's for Gloria the Cop."

I strolled the half block toward the deli, enjoying the fresh air, then crossed to the opposite corner. The bell above the door jangled merrily when I entered.

Barnes's usual turned out to be a Rachel—pastrami and coleslaw on rye with Russian dressing. How did I not know that before?

It looked messy but delicious, so I ordered two.

Once the owner, a short, stout, gray-haired gentleman with a slight Brooklyn accent, realized I was Gloria the Cop's boss, he regaled me with stories of his family. Apparently, making admiring noises over pics of his grandchildren was part of the price one paid for an extra helping of pastrami. But only if you were connected to Barnes. The guy had hardly said ten words to me in the six months I'd been getting lunch here, until today.

Finally he handed over a white bag that smelled like dill pickles. "Here ya go, Chief. I'm Maurie Bernstein, by the way, but most people call me Mr. B."

"A pleasure to formally make your acquaintance, Mr. B." I was chuckling under my breath as, bag in hand, I stepped out onto the sidewalk...and spotted Sam across the street.

I froze.

His head was turned away from me, but I knew that khaki uniform shirt and sandy hair. And the way he held his shoulders, as he leaned down a little to talk to the woman beside him. She didn't look like the same woman I'd seen him with this morning.

Indeed, she resembled me, slender and dark-haired.

I shook my head. Had I landed in some kind of alternate universe, and I was watching myself and Sam walking down the street?

I lifted my foot to step off the curb. A horn blared, and a delivery truck whooshed by, going a good ten miles over the speed limit.

I almost lost my grip on our lunches. Wrapping my fingers more firmly around the rolled-over top of the bag, I looked across the street. Sam and his companion were gone.

I shrugged and walked back to the office.

On the third floor, I discovered the source of the pickle fragrance. Mr. B had included two fat dills with the sandwiches.

Leaving my door open, I sat at my desk and unwrapped my sandwich. It was huge. I wasn't at all sure I could get my mouth around it.

I'd barely succeeded and was chewing slowly, groaning with pleasure at the tart and sweet combo of pastrami, slaw, and Russian dressing, when I spotted a broad-shouldered man in a khaki uniform entering the bullpen. He lifted a hand, smiled, and waved at me.

This was definitely Sam. In his other hand was a large brown paper bag.

He was waylaid halfway across the big room by Cruthers. The detective said something to him, and they both laughed. Apparently the something was a joke.

Being a good detective, I detected that the big bag was probably lunch, for both of us. Most likely Chinese food, from the fragrance wafting my way.

Dang, I wish he'd called first. I put down my sandwich and quickly wiped coleslaw juice off my chin.

Wait a minute. How did Sam get the Chinese food in the short time since I'd seen him on the street?

I closed my eyes, recalling. No, he hadn't had anything in his hands. I mentally ran through the shops on that side of the street—no Chinese carryout nearby.

Hey," Sam said, and I opened my eyes.

He stood in my doorway. "Guess I should've called to see if you'd already eaten."

"I've just started. Um, want half? I'm not sure I can eat all of it."

"Sure. We can have the Chinese for dinner."

"Put it in my mini fridge." I gestured toward my bathroom door.

The tiny room, cut out of a corner of my office, held a toilet, a minuscule shower, and under the equally petite sink was a pint-sized refrigerator.

Sam popped in there and came back out without the bag. He sat in the comfy visitor's chair.

I handed him half of my sandwich and a fistful of napkins. "Warning, it's sloppy."

He took a bite, chewed, and smiled, his blue eyes twinkling. He swallowed. "It's great."

We ate in silence for a few minutes. I kept my body language casual, relaxed. Some days, it pays to be a cop. We learn how to fake different emotions—and the lack of any emotion—while interrogating suspects.

I opened my mouth, then hesitated. I was really crappy at this relationship stuff. But so far, Sam had been very tolerant of my social awkwardness.

"Hey," I managed to get out in a casual tone, "I thought I saw you on the street downstairs earlier."

"How much earlier?"

"About ten minutes ago."

He glanced at his watch, a black plastic sports model. "Yeah, I guess that's about when I parked out back."

In other words, in the municipal parking lot. Then he could've come around the front of the building...but again, where was the bag of Chinese food?

"Who was the woman?" I blurted out.

He paused, his sandwich halfway to his mouth. "What woman?"

"You were having a conversation with her. She looked a little like me."

He shook his head. "Only women I've talked to today are you and Doris." His dispatcher at the Clover County Sheriff's Department.

I shrugged, deciding to make light of it. "I wondered at the time if I was caught in some sci-fi movie, and I'd been transported to an alternate universe."

He chuckled. "Hope *I* spot this doppelganger of mine. Now I'm really curious."

"I'll give him your card next time I see him."

He chuckled again and polished off his half of the sandwich.

I paused, my last bite between my fingers. "You might want to take some of the Chinese with you. With the mayor's shooting, I may or may not be able to get away at dinnertime."

"That's okay. I'll come into town later and eat with you here."

It's what we often did—ate meals at my desk, or sometimes his desk. It was the only way to assure we got at least some time together.

But today, the arrangement made me uncomfortable. Sam didn't sound like he was lying about the woman, and his body language was relaxed, not at all defensive. He'd never lied to me before.

Still, I wasn't sure I wanted to see him again today. "Um, call first," I said. "I may not even have time to slow down to eat."

He stood, giving me a grin and a small salute. "Later, Chief."

I smiled back.

Watching him saunter off across the bullpen, I told myself he was too much of a distraction right now. I needed to focus on the two cases on my plate, both of them time sensitive.

When he called later, I'd probably say no to dinner, even if I did have time to stop and eat.

CHAPTER FOUR

Barnes had three of the background checks done by four p.m.—Alfie Taft, Juan Alvarez, and the victim, Miguel Navarro.

Taft was a member of a gang called The Pillar. I'd never heard of them before. Barnes's report said they had white supremacist leanings. That fit with the swastika tattoo on his hand.

But wait a minute. Hadn't Alvarez implied that these guys were from the same gang that had tried to recruit him? What was a white supremacist gang doing recruiting Latino kids?

Barnes had included a photo of their gang tat, three tall rectangles. The one on the left was solid black, on the right solid brown, but the middle rectangle was twice the width and half again the height of the others. It was a black outline, bare skin inside.

A half-baked thought niggled at the edge of my brain. *Not again!*

I tried to haul it out into the open. All I got was the sense that I'd seen the tattoo before, and not just on the two clowns this morning. I'd seen it standing alone, on somebody else.

But that's all I could dredge up.

I moved on to the report on Juan Alvarez, which was quite sparse. He was indeed, a third generation Cuban-American, an only child. As he'd claimed, he had no prior record. And he was a good student, in the running for a partial scholarship to the University of North Florida, before that fateful night last May.

Barnes had added a note at the bottom that there had been an SAT test scheduled at Bennett High School the morning after the Navarro homicide. She was checking to see if Juan actually showed up for it.

Miguel Navarro was only a couple of years older than Alvarez, just eighteen when he was killed. And he also had no record. Not even minor kid stuff like shoplifting, which was sadly all too common among kids who grew up in his section of town—one of the poorest neighborhoods in Starling.

Also a decent student, straight Bs in high school, and no indicators that he'd been using drugs, although he could've been good at hiding that.

I sat up straighter when I read that he'd filed a harassment complaint nine days prior to his death. *Very* unusual for that part of town, where folks avoided the police as much as possible.

The next day he'd withdrawn the complaint. Then a week later, his older sister reported being sexually assaulted. She couldn't identify her two assailants, who had grabbed her from behind and never let her see their faces.

Navarro had accompanied his sister to the police department. He'd told the officer taking the report that he thought the sexual assault was reprisal, because he'd been approached by a gang but had refused to join.

The next night, he was killed.

I sat back in my desk chair and blew out air, my chest heavy. These young people had tried to do the right thing by reporting crimes to the police, and what had the Starling PD done?

And the Navarro saga sounded an awful lot like Alvarez's story.

"Barnes," I called out.

She popped into my open doorway. "Yes, Chief?"

"What was the name of the gang that approached Navarro, that he thought was responsible for his sister's attack? And which detective was assigned to the SA case?"

She pursed her lips. "I don't remember. Lemme check it." The sound of her printer whirring, then she was in my doorway again, her eyes on a sheet of paper in her hand. "That's odd. The report doesn't say which gang. And I don't see any notations or reports on the investigation."

If there even was one....

"Who took the report?" I asked.

"Sergeant Lewis."

I thought I'd stifled my groan fairly well, but Barnes had good ears. She gave me a lopsided half-grin as she handed me the printed-out report.

I scowled at her before glancing over the page. It was pretty skimpy on information. "Is Lewis on duty now?"

"Came on at three. You want him in here?"

"At his earliest convenience," I barked.

She disappeared and her brother took her place in my doorway. Barnes and Bradley were half-sibs. They got along well but had little in common, besides police work and always being impeccably dressed. She was short and solidly built, with straight, dark hair and brown eyes. While he was tall and slender—he had a good foot on me—with lighter brown, wavy hair and blue eyes.

I motioned Bradley into my office. Today's sartorial splendor included gray slacks with a knife-sharp crease and a navy blazer.

He settled in the comfy chair. "I figured you'd want a recap of where we are." He waved a hand in the direction of my computer. "I mean, it'll all be in the reports but..."

Something about his gesture toward the monitor triggered a moment of *déjà vu*, and the gut sense that it had something to do with one of my niggly feelings.

Sheez Louise, am I losing it? Now I was having a *gut* feeling about my *niggly* feelings.

Barnes was in my doorway again, this time leaning a shoulder against the jamb, pad and pen in hand, taking notes. Said notes were usually for her own benefit, since I had a good memory and would get the info in writing later, via the detectives' reports.

But this time, as Bradley wound down, I had to admit to myself that I hadn't heard a word he'd said. Maybe I'd quiz Barnes after he left—pretend I was testing her information-processing abilities. Yeah, that sounded good.

"And by the way," Bradley added as he rose from his seat. "We have a new dispatcher starting tomorrow. Jenny decided not to come back from maternity leave. She's staying home with her baby for a while."

I nodded, and he left.

Barnes took his chair.

"Summarize the report Lieutenant Bradley just gave me."

She blinked, once, then looked down at her pad. Her summary was succinct.

And I could summarize what she had said in one short phrase. We had bupkis in the mayor's case.

The only fresh information was that the bullet from the driver's shoulder was a hollow point, designed to do maximum damage by fragmenting inside the body. There were some markings on the cartridge end that the lab might be able to match to a specific gun barrel, once we had the gun. But it was an 8mm, a common rifle caliber.

"Any word from Wellbourne?" I asked.

"Other than she's bored to tears? She said the mayor has stuck to his office all day, and the only 'excitement,'" Barnes made air quotes, "is when she follows him down the hall to the men's room."

"She doesn't go in with him, does she?"

"No."

"Hmm, maybe she should, or rather... Call her and tell her to send the uniform who's assigned as his driver to go in with him."

Barnes made a face I couldn't readily interpret. Maybe she was imagining having to watch Mr. Mayor pee.

I suppressed a shudder.

"You really think somebody's out to get him?" she asked. "Couldn't the shooting yesterday have been a random thing? Or a mistake—they were after someone else."

"I might believe that if we were in Jacksonville or Orlando, but *Starling*? We don't usually have drive-bys here, do we?"

"Occasionally, but not often. And they're usually in the poorer sections."

"Speaking of which, get me an updated list of the gangs operating in Jacksonville and Starling. And tell Wellbourne that after they take the mayor home, if he's not going out again later, she and the driver can go home as well. But she should check the mayor's house thoroughly before letting him go in."

"She'd probably think of that herself."

"Probably, but figure out a diplomatic way to remind her."

Barnes nodded, got up and left.

I normally wouldn't be micro-managing a detective like that. It wasn't even my job to supervise them, it was Bradley's. But I was keeping a close eye on Wellbourne, for two reasons.

One, she was a rookie detective, on loan from the FDLE, and I didn't want to have to explain to her boss, Dot Wilder, how I'd let something happen to her on my watch.

And two, if she turned out to be a good detective, I was going to try to discreetly steal her from the state agency.

My computer pinged, indicating an incoming email. It was from Barnes, with the last of the background checks attached, on Thompson. But it gave me nothing new, except that he was a member of the same gang as Taft.

I squinted at the mug shot and was able to make out the three columns of the gang tat among the other clutter of ink on the guy's neck.

Again, the niggly feeling. And again, it refused to coalesce into a full-blown thought.

"Arrrgh," I growled.

Barnes popped into my doorway. "You say something, Chief?"

I shook my head.

A throat clearing behind her. Lewis's face appeared above her shoulder. "You wanted to see me, Chief?"

I wiggled my fingers to indicate he should come in. Barnes stepped aside and waited.

I tilted my head to one side, the signal that she was to leave rather than sit in on this discussion.

She pulled the door closed behind her.

Lewis strolled over and plopped down in the comfy visitor's chair.

I gritted my teeth, my expression carefully neutral. "At ease, Sergeant."

He sat up a little straighter, but then shrugged, his navy uniform shirt pulling snug across his shoulders. He was of medium build and height, brown eyes, and dark, short hair. A very average-looking guy, if you ignored the perpetual slight sneer on his face. "We've never been all that formal around here."

I knew that was a challenge, not an apology, but I let it go. I slid the report on Maria Navarro's SA across the desk.

He leaned forward and picked it up, glanced at it. "Yeah, okay. What about it?"

"What was the name of the gang harassing the brother?"

"He didn't say."

"Did you ask?" I said slowly.

"Yeah. He said they were always careful to avoid saying the name of the gang."

That struck me as odd. Gangs usually flaunted their identities, especially with new recruits. It would either impress them or intimidate them.

"Are you familiar with the gang called The Pillar?"

His eyebrows went up a notch but otherwise he didn't react. "Yeah, I've heard of them. They're not active in Starling, but they're in Jacksonville and Raiford prison."

"Well, it's looking like they are becoming active here. I suspect they were the gang trying to recruit Navarro, and they may have been going after at least one other Latino kid." I didn't mention that said kid was Alvarez, accused of felony murder in the Navarro homicide case.

"Good to know. I'll tell my men to keep an eye out for them."

I wasn't sure which grated more, the *my* or the *men*. They were my people, not his, and there were several female officers on the force.

I kept all of that to myself. I so wanted to put this guy in his place, but I knew that would actually give him satisfaction, knowing that he'd gotten to me.

"Dismissed," I said in a brisk tone.

He stood, gave me a salute along with a smirky half smile, and left.

I checked my watch—silver-toned with a man-sized face I could read at a glance. Five-thirty. I rarely left this early, but it had been an intense day. And my people would call me if there were any new developments.

I shut down the computer, gathered my things, and walked out of my office, my mouth open to announce that I was going home to my cat.

"I've been working on that list of gangs," Barnes said, an eager note in her voice. "There are thirty-one that are active in Jacksonville, but I haven't found any that are based in Starling. We get spillover from Jax, though, on the east side of town."

"Where the poorest neighborhoods are," I commented.

She nodded. "Five gangs in particular, including The Pillar. They run the gambit from white supremacists to predominantly Black or Latino."

"Good work. Send all that to my email and call it a day." I could hardly expect her to work late if I wasn't staying.

She grinned, quickly tapped a few times on her keyboard, then began rummaging in her desk for her own belongings.

As we walked out together, I watched her out of my peripheral vision. What was I going to do in two weeks, when we reached the six-month mark from when I'd pulled her out of the rookie pool?

My intention had been to rotate rookies through the position—those who were interested in eventually becoming detectives—to give them an inside look at how investigations were handled. But it wasn't my job to train rookies. We had experienced officers who were much better at it than me, or at least more patient.

And how likely was it that the next rookie assistant I recruited would be anywhere as efficient as Barnes was? I tried to imagine doing my job with someone other than Barnes at her desk. I couldn't visualize it.

I shook my head slightly.

"Chief?" she said, a question mark in her voice.

"Nothing. I was trying to remember what I have in my fridge. I'd rather not go grocery shopping tonight."

—◆—

My cat was no longer the little ball of white fluff we'd found at a crime scene last October. But the name Sam had given her, Pipsqueak, was still appropriate. She was slender and small boned.

And determined to trip me up as she wound around my legs. I managed to gently shake loose from her, then dropped my laptop case on my old leather sofa, and made my way to the kitchen for a much-needed glass of wine.

She had an automatic feeder in the room I euphemistically called my study—which contained exactly one bookcase and a whole bunch of cat paraphernalia Barnes had bought. But I also kept a small dish for her in the kitchen, into which I now dropped several cat treats.

That kept her amused long enough for me to slip out of my shoes, pour my wine, and return to the sofa.

I tossed my suit jacket over its back and plopped down, too tired to even change my clothes. I'd take a shower in a few minutes, I told myself, as I sank into the soft black leather.

Why was I so tired? Yes, a lot had happened today, but I'd left at a decent hour, after only a ten-hour workday. Relatively short for me.

An image popped into my mind of Sam's khaki-covered shoulders across the street, his head bent down to speak to the woman beside him.

What the hell is going on with that?

Did Sam actually have a doppelganger?

As if on cue, my personal cell phone rang, Sam's name on the screen.

I sighed. I couldn't duck him forever, and I really didn't want to. I just didn't need this extra stressor right now.

I sighed again and accepted the call. "Hey."

"Hey yourself." His voice neutral, neither cheerful nor...something else. "I tried your private line but nobody picked up."

"Barnes and I left relatively on time for a change," I said, then realized my *faux pas*. "I brought work home though."

"How about the Chinese?"

"Wha'?" I said lamely.

"The carryout. Did you bring it home?"

Did he sound pissed? I couldn't tell.

"Um, I forgot all about it."

"No problem. We can heat it up for lunch tomorrow." Now he sounded cheerful, but was it fake cheerfulness?

What was I doing, dissecting his voice like this? Why was I suddenly paranoid about his mood?

"I could grab a pizza in a little bit," he said, definitely cheerful now, "and bring it over. How long do you think you'll need to work?"

"Huh?"

"On the stuff you brought home?"

"Um, an hour or two, maybe."

"Judith, are you okay?" His rich baritone was now full of concern. "You sound kinda off."

"No, I mean yes. I'm fine. Just distracted. It's been a complicated day."

An ironic chuckle. "Yes, it has been that."

The rumble of that chuckle had something loosening in my chest. My muscles began to relax. What was I thinking? This was Sam. Whoever his look-alike might be, it didn't matter. I trusted this man.

"Give me an hour," I said. "Whatever isn't done by that point can wait until tomorrow."

"See ya then." He disconnected.

I struggled up off the soft leather sofa, suddenly not as tired as I had been.

I noted the time on the driftwood wall clock, handmade by my cousin Paulie years ago, when he'd gone through what he called his "crafty stage."

It was six-ten.

"I'm taking a shower," I announced to the cat.

Twenty minutes later, I was clean and comfy in the beige silk lounge outfit Sam had given me for Christmas. We'd only been lovers for a few weeks at that point, and he'd apologized for the intimate nature of the gift.

"But," he'd said, "I thought of you the second I saw it and imagined how good it would look on you."

Now, I checked myself out in the floor-length mirror on the back of my bedroom door. He'd been right. The loose-fitting pants and shirt-like top flowed whenever I moved, transforming my stick-like, almost boyish body into a tall and willowy woman.

I fluttered my eyelashes at my reflection, then laughed at myself and ran a hand through my still damp, short hair.

With time to kill, I booted up my laptop on the breakfast bar that separated the kitchen from the living room. I read through the background checks again, but nothing new jumped out at me.

I zoomed in on Taft and Thompson's mug shots, the profiles that showed their necks and the tattoo of The Pillar gang.

The pillars were superimposed on other tattoos, of snakes and vines and such.

I double-checked their ages. They were thirty-six and thirty-seven. On the old side for gang members, who rarely made it past thirty. Both had spent some of those years in prison.

I pulled over my grocery list pad, flipped to a blank page, and made notes for things to check out tomorrow. Like if they'd had any gang affiliations before The Pillar. And what the hell did the three columns stand for?

My doorbell rang, and Pipsqueak let out a loud screech of a meow.

"What, you think you're a watchdog now?" I said to her, as I rose to get the door.

Sam, in jeans and a light blue sweatshirt that matched his eyes, strode into my apartment, pizza box in hand.

I sniffed appreciatively. "Smells good."

"Me or the pizza?" he teased.

I grinned. "Both."

He unceremoniously dropped the pizza box on the arm of the sofa and took me in his arms. Warm lips grazed mine. "I probably shouldn't do this," he whispered, "because I'm famished."

My lips curved upward under the slight pressure from his. "For me or the pizza?" I mumbled.

He chuckled, a low rumble in his chest, pressed against mine.

The cat wound around my ankles, meowing. Without letting me go, Sam kicked the apartment door closed before she could escape.

Then he increased the pressure on my lips and pulled me closer.

My insides melted as heat coursed through my body. Why had I doubted this man?

The doubts tried to reassert themselves. I firmly shoved them away, letting my lips part.

Sam accepted the invitation and deepened the kiss.

The heat was joined by a tingling sensation, and I felt a little lightheaded. I wrapped my arms around his broad shoulders. *To steady myself*, I told myself.

Who am I kidding? I wanted this man. Right. Now.

And I was perfectly okay with room-temperature pizza.

CHAPTER FIVE

I jolted upright, a sense of urgency shooting adrenaline through my system.

I was in my bedroom, the soft green glow from my alarm clock the only light. But it was enough to assess that everything was normal.

Except for the man in my bed. And that was becoming close to normal.

The image in my mind's eye, a remnant from a dream, was beginning to fade. I chased it, sensing it was important.

To what? A case? Which case?

Diaz! What's a diaz...a name? Who's Diaz? The guy in the mug shot in my dream? Maybe.

I looked around again. All was as it should be.

A soft meow from the other side of the closed bedroom door. Pipsqueak did not like being locked out of my room. But she tended to be an annoyance when one was trying to make love.

I smiled a little as warmth filled my chest...at the thought of Pipsqueak? Or of making love with Sam? I wasn't sure which, maybe some of both.

I felt around on my nightstand for the pad and pen I kept there, for this express purpose. Finding them, I scribbled *DIAZ* in block letters. My brain would sort it out in the morning.

I returned the pad to its spot and sank back against my pillow, now fully awake. I sighed.

Sam stirred, turned on his side toward me, and dropped an arm over my stomach, all without waking up.

I resisted the urge to wiggle out from under the weight of that arm. It was both comforting and confining, anxiety-provoking.

Damn it to hell! When would this good thing that was happening in my life stop making me anxious?

It's not like I'd never dated before. I'd even had a couple of long-term boyfriends—that is if you considered six months long term.

And I'd really liked one of them. We'd been best friends as well as lovers.

Liked? Not loved?

No, I hadn't loved Gregory. I'd only liked him a lot. I'd found him great company. And we got each other, except he wasn't a cop. He didn't get that part of me.

And that's a huge part of me.

Some days, it was all of me. But was that because I didn't have anything else in my life?

Being with Sam was so easy. Even easier than with Greg. But was loving another law enforcement officer only making it easier for me to be consumed by law enforcement 24/7?

Wait, *loving*? My stomach hollowed out. Sam's arm grew even heavier.

I gently eased it aside. He didn't stir.

His warm breath tickled my ear. Part of me wanted to roll over on top of him and get something started.

Another part wanted to bolt from the room.

I considered compromising by carefully edging out of bed. Then I imagined the conversation that would follow once Sam realized I was gone. And he would.

I did none of those things.

Instead, I lay there, willing myself to go back to sleep. Eventually, my tired body and brain complied.

———◆———

The next morning, I sat at my desk staring at the mug shot of Ricardo Diaz, one of several ex-cons we had looked at for a series of smash-and-grab robberies last December.

There was the tattoo on his neck of the three columns—the tat for The Pillar gang. But this guy's name and his beige skin tone both begged the question of why he was in the same gang with two white supremacists.

"Well," I said to the image on my computer monitor, "I think you are the reason for at least two of my niggling feelings."

I scrolled to his current address, wrote it down, then called out, "Barnes, you busy?"

Her head appeared in my doorway. "Not very. What's up?"

"Let's take a little drive."

I drove. On the way, I brought up what I suspected would be a touchy subject, hoping that it would be less awkward in the car, where I had an excuse not to make eye contact.

Coward, I thought.

"Barnes, you know we're coming up on the six-month mark."

She shot me a confused look. "Of when you started?"

"Yes. *And* of when you became my assistant."

I sensed her stiffen in the passenger seat.

"I had intended for it to be a position rookies would rotate through," I said, "to help them learn the department and law enforcement more quickly."

A beat of silence. "Can't we make it a one-year rotation?" Her voice was shaky, hesitant.

I swallowed a sigh and answered her question with one of my own. "What's your eventual goal in the department?"

I watched her out of my peripheral vision. Her eyes darted toward me, then away again.

"Um, to become a detective."

"Like your brother."

"At least as good as him." No hesitation this time.

I glanced over. Her cheeks had reddened.

I chuckled softly. "Do I sense a little sibling rivalry?"

"Um, that didn't come out right. I don't know that I could be better than him, but... Well, I've always looked up to him, tried to be as good as he is at...things."

I flashed her a smile. "I get it."

I thought about my cousin Paulie. He was a year and a half older than me, also an only child, and the closest thing to a sibling I had. As a kid, I'd always struggled to keep up with him, sometimes literally as his stride was almost twice the length of mine.

But at some point, we'd switched roles. I'd skyrocketed up the ladder at Baltimore County PD—making detective, then sergeant, then lieutenant—while he'd floundered. Late forties, actually getting scary close to fifty, and he still hadn't "found himself" completely.

Last I'd heard from him, he was job-hunting. Again. He'd mentioned that, like me, he was trying for a warmer climate.

When had he begun to imitate me instead of the other way around?

Barnes cleared her throat, yanking me out of my reverie. "Um, can we make it a year's rotation?" she asked again. "Please."

I sighed, out loud this time. "I'll think about it."

Face it, Anderson. You're not really in the mood to break in a new assistant anyway.

Diaz had a fourth-floor apartment in the red-light district of town. He stood in the open doorway, blocking our way. "Whadaya want?"

"Just a short chat," I said, trying not to wrinkle my nose at the odorous fumes emanating from his kitchen area.

"I was about to go out," he grumbled. His beige skin had lost its prison pallor, tanned some by the Florida sun. His chin now sported a goatee, and, under his long sleeved, button-down shirt, he wore a dark green turtleneck that partially covered the tattoo on his neck. Despite the state of his place, he was clean and neat, his long straight hair pulled back in a ponytail.

"On your way to work?" I asked.

He nodded, his expression conveying that he begrudged me even that much information.

"We'll walk with you." I gave him a pleasant smile. "Don't want to make you late."

He nodded again, still with the begrudging look, and Barnes and I headed toward the elevator.

"Stairs," he said. "That thing don't always work right. It's got me stuck a couple of times."

And no doubt he wanted to be stuck in an elevator with two cops about as much as we wanted to be stuck with him.

We went down the fire stairs single file. Once out on the street, I fell into step beside him, Barnes trailing right behind.

"I wanted to ask you about your tattoo," I said.

He yanked at the collar of his turtleneck, pulling it up higher. "What about it?"

"It's a gang tat, correct?"

His eyes darted around. "Yeah, what of it?"

"You got it in prison?"

"Yeah."

"Funny though, I've run into a couple of other fellows from that gang, and they were white supremacists. Must be a very tolerant gang."

He snorted. "I was told to join up or die, so I joined up, even though they were all lily white. They said this was their new 'diversity plan.' And then they laughed hysterically, like a bunch of little boys, nudgin' each other and gigglin'." His voice dripped with disdain.

"What happened after that?" I asked.

He shrugged. "They pretty much left me alone, and so did the other gangs inside. I figured then that I'd made a good deal."

"And now?"

"Employers don't like neck or face tats. Arms are okay, but too much ink makes the customers antsy. I'm savin' up to have the tat removed."

I nodded. "Good idea. How much does that cost these days?"

He glanced down at his phone and picked up his pace. "Depends on where you go. On the street, it's not much. But somebody who knows what they're doin', it's a few hundred. A friend a mine had one removed, paid fifty bucks, and ended up with an infection. Almost lost his arm."

I grimaced.

"Yeah," Diaz said. "I'm savin' for the guys who know what they're doin'."

"The gang hasn't been in touch with you since you got out?"

He shook his head. "And I'm hopin' it stays that way."

"Who recruited you?"

He blew out air, slowed his pace slightly. "These two guys. They went by Snake and Bugeye inside, don't know their real names. They was big and ugly so I didn't ask questions, just went along with gettin' the tattoo."

"Anything else you can tell us about the gang?"

He shook his head again.

"Do you know any other non-white members?"

Another head shake.

I stopped, put a hand lightly on his arm to halt him as well, and handed him my card. "Thanks very much for your help, Mr. Diaz. If you think of anything else about that gang, let me know. Or if they contact you."

He gave me a lopsided grin. "No cop's ever called me *mister* before."

I gave him a small smile in return. "Always a first time."

A slight nod, and he took off at a trot. A half block farther down, he turned into a convenience store—no doubt, his place of employment. I noted the name, Uncle Joe's.

We were almost back to my car when both our phones buzzed. Mine was a text from Bradley. *There's been another attempt on the mayor. In Holly Park.*

"That's only one block over," Barnes said. She'd apparently gotten the same text. "It may be faster to run there."

"You go. I'm moving my car. I leave it here, it'll be stripped by the time I get back."

"Good point." She took off.

—◦—

By the time I'd parked in the small lot attached to Holly Park, there was a significant police presence.

Good thing, since a crowd of looky-loos was already gathering, along with at least one member of the press—Stuart Frost, the young man who had replaced my old nemesis, Marly Davis, at the local newspaper.

Davis had managed to get herself killed last fall, despite my warning that her "source" was probably the very serial killer we were seeking and she was reporting on.

A twinge of guilt. I reminded myself that I *had* warned her.

I plowed through the crowd, holding my badge up, and ignoring Frost's shouted questions.

"Chief," he called out, "who killed the mayor?"

I winced but didn't look his way. At least Marly couched her suppositions as just that, *not* assumptions of fact.

I presented myself to the uniformed officer at the gap in the police tape that was the entrance to the scene. From the zits on his chin, I figured he was a rookie.

Good lord, they're getting younger every year.

While he laboriously recorded my information, I glanced over his shoulder. My people had taped off most of the park, but the majority of the activity was by a clump of trees in one corner.

Impatiently, I nudged past the officer and took off in that direction.

Barnes met me at the edge of the trees. "Mayor was hit this time, but it doesn't seem to be life-threatening."

The mayor's raised voice, coming from the thicket, affirmed that. He sounded livid, but very much alive.

We stepped between some trees and came out into a clearing. There were several stone benches scattered around it. At first, I thought the bent-over figure on one of them was the mayor.

But then I realized that Mr. Mayor was on the gurney that the paramedics were steering through the trees on the other side of the clearing, headed for the parking lot beyond.

Bradley jogged over to us, Wellbourne in tow. "Looks like the shooter's long gone," he said. "I've got uniforms searching the park for any clues where he was hiding, and anything else they can find."

"And where were you when this went down?" I demanded of Wellbourne.

Her light brown skin turned a tad ashen under the scattering of freckles over her nose and cheeks. "Standing outside the trees. The mayor insisted." Her high-pitched voice sounded like a sixteen-year-old's. "I heard two shots and ran in." She gulped. "He was on the ground."

"Where was the driver?" I snapped.

She tugged the end of one of the red-brown spiral curls that adorned her head. "Mr. Mayor made him wait by the car. Said he was afraid it would be vandalized in this part of town. He tried to get me to stay there too."

The first part of that sounded reasonable. The last part, not so much. Why would he try to ditch Wellbourne?

Anxiety clouded her brown eyes.

I relented. "You didn't do anything wrong. Worst part of protection assignments is getting the person being protected to cooperate."

I pointed my chin toward the bent-over figure. "Who's that?"

"Councilman Hayes," Wellbourne said. "He showed up a few seconds after the shots. Almost fainted when he saw the mayor. I told him to wait there on the bench until someone could interview him."

"You want to do the honors, Chief?" Bradley asked.

I nodded, and he turned to Wellbourne. "Make sure the uniforms have the contact info on anyone who heard or saw anything."

"You got it, Lieutenant." She trotted off.

I gestured for Barnes to follow her and help with the canvassing. Bradley and I headed for Mark Hayes's bench.

He jumped up when he saw us coming.

"Dear God," the councilman spluttered. "He..." A glance over his shoulder toward the spot where the mayor had apparently fallen. He swayed on his feet.

"CS team is on their way to go over the clearing," Bradley whispered in my ear. "I've got the mayor's cell phone, in an evidence bag." He patted his suit jacket, where the inside pocket would be.

I nodded, then said to Hayes, "Councilman, what happened to bring you here today?"

"I, uh, got a call, from the mayor's assistant, telling me to meet the mayor here."

"His admin?" I asked.

Hayes shook his head. His face was pale, his normally well-groomed dark hair sticking up in places. He ran his fingers through it now, and tugged, thus explaining the random tufts. "No, the other one," he said. "The new guy."

"Did he say why you were meeting in a park?"

"I asked, but he said he didn't know. That the mayor had just asked him to call me."

Hayes swayed on his feet again. I gestured toward the bench, and he sank back onto it.

Only now I was hovering over him. Not the best way to conduct an interview with one's superior. I considered crouching down but wasn't sure my knees would cooperate.

Hayes apparently figured out the awkwardness of it all and scooted over on the bench. I sat beside him, and Bradley, ten years my junior, crouched in front of both of us.

"Do you have any idea why the mayor wanted to meet here?" I asked.

Hayes's gaze darted around the clearing, then landed back on Bradley. "Um, perhaps we should speak alone, Chief."

The lieutenant cocked his head toward me, silently asking if I wanted him to get lost.

But I had a feeling where this was going, and I wasn't willing to convey to Bradley that I didn't trust him. "You were thinking it had something to do with more corruption in my department," I said.

Hayes nodded. "That's what I assumed, that he wanted to talk about something, um, sensitive like that."

I was dying to ask if Hayes had some reason to believe there was more corruption in SPD, other than what we'd already ferreted out. But now was not the time or place.

"So, what did you see or hear when you arrived here?" I asked instead.

"The mayor's car and driver in the parking lot. The driver was standing outside of it, so I assumed the mayor was already in the park. I was walking in on the main path toward the building, when I heard..." He trailed off, swallowed hard.

The park's small building held a minuscule display of artifacts from the original Indian inhabitants of the area and the early white settlers. And restrooms. No offices and no one in charge. A caretaker opened and closed the building at the beginning and end of the day.

Our crime scene guys would have to go over everything in there as well. I wondered how many drug deals went down in its unmanned corridors, and no doubt teenage lovebirds found the darkest corners on a regular basis.

Bert and Ernie would not be happy.

The councilman was visibly trying to gather himself. "I heard the shots and began to run back toward my car. The mayor's driver ran past me, headed for the woods. Um, so I followed him."

"What did you see?" Bradley asked, his voice neutral.

"Only the mayor, lying there. I, uh, thought he was dead." He took a deep breath. "Agent Wellbourne was checking his pulse, and the driver was on his phone, I assumed calling 911."

"Did you see anyone else in the park?" I asked.

"No, which I thought was surprising when I first got here. I mean, it's a nice afternoon, not too chilly."

"Anything else you can think of?" Bradley asked.

Hayes shook his head.

I nodded, and Bradley handed him his card. "If you think of anything, call me, and we'll need a formal statement from you later this afternoon."

Hayes took the card. Still seeming a bit shaken, he rose and started out of the clearing.

"Lieutenant," came from beyond the trees.

Bradley and I jogged in that direction. Hayes slowly trailed after us. Barnes was hoofing it toward us from the other side of the park.

Two uniforms stood beside a bush. "Look what we found," one said, pointing at the ground under it. In a nest of leaves rested a rifle—an old-fashioned one, with a wood stock, black metal barrel and bolt handle.

"The leaves were covering it," the uniform added.

A gasp from behind us. We whirled around. Councilman Hayes was once again swaying on his feet. Barnes grabbed an arm to steady him.

"It's a German M-mauser," he stuttered. "My grandfather brought one back from the war."

"Which war?" Barnes asked.

"World War II."

I stared down at the gun, a bad feeling in my gut. I pulled out my phone and snapped my own picture of it.

"Where's your grandfather's gun?" I asked the councilman.

"Um, on the wall in my study... In a rack I, uh, made for my dad. In wood shop my senior year of high school."

I nodded. Why was Hayes giving me more info than I needed? Was he just babbling because he was rattled?

But the info had the ring of truth. Hayes was about my age—they would've still had wood shop in his day.

My gut continued to churn. This was no niggling thought, it was full-blown suspicion.

And if I'm right... I shook my head slightly.

"Show me your gun rack," I said.

CHAPTER SIX

"My car?" The councilman's voice was shaky.

I had just suggested he ride with me. He seemed too unsettled to be driving, not to mention he was now a prime suspect for attempted murder.

"Do you mind if Officer Barnes drives it home for you?" I asked. "She's a good driver."

He shook his head, but said, "Yes, that's fine. Thanks."

He was quiet—staring out the passenger window—during the ten-minute drive to his place, in a much fancier part of town.

The house was more a mini-mansion, old and sprawling but well kept. It had once sat well back from the road, until a street-widening project had taken two-thirds of the front yard.

He unlocked the front door, but I held out an arm in front of him. I doubted anyone was in the house, but one couldn't be too cautious.

"No one's home," he whispered. "My son is in school."

That would be his youngest. The other two lived on the campus of the University of North Florida in Jacksonville.

I nodded and pulled my Glock from its waistband holster at the small of my back. It took only a few minutes to clear the house. Then I led the way to his study.

He gasped at the empty slot in the gun rack on the wall, but I wasn't the least bit surprised.

"You didn't notice it was missing?" I asked.

He shook his head.

"When's the last time you handled it?"

"Years ago. I, um..." He eyed the Glock still in my hand but down at my side. "I'm not fond of guns. I keep it as a reminder, of both my grandfather and father. He...Dad, that is. He was very proud of his father's service in the war."

"And I suppose someone has cleaned in here recently?" There was no sign of dust.

"Nanette," Mark Hayes said. "She comes in twice a week."

"I'll need her fingerprints," I said, as I holstered the Glock, "and yours, for elimination purposes."

He nodded and swallowed hard, his Adam's apple bobbing in his throat.

"Who else might have been in this room recently, besides you, your kids and Nanette?"

He shook his head again, but I wasn't sure if it was a negative answer to my question or an expression of shock and confusion. His eyes were a little glazed.

I braced myself to catch him, should he faint, and asked, "Was the gun loaded?"

"I...uh, I..." he stuttered, "I don't think so."

"You never checked it?"

"No. Um, there's a box of ammunition for it around here somewhere. Grandpa had intended to do some target practice with it, but he never got around to it." Hayes gestured vaguely toward the other gun in the rack, a long-barreled Winchester. "He was a deer hunter, before the war, but I don't think he picked up a gun ever again, after he came home."

"Any ideas where that box of ammo might be?" I asked.

"No." Then he seemed to pull himself together. "This was my parents' house," he said in a firmer voice, "and my grandparents before them. I just remember Grandpa talking once or twice about how he'd always intended to test that rifle out."

I waved a hand in the air. "But you've remodeled the house."

Hayes grimaced. "More like redecorated. Painted and changed out some furniture. Karen..." he hesitated over his dead wife's name, "...she liked a more modern style."

Still, I thought, resisting the urge to shake my head, *at some point you handled that gun, took it off the wall to paint, then rehung the rack.*

And it hadn't occurred to him to check if it was loaded? The most dangerous situation sometimes was a gun in the hands of someone who knew nothing about them.

"I take it that you've never cleaned either rifle," I said.

"No." He eyed the Winchester as if it were a snake.

"Do you mind if I have my CS team come in here to check for fingerprints and such?" I wasn't sure what I would do if he said he would mind. I'd really hate to have to seek a search warrant for the house of the chair of the city council, who had the power to fire me if he so chose.

"Of course. Whatever you need to do," he said.

"Good. I'll have a couple of uniforms search for that ammo box also. They'll be careful not to disturb too much."

He nodded. "Sure, okay. But could we do that before my youngest comes home? He, um, he's still dealing with his mother's..."

"Sure. I'll have Barnes start searching now, and send over someone to help her, plus one of the CS guys."

That meant processing the park would take forever, with only one crime scene tech to supervise. Would it be crass to bring up the need for more support staff?

Probably not the best time.

Instead, I asked, "Can you think of anyone who would want to set it up so it looked like you shot the mayor?"

He stared at me for a few seconds, his mouth slightly open. Then he swallowed hard. "No."

"No enemies? I mean, you're a politician. Surely you've pissed some people off along the way."

He snorted softly. "Only Mayor Daniels, and I doubt he arranged to have himself wounded in order to make me look bad."

"Okay," I said. "I'll need you to stop in at 3MB and give a formal statement later today, okay?"

He nodded again, his gaze flitting around his own study as if he'd never seen it before.

Once outside in front of the Hayes's house, I took a deep breath. I didn't believe for a New York minute that Hayes had shot the mayor.

He was a gentle man, almost self-effacing. If left to his own choices, he likely would've become an accountant or a veterinarian, or maybe a teacher. But he'd been born into a well-to-do, powerful family, with a mother who had strong ideas about what her sons would do for a living.

Mark Hayes had bent to her desires and become a lawyer, then a politician. And he'd married a woman as ambitious for him as his mother had been.

But he seemed to be legitimately dedicated to helping the City of Starling. And my instincts said he wasn't capable of shooting a gun at another human being, maybe not even at an animal. Especially not at an animal.

But my instincts didn't have a great track record lately. I'd trusted the wrong people more than once in the last six months, and distrusted others who'd deserved better.

Then again, this time my instincts were probably right. Mark Hayes was not a stupid man. Why would he use an unusual weapon that could easily be traced back to him, and even leave the gun at the scene?

A throat clearing nearby. I startled a little.

"Sorry, Chief," Barnes said, from beside my car in the parking area. "Um, where to now?"

"Get out your phone and look up a German Mauser rifle from World War II. Can one still get ammo for it?"

She pulled out her phone and poked at it a few times. "Yes, it takes 8mm cartridges, like a lot of hunting rifles."

The same caliber as the shots fired yesterday in front of the municipal building.

"I need you to stay here," I said, "and search the house and property. You're looking for a box of that ammo and anything else suspicious. Call the watch commander and ask for somebody to help you."

She nodded and headed for the house.

I climbed into my car. But before I started it, I texted Bert Deming, the senior member of my CSI team. *Can you check the rifle and see if it's been cleaned lately?*

Sure thing.

Seconds ticked by. I drummed my fingers on the steering wheel, trying to figure out what I could do next that would be most helpful.

My phone pinged. *It looks pretty clean,* Bert texted. *But it's been fired at least once since the last cleaning. Smells like it was fired recently. Only one round in the magazine.*

Thanks. I need one of you to go over Councilman Hayes's entire study for fingerprints, and look for trace evidence around the gun rack. Now, before his youngest comes home from school.

I'll send Ernie over right away.

Barnes is there. She'll show him where things are. I want to know who has been in that room.

You got it, Chief.

I pointed my car toward Shands-Starling Hospital. My next move, I'd realized, should be to check on the mayor...and interview him.

I groaned.

At the hospital, the mayor was hopping mad.

Well, he wasn't doing much hopping, since he was confined to bed, one arm in a sling and wearing a too-large hospital gown, which very likely would fall off his skinny shoulders if he tried to hop.

But he was royally pissed—red faced and spitting a little as he yelled at me.

"What the hell have you been doing, Chief? Why didn't you find this bastard before he got another shot at me?"

Heat and pressure built in my chest as several retorts crossed my mind. I ignored all of them and tamped down the anger. "What were you doing in that clearing at the park, Mr. Mayor?"

He spluttered, his face turning even redder. "None of your business."

A surge of heat. I clamped my mouth shut for a second, lest my thoughts escape.

"Sir," I said in the mildest of voices, "I'm afraid it is my business, since it's my job to find out who shot you."

"If you'd been doing your job, you would've had the asshole in custody by now."

"Sir," I said, through clenched teeth, *"why* were you in the park?"

He scowled, but this time he answered, "To meet someone."

"Who and why?"

"Mark Hayes, and I don't know why. He said he had to talk to me away from the municipal building, where we wouldn't be overheard."

The pressure in my chest moved southward and morphed into a churning feeling in my stomach. "Hayes set up the meet? He called you?"

"That's what I said, wasn't it?" he snapped.

"You talked to him directly?"

"No, I got a message that he'd called."

"Message from who?"

"From my assistant." His voice had lost none of its sharpness.

"Your admin?"

"No, from Pete McAllister. He left a note on my desk."

"You're sure it was McAllister's handwriting?"

"Yes, of course." He glared at me.

I paused, half closed my eyes, and took a deep breath. "Tell me about McAllister. How did you happen to hire him?"

The mayor bristled, which was kind of comical since the hospital gown had slipped off one shoulder. Turns out, he has very hairy shoulders.

I stifled a giggle and waited patiently, stone-faced.

"I needed more help," the mayor finally said.

"Okay, but why him?"

"We, uh, ran into each other at a party a few weeks ago, at the governor's mansion. He said he'd done some political consulting, but was between positions at the moment."

"Political consulting?"

The mayor looked away, stared at a piece of machinery near his bed. It wasn't hooked up to anything—not exactly the most fascinating thing to look at. "You know," he said, "helping with decision making, being a sounding board, that kind of thing."

Uh, huh. I'd bet my next three paychecks this "assistant" was a campaign manager in disguise, so the mayor could get the city to pay his salary.

But now at least his presence in the mayor's entourage made sense.

"So, what exactly did this note say?" I asked.

"That Hayes wanted me to come to the park and meet him in those trees, with nobody else in earshot."

Hmm, and Hayes's story was that he got a call from McAllister, saying the mayor wanted to meet him privately at the park.

I decided I wasn't quite ready to share that tidbit with the mayor. He would immediately question his staff member, and I wanted to get to McAllister first.

"Where is Mr. McAllister at the moment?" I asked.

"Back at the office, holding down the fort. I've temporarily put him in charge." He waved his uninjured arm in the air. The hospital gown slid farther down his hairy, scrawny chest.

I wasn't sure whether to laugh or gag. Terrified I'd do one or the other, I muttered, "Feel better soon," and got the hell out of there.

Coming out of the mayor's hospital room, I stopped the nurse who was going in. "Was the mayor wearing his Kevlar vest when he was shot?"

"Don't know. The paramedics would've taken it off if he was. Ask them."

I nodded my thanks to her, deciding it wasn't that important—and I already suspected the answer was no.

Damn macho male.

I headed out to my car, contemplating why Mr. Mayor would have put McAllister in charge temporarily. According to the city charter, Mark Hayes was next in the pecking order, should the mayor be unable to perform his duties.

But he and Hayes rarely saw eye to eye, so Mr. Mayor probably wasn't officially relinquishing the reins of the city government.

My phone buzzed as I was about to start my engine.

"Found the ammo," Barnes said without preamble. "Out in a shed behind the house. Councilman Hayes thought it might be back there. The shed was his grandfather's and then his father's workshop, but nobody's used it for years, except for storage."

The sound of air being sucked in quickly. "And get this, the whole place was pretty dusty, except the floor had been recently swept. The ammo was in a drawer in the workbench."

"And whoever found it there," I said, "realized they'd left footprints in the dust on the floor, so they tidied up."

"Yup," Barnes said, satisfaction in her voice. "Five cartridges are gone from the box."

The four shots fired and the one left in the magazine.

But wouldn't the person who'd taken the gun test-fire it first to make sure it was in working order? I certainly would. Indeed, a gun that old, I might have rigged it to pull the trigger from afar, just in case it exploded.

But Hayes wouldn't think of all that, an annoying voice in my head said.

Shoving that thought aside for now, I asked, "Find anything else interesting?"

"Not so far. The place is pretty neat for a house where two males live, one of them a teenager."

I nodded, not surprised. Karen Hayes had been a neatnik. No doubt, the biweekly maid was still following her strict orders to keep the place immaculate.

"Meet you back at 3MB," Barnes said, "once we're done here." She disconnected.

Back at the municipal building, I hit the five button instead of three in the elevator.

Bonnie Burke, the mayor's admin, wasn't at her desk, and his office door was slightly ajar.

I nudged it open and stepped inside.

Peter McAllister sat in the mayor's chair, rummaging through the drawers in the desk.

He looked up and startled, his eyes going wide.

CHAPTER SEVEN

"Chief, what a pleasant surprise." McAllister's tense body language belied those words.

"Sorry to bother you," I said. "I know you have your hands full. However, the sooner we figure out who's going after the mayor, the sooner things can get back to normal."

He visibly relaxed. "Yes, of course. What can I help with?"

"It seems you're at the center of this meeting at the park." *The meeting that set the mayor up to be shot.* I left that part out.

Instead, I said, "Councilman Hayes claims he received a call from you, on behalf of the mayor, asking him to come there, by himself."

"Uh, yes, I made that call." His face remained turned toward me, but his eyes flicked away for a second.

"And the mayor says," I continued, "that he went to the park in response to a note on his desk, in your handwriting, saying the council chair wanted to meet with him there."

His eyes had gone wide again. "I wrote no such note."

I tilted my head slightly, giving him my best skeptical look. "The mayor seemed pretty convinced it was from you."

McAllister pushed up from his chair. "*I* didn't write any note, and nothing like that was here." He gestured toward the papers strewn across the top of the desk.

I took a step toward the trash can next to it, and reached for it the same time as McAllister did.

He chuckled. "Great minds think alike."

"Yup." I held his gaze and my grip on the can.

He let go and pointed to a credenza along one wall. "You can dump it there."

I gently tipped the can over the shiny wooden surface. Several pink phone message slips, a crumpled piece of white paper, and a banana peel fell out. I looked to make sure that was all.

McAllister started to reach for the white clump of paper. I blocked his hand.

Slipping on blue nitrile gloves from my pocket, I picked up the paper and uncrumpled it on the credenza top. On it were several scribbled paragraphs, the beginnings of a speech.

I examined all the pink phone messages. None were from Mark Hayes.

"Who's had access to this office since the mayor left for the park?"

"Mainly me and Bonnie, but we don't keep anything locked during the day. It's not like the City of Starling has top secret documents lying around." His chuckle sounded more forced this time.

"Uh, huh." I pointed to the top of the desk. "May I?"

"Um..." He scrambled back behind the desk, ruffled through the papers. "Yeah, okay. Nothing here you can't see."

A statement that somewhat contradicted his earlier comment about no top-secret documents. I made a mental note to talk to Bonnie about keeping doors to vacant rooms locked, especially the mayor's office.

McAllister stepped back with a help-yourself gesture.

I leaned over slightly and sorted through the papers. Nothing even vaguely resembling a "meet me at the park" note.

I took out my phone and called the mayor's cell.

"Chief, whada ya want?" he barked in my ear, his voice sounding a little slurred.

I should've apologized for bothering him, but the hell with that—I was trying to save his life. "Mr. Mayor, what size and color was the note?"

"Wha' note?" Definitely slurring his words.

"The one on your desk telling you to go to the park."

"Oh, yeah. It was yeller, lined, like froms a legal pad. Block letters, s'way McAllister writes."

"Ink color?" I asked, to be thorough.

"How da hell woulds I know? Black, I guess."

"Okay, thanks." I was about to ask about the order to McAllister to call Hayes, but realized I should've led with how he was doing. "How's it going?"

"My detail's drivin' me home. They was givin' me all them drugs at the hopspital." He seriously mispronounced *hospital*. "I dint like it."

"Okay. Is Agent Wellbourne with you?"

"Yesh, wanna talk ta her?"

"Yes, please."

"Chief." Wellbourne's high voice.

"Does Mr. Mayor look as stoned as he sounds?"

"Yes."

"Do you think it's just the painkillers they gave him at the *hopspital*?"

She snorted softly. "Maybe."

"How did they administer those painkillers?"

"IV."

"So anyone looking like a nurse or doc could've maybe slipped something in there."

"Possibly."

"Take a little side trip, to the nearest Jacksonville ER. Ask them to be discreet about it but get them to draw blood. Make sure what's in his system is appropriate and not excessive."

"He's not gonna like it," Wellbourne whispered.

"Tell him you are following my orders."

"Got it, Chief."

I disconnected. McAllister was once again sitting in the chair behind the desk. His face had paled under his tan. Only his neck was red.

What did that mean? Was he scared or angry? And if scared, about what...the mayor's safety? Could be. Or for his own job.

I glanced over the papers on the desk again. No sheets from yellow legal pads.

"Did you give my people your formal statement about the first shooting yet?" I asked.

"Um, no. It's been a bit hectic." Another forced chuckle.

"Okay, but I need the name and number of your dermatologist."

He nodded, leaned forward to pull out his wallet, and extracted a business card. "Keep it," he said, handing the card over. "I've got her number in my phone. Um, you think someone tried to poison the mayor?"

"Just being extra cautious." I started to turn away.

"So, back to the note," he said, "maybe somebody forged my hand-writing?"

I shrugged. "Can you think of anyone around here who might want to do that—set the mayor up and implicate you?"

He shook his head. "But then, I don't know all the players that well yet. I am wondering though, if the mayor's instructions to call Mr. Hayes were in response to the note, you know, to confirm the meeting. Now that I think about it, he didn't say *ask*, he said *tell* the councilman to meet him in Holly Park."

"That's possible. Keep your eyes and ears open. If you notice anything the least bit off, let me know."

He gave me a small salute. "Will do."

"Thanks for your time."

Back in my office on the third floor, I put in a call to McAllister's dermatologist. Checking alibis would usually fall to the newest of the detectives, either Wellbourne or Collins. But the former was with the mayor's detail and the latter was canvassing the neighborhoods around the park.

And I was too antsy to review incident reports, the task I should be doing. They would have to wait.

I was told the doctor was unavailable but would call me back during a break between patients.

"How soon?" I asked.

"About twenty minutes."

I hung up, then twirled a pen through my fingers like a mini baton. *What a mess.*

The note—which had supposedly been on the mayor's desk and now had conveniently disappeared—indicated that the attacks were an inside job. Or at least an insider was aiding and abetting whoever was after Mr. Mayor.

And McAllister's explanation worked. The mayor might have told him to call Hayes, meaning it to be a confirmation of their meeting. Only Hayes didn't know what it was about and thought the mayor was initiating the meeting.

I needed to ask the mayor if he told McAllister to call Hayes, just to complete that circle. But that would have to wait for another time. Right about now, some poor soul in a Jax ER was getting an earful as he or she drew blood for a tox screen.

With nothing more to do at the moment regarding the mayor, my mind turned to Alvarez's felony murder case. I picked up my phone and called Derek the Geek, aka our sole computer tech specialist.

"Good morning, Chief. What can I do for you?"

I glanced at my man-sized wrist watch. It was only eleven—still morning, surprisingly.

"Good morning. I need some financial info on a street gang called The Pillar. They're white supremacists, but lately they've been recruiting Hispanics. I'm trying to figure out why. They're mostly active in Jacksonville and Raiford prison, but it's looking like they're trying to make inroads into Starling."

"You got it, Chief. I'll see what I can find out."

Bradley appeared in my open doorway as I disconnected. Barnes followed him into my office.

Bradley started off with his report, which sadly didn't take long. The search of the park had produced nothing, not even the second bullet. It could be lodged in a tree somewhere, or in the ground, or two blocks over in the wall of a house. The canvas of nearby neighborhoods had also produced nada.

I asked, "What do you think of the councilman's comment that no one was at the park when he arrived?"

Bradley shrugged. "It's mainly drug dealers and hookers who hang out there now, and mostly at night."

I grimaced. "Once this case is resolved, we should give some thought to how to reverse that, somehow clean up that park for legit uses again."

"It's also possible," Barnes said, "that someone put out the word for folks to avoid going there this morning."

Bradley raised an eyebrow but gave a slight nod. "Since it is mostly low-lifes who use that park now, there could've been word on the streets to avoid it, and law-abiding citizens–"

"And the police," Barnes inserted.

"...would be none the wiser," Bradley finished.

"Do another canvas of the area," I said, "asking specifically if anyone warned them to stay away from the park this morning."

Bradley nodded, slouching some in the comfy visitor's chair.

I told them about the mayor's disappearing note and the phone call from McAllister to Hayes.

"And you believe the councilman, that he did not initiate the meeting?" Bradley's tone was carefully neutral.

I sighed. "For now, I do."

"Did the mayor confirm that he asked McAllister to make the call?" he asked.

"Not yet." I opened my mouth to fill him in on the mayor's current state when my phone rang. The dermatologist's name appeared on the caller ID screen.

I punched the button for speaker, to save me having to repeat what she had to say to the others. After exchanging greetings, I asked, "Can you confirm, Doctor, that Peter McAllister was at your office yesterday morning for a yearly exam?"

Silence for a beat. "I can't comment on the purpose of his visit." Her voice was clipped.

I didn't take it personally. She was a busy woman.

"But yes, he was here," she continued. "His appointment was for ten-thirty. I was running a little behind. It was more like quarter of by the time I saw him, but it was a quick–"

She paused. "He was out of here a few minutes after eleven."

And the attempt on the mayor's life had occurred at ten minutes before eleven.

"Is there a problem, Chief Anderson?" the doctor asked.

"Oh no, just routine. Thanks for your time, Doctor." I disconnected.

"Interesting that she had all those details at her fingertips," Bradley commented.

I shrugged. "I told the gal the purpose of my call when I left the message earlier. She's probably the uber efficient type and looked up the time of his appointment and such for the doc." I gave Barnes a teasing glance. "Maybe I should try to recruit her, now that I have a line-item for a department clerk in the budget again."

I expected a smile or maybe a mock glare. I got a hurt look.

Oops, not something she's willing to joke about.

"Wellbourne called," Barnes changed the subject, "when you were on the phone earlier. They're keeping the mayor overnight in Jacksonville. The dose of painkillers was correct, but he's a small man. The ER doc thinks he may also be overly sensitive to sedating drugs. Some people are. Wellbourne's gonna sit outside his door tonight."

"Which brings us back to your question," I said to Bradley. I told him about the mayor's stoned status. "So confirming that he asked McAllister to make that call will have to wait."

Bradley nodded and stood. "Bert's gonna run the ballistics tests on that Mauser this afternoon."

"Good," I said.

"Oh, and the new dispatcher is starting tomorrow, but he's in today to fill out the HR paperwork. I suggested he stop up here to say hi to whoever's around, get to know some of the names and faces of the officers he'll be talking to when on duty."

"A *him*?" I asked. Women outnumbered men as dispatchers almost three to one.

"Yes, but my gaydar was tingling when I ran into him downstairs."

I raised my eyebrows at him. "Gaydar?"

He chuckled. "Hey, *I* can say it, even if you can't."

"Yeah," I said, "but even you need to watch who you say it in front of."

Barnes rolled her eyes, and brother and sister trooped out of my office.

I sat back in my desk chair and stared into space, contemplating the two cases.

Not much to be done on the mayor's case at the moment, not until we had some results—from the mayor's doctors, the ballistics tests and/or the new canvas of the neighborhoods.

Should I try to talk to Patterson, the detective who'd arrested Alvarez, and who'd taken a plea deal on bribery charges related to another case? Could I trust anything he said?

And would the ASA get bent out of shape if I talked to him? He was a key witness against my predecessor, John Black, who was also charged with accepting bribes.

I ground my teeth. *Damn it!* I hate complications like this. I had to be able to do my job, without being hamstrung regarding who I could or couldn't talk to.

My stomach growled. I shoved myself to a stand. Finally a problem I could take care of right now. *Lunch!*

Heading out of my office, I was about to ask Barnes if she wanted anything from the deli, but paused at the sight of several officers and detectives gathered around a stranger in the bullpen. All I could see was the back of a blond head and the line of the guy's shoulders, but he looked vaguely familiar.

Here I go again, seeing people I think I recognize.

Then the stranger turned sideways, and my heart ratcheted up a notch. "Paulie?"

He turned toward me and his face lit up. "Hey, Cuz!"

———◄O►———

We sat in my office, the blinds closed but the door ajar, inviting my people to knock if they needed me. Fat tuna sandwiches from the deli sat in front of each of us, but we were not eating very fast. We were too busy catching up.

"So, what made you decide to become a dispatcher, and in Florida yet?" I took a bite of my sandwich, savoring the little zing in the tuna salad. How did they do that? Pickle relish maybe?

"I saw an ad for an online course," Paulie said. "Only nine weeks. But they turned out to be pretty intense weeks."

He took a quick bite of his sandwich, chewed and swallowed. "As to why Florida, the climate for one. And the pay for dispatchers is fairly good, and it'll go farther here in north Florida. Cost of living's lower than in Maryland."

"Both factors in my move down here as well," I said. I opted not to point out that Florida was less tolerant of gays than Maryland. He would already know that.

"And," he continued, a twinkle in his eye, "when I saw that there was an opening here in Starling, that was the clincher. I'm still trainee status until I take the exam, though."

We ate in silence for a couple of beats, while I digested the idea that my cousin was now living in my city, and working in the same building as me. I wasn't totally sure how I felt about that. I loved Paulie, but he was easier to take in small doses.

"How's your mom doing?" I asked. "I haven't talked to her in a while."

"She's okay. Slowing down some now that she's in her seventies. And she's not happy about me taking this job. It's too far away from her."

I smiled. "Maybe we can talk her into moving down here too."

"That'd be cool." Paulie waved a dill pickle spear at me. "You broach the subject though. She listens to you better than she does me."

"Hey, speaking of you being down here, we need to set a few ground rules."

Paulie arched an eyebrow. He was a little older than me and a head taller. But his face was wrinkle free. He looked more like thirty-nine rather than forty-nine. His body was lean, his shoulders the top of a V that slimmed down to a narrow waist, almost nonexistent hips and slender legs.

"No calling me Cuz around here. I'm Chief."

He smiled. "Got it."

"No references to our family relationship at all. You don't want it to appear that you got the job because of me." And I didn't want to be accused of nepotism. I was even a little concerned about conflict of interest. The dispatchers worked directly for the city and Jan Richards was the head dispatcher, but I was unofficially her supervisor.

Did she even know Paulie and I were related? We had different last names. Should I tell her?

"No prob," Paulie said, bringing me back to the present conversation.

"Where are you staying?" I asked.

"In a hotel for now. I was gonna go apartment hunting this weekend."

I hesitated for only a second or two, but it was long enough for him to catch it. He held up his hand as I began, "You can stay with–"

"No, I can't. You are the biggest privacy nut I've ever known. We'd make each other crazy in twenty-four hours or less."

"I'm not that bad, and I'd never hear the end of it from Aunt Jean if I left you in a hotel."

"Well, I guess, but only until this weekend. And Cuuuzz..." He dragged out the word. "I have a ground rule of my own."

"What's that?"

"I'm Paul. Only you and Mom still call me Paulie, and I always feel like I'm five years old when you do."

My private line rang. Smiling, I reached for the receiver without checking caller ID. "Of course. I guess it's time to let go of that nickname...Hello."

"Ask him about the woman." A whisper.

I froze. "What? Who is this?"

"Ask him." I didn't recognize the low voice. It could be male or female.

But I had a strong suspicion who *him* was. My heart stuttered in my chest.

I jumped to my feet. "Who the hell is this?"

"And ask him who was the father of Caroline's baby?"

"Caroline?" *Caroline Baumann?* A murder victim last fall, one of Sam's cases.

Bile rose in the back of my throat. "What are you talking about?"

No answer. The line had gone dead.

CHAPTER EIGHT

"Who's Caroline?" Paulie asked.

I flopped back into my chair, willing my racing heart to slow down. "A dead woman."

My cousin's eyes went wide. "A dead woman?"

I held up my index finger in a wait gesture and called Derek.

"Hey, Chief. I–"

"Can you trace a call that just came in to my private line?"

"I can try. Back to you in a sec."

He disconnected.

"Barnes," I yelled.

She popped into my doorway. "Yes, Chief."

"I thought you were changing the number on my private line." My tone was sharper than I'd intended.

Her face fell. "Damn! I put in a request for it, but then with all that's been happening..." She trailed off. "I'm sorry."

I waved a hand in the air. "It has been crazy, but get it done. Now."

"Yes, ma'am." She disappeared.

It was a sign of how rattled she was that she'd *ma'am*ed me. She knew better.

I let it go.

"Sooo," my cousin said, "what's going on?"

I took a deep breath and blew it out, as I tried to decide how much to tell him.

Paulie's presence complicated things that evening, on several levels.

I'd ended up telling him very little, although I had admitted to having a new love interest.

My cousin had leaned forward in his chair, his face eager. "When do I meet him?"

"This evening," I'd replied. "God willing and the bad guys behave. We're supposed to meet for dinner later."

Now we sat around the table at our favorite steak house, while Paulie, uh, Paul told embarrassing stories about me from our childhood.

Over dessert, he said, "Did she ever tell you about the time she mooned a coach in high school?"

Sam chuckled and gave me an admiring look. "No, but somehow I'm not surprised."

"Not surprised that I did it," I said, "or that I didn't tell you?"

"Both."

My cousin opened his mouth. "Well, she–"

I held up my hand. "Enough, or I'll start telling stories on *you*."

Sam chuckled again. The waitress brought the bill, and Paulie, uh, Paul made as if he were reaching for his wallet.

"I got it," Sam said. "Consider it a welcome-to-Florida dinner."

I let it go, but I needed to warn Sam that Paul could be a bit of a mooch. I was hoping I would really be able to eject him from my apartment in the "few days" he had promised it would take to find his own place.

Paul thanked him, and we all rose. Outside, I handed my cousin my car keys. "I'll be along in a minute. I want to walk Sam to his truck."

Paul wiggled his eyebrows suggestively and headed for my car.

Arm in arm, Sam and I strolled in the direction of his small silver pickup. "You know those sightings I've had of your doppelganger, I think they were set up."

"Oh yeah?" Sam said.

"I got a call this afternoon, on my private line. A whispering voice saying I should ask you about the woman."

"What woman?"

"Each time I've seen your look-alike, he's been talking to a woman, but different ones. Different hair color, height." I paused, took a deep breath. "The voice also said to ask you about Caroline. Was she pregnant?"

Sam froze in mid-stride, then turned toward me. "Yes." His expression was grim. "Nine weeks. I was discreetly checking that out, to see if maybe an unhappy dad-to-be had killed her, when we discovered the connection to your case."

It wasn't in the autopsy report," I said.

"It was. I took out that page before I copied the report to bring to your office."

I pulled my hand loose from his elbow. "Why didn't you tell me?"

He and Caroline Baumann had dated briefly a few years back, and he had sworn to me it was long over before we'd met.

But was that true?

Sam shrugged. "It didn't seem relevant at that point, and I felt I should preserve Caroline's privacy. Nothing was to be gained, say, if her kids found out."

"How could she have gotten pregnant?"

Sam gave me a half smile. "Probably the usual way."

"No, I mean, she was in her late forties."

He shrugged again. "But apparently *not* post-menopausal yet."

I stared at him for a moment.

Another half smile. "I can hear the gears grinding in there. No, the baby was not mine. We'd only had sex once, many years ago now. I'd thought she would relax after that, open up more. But she remained secretive, and I wasn't willing to deal with that."

I nodded but didn't say anything. I was processing, trying to decide if I was going to let that seed of doubt the phone-caller had planted take root.

Sam shook his head slightly. "I get more than enough chances to dig through what people *aren't* telling me in my work. I want a relationship to be easier than that."

I snorted, and somehow the tension was broken. "Since when are relationships ever easy?"

His smile was full-sized this time. "True. But keeping secrets makes them far more complicated."

I took his arm again and we walked the last few steps to his truck. He made a show of looking Paulie's way, making sure he wasn't watching. Then he led me around the truck to the other side.

Wrapping his arms around my waist, he pulled me close. "I don't suppose I could convince you to ditch your cuz and come out to my place."

I sighed. "Maybe tomorrow night, but it seems rude to leave him alone tonight."

"I know, but I thought it was worth a try." And he kissed me. A soft chaste kiss...that slowly deepened, sending currents of electricity shooting in all directions inside of me. Heat built in my core.

He let me go. "That's to remind you of what you'll be missing."

I mock slapped his arm. "I'll see you in the morning. I'm coming out to the jail to talk to Patterson."

"Ah, about that felony murder case," he said. "Stop by my office afterwards."

"Will do." I stood on tiptoe to kiss his cheek.

But he turned his head and captured my lips with his again.

I was about to melt into a puddle on the asphalt by the time he let me go.

Another cold front had blown through in the middle of the night, dropping the daytime temperatures into the high fifties, and separating the native Floridians from the Northern transplants. The latter, like myself, still thought this was a balmy day by comparison to February weather up north. My only concession had been to wear my wool pantsuit, instead of one of the cotton or linen ones. But I'd felt no need for outerwear. Indeed, I'd only worn my winter coat twice so far this year.

I pulled into the municipal lot, spotted Mark Hayes climbing out of his car, and noted he was wearing an overcoat. Smiling, I shook my head slightly. *Thin-blooded Floridian.*

While pausing by his still open car door, he actually pulled gloves out of his coat pocket. And something else fell out, landing on the pavement.

A female officer, on her way to the back door of the building, called out, "Sir, you dropped something."

I walked over as he was thanking her. He bent down to get the object and handed it to me. "This was on my car hood this morning when I came out of the house."

It was a cell phone, a rather basic-looking one.

"I was gonna bring it to your watch sergeant. Could y'all see if you can find its owner?" Hayes asked. "They're probably frantic by now. I know I would be if I lost my phone, with all its contacts and my calendar."

"Sure," I said. "We can try. I wonder how it got on your hood."

"I usually turn my car around in the parking area, so I'm pointed outward in the morning. In recent years, traffic's gotten pretty heavy on my road during rush hour. It's a lot easier to be able to pull out."

I nodded, my heart aching some at the thought that his parking area, which extended the short distance from his garage to the street, was pretty empty now, with his late wife's car gone, and his two eldest children living on campus at UNF. Lots of room to make a K-turn.

"I'm guessing," Hayes continued, "that somebody put their phone down for a second to do something, maybe tie their shoe, and then walked off without it."

I promised the councilman that I'd turn the phone in for him.

On the third floor of the municipal building, I approached the watch commander's desk. Sergeant Lewis was on duty, which was a bit unusual. Normally either Armstrong or Johnson worked days, but the three of them tended to switch around as needed, to cover when one wanted time off.

Lewis was on the phone, the receiver tucked between his shoulder and chin as he shuffled through paperwork.

I dropped the cell phone on his desk and grabbed a pad and pencil from amongst the litter of papers. I wrote, *Lost in front of Councilman Hayes's house. Find its owner, please, if you can.*

He nodded without looking up. "Yes, sir, I understand," he said into the phone. "But we don't have any way to get rid of the squirrels in your attic." He glanced at me and rolled his eyes. "You need to call an exterminator."

We exchanged a small grin as I turned away.

And with that slight warming of the ice between the sarge and myself, I decided my day was off to a good start.

It was mid-morning before I could shake loose and head for the county jail, where my former detective was now a long-term guest.

Patterson had struck a sweetheart deal with the Assistant State Attorney's office, two years for corruption and bribery with one year suspended. To be served at the county jail, since it was dangerous for former law enforcement to be sent to prison. With good behavior, he'd be out in time to see his daughter graduate from high school.

All that was in exchange for his testimony against my predecessor, Chief John Black, who had been the center of the corruption in the department—passing on some of the bribes he'd received to certain of his underlings, including Patterson.

Ironically, Black was out on bail, pending his trial, while Patterson was locked up.

At the jail, I sat again at the large metal table in the Army-green room.

When the prisoner was brought in, I waved the guard away as he began to handcuff Patterson to the ring welded to the table.

The guard hesitated. I flashed my badge, and he nodded and left.

"Hey, Chief," Patterson said, looking sheepish. His rugged face was pale, and the orange and white striped jumpsuit hung off his frame. His dark hair had grown some—a little past his collar now—with more streaks of gray than had been there a few months ago.

"This is not a social call," I said, my voice stern. "I need to ask you about a case you caught last summer, the Navarro homicide."

He turned away slightly, swallowed hard. I wasn't sure what that meant. Did he care so much about my opinion of him that he was upset, or maybe embarrassed, by my tone? Or was there something hinky about the case?

"That wasn't my case originally," he said, his voice neutral. "Sergeant Lewis had rounded up two suspects. They both had extensive records. He'd already talked to them before I was given the case. They'd confessed and given up the third guy."

"And you interviewed and arrested Alvarez."

He glanced sideways at me. "I interviewed him. He didn't have much of an alibi, but I was inclined to believe him. But the ASA insisted he wanted to prosecute him on felony murder."

"Seems harsh."

"Yeah, and I said so at the time. I was reminded I was just the cop, not the prosecutor."

"You said he? Not Brenda Stone?"

"No, the guy before her, Newhouse. She came on board shortly before you did."

*Hummph...*and I'd thought Stone was a pain to deal with.

And suddenly one of those damn niggling thoughts jumped up and started waving its arms around. I paused, dragging it farther out into the light.

"We told him..." The answer one of the gang members had given when I'd asked who initiated their plea deals, them or the ASA. The *male* ASA, i.e., Newhouse.

"Was ASA Newhouse chummy with Black?" I asked.

"Not really..." Patterson trailed off. Then he turned to look straight at me. "But now that you mention it, Newhouse fluctuated between lenient and being a hard-ass. You never knew what to expect from him."

So he could've been in on things with Black, going easier on those who were paying bribes and coming down harder on the poor schmucks who weren't able to grease palms.

A pang of sadness. Normally, I would say all that out loud, using my detective as a sounding board, getting his feedback on the theory. But in this instance, I had to keep my thoughts to myself. Patterson was not one of *my* detectives anymore.

"Anything else you can tell me about the case or Alvarez?"

He thought for a moment, then slowly shook his head. "Are you looking into it because I was the lead detective? I swear to you," he held up his right hand, "I didn't take any bribes related to that case."

"Yes and no. Alvarez contacted me, claims he's innocent. And I can't really trust any arrest that was made on Black's watch, can I?"

He hung his head. "Sorry, Chief. You can't imagine how much I regret getting sucked into that mess."

I sighed softly and stood. "Yes, I know. If you think of anything else about that case that seemed at all off, let me know."

"Will do, Chief."

The guard entered, and I headed for the door. There I turned. "Take care of yourself, Patterson."

He gave me a weak smile. "I'm tryin', Chief. Thanks."

I wanted to talk to Alvarez again but not be obvious about it. Knowing that the police were revisiting the case might make The Pillar gang nervous.

I'd called Sam earlier to confer. We'd decided he would have the kid brought to the sheriff's office, where I could talk to him more discreetly.

I settled into a chair in the department's sole interview room. Sam himself brought Alvarez to me, in handcuffs and ankle chains. He sat the kid down across from me and raised his eyebrows in my direction. A silent question—did I want him to stay?

I shook my head slightly.

"How you holding up, Juan?" I asked in a sympathetic voice, as Sam exited the room.

He shrugged. "Okay, I guess."

"First, let me tell you that I am revisiting your case."

His body language shifted from vaguely sullen to excited. He leaned forward. "You believe me then?"

I held up a hand. "Slow down. Yes, your story sounds credible." I didn't tell him that it was strikingly similar to the victim's story. I doubted his public defender even knew that yet. They had a tendency to wait until the trial was imminent before they even looked at the discovery info.

I understood that their caseloads were horrendous, so why waste time on a case that might not make it to trial. But sometimes there was info in the case file that would obviously clear their clients—who were often languishing in jail until their trial date, unable to come up with bond money.

"So I am looking into it. But I have more questions for you." I paused a beat. "Did you know the name of the gang that was trying to recruit you?"

He tilted his head to one side. "Now that you mention it, I didn't hear their name until after I was arrested, when I was told that two members of that gang had said I was there, you know, when Navarro was killed. The guy showed me their mug shots. I told him I didn't know them, but he thought I was lying because..." He dropped his gaze to the table in front of him.

"Because why?" I prompted after a half-beat.

"Probably because he saw something in my face," Alvarez lifted his head and made eye contact, "when I recognized the tattoos."

"On their necks?"

"Yeah, the three bars standin' on one end. They were the same as tattoos on the guys who'd been harassing me."

"I want to hear more about that, but first, you say the guy showed you the mug shots. The detective?"

"No the prosecutor guy."

"The Assistant State Attorney?" I tried but was unable to keep all the incredulity out of my voice.

"Yes, but I can't remember his name."

ASAs didn't normally participate in interrogations, especially for something as low level as a drug deal that went wrong, even if it did end with a homicide. This previous ASA, Newhouse, may have been on the take himself. But there was also the possibility that he was onto something with this gang, so he took a more hands-on interest in this case.

"Juan, tell me about the guys who were harassing you."

"They had those same tattoos. I didn't realize they were the gang's tats until I saw them again on the mug shots. One of the guys had it on his neck but the other one had it on his shoulder." He patted his own shoulder, just above the bicep muscle. "And he had a sleeveless tee on most of the times I saw them." He paused for breath. "At first they were nice enough. They said they were trying to have more diversity in their group. I think they might have even called it a club at first."

"You weren't aware that the gang is known to be into white supremacy?"

His jaw dropped. "No. Really?" His voice squeaked a little.

"Really," I said.

He blew out air. "Well, that explains something. They got funny looks on their faces and avoided looking at each other when they talked about diversity."

"Funny in what way?"

"Now that I'm thinking about it, like they were trying not to laugh."

I nodded. That fit with what Diaz had reported. "When did they start trying to recruit you?"

"In mid-April. I remember because it was right after we got back from spring break." His face had a far-away look. He shuddered. "When I kept telling them I wasn't interested, they got nasty, threatened me. And then they asked if I had any siblings. I told them no, and they said, 'Well you must have parents, grandparents?'"

His eyes went wide, but he was still staring into space. "When they mentioned my *abuela* I got really scared. I told them I was leaning toward joining them but I'd have to give it some more thought. They said I had a week."

His face cleared and he looked at me. "But they never came around again. I figured I was off the hook."

Until they set you up for felony murder. I kept that thought to myself.

"And that night in May, you were home alone the whole time?" I asked.

He nodded.

"You never went out at all?"

Something flickered in his eyes, and a couple of seconds went by before he said, "No. I was in for the whole night, studying."

I frowned at him. "You better be telling me the truth, Juan. If I go to bat for you and you really did this, I'm not gonna be a happy camper. I'll be coming after your hide!"

Another flicker, more pronounced. I was pretty sure it was fear.

What is he not telling me?

He shook his head. "I swear, I was in all night. I was nowhere near the riverwalk that night."

Hmm... I stood. "Okay, I'm, still working on this, but I might not be able to come see you again. I don't want to draw attention to the fact that the chief of police is taking an interest in your case. So, sit tight, keep your nose clean, and I'll let you know what's going on when I can."

He nodded vigorously. "Thanks, Chief Anderson."

I held up a hand. "Don't thank me yet."

———◦———

Fifteen minutes later, Alvarez was on his way back to the jail, and I was sharing lunch with Sam at his desk. He'd gone out to one of the few fast-food joints in Clover County and brought back burgers and fries.

My stomach rumbled happily at the smell of hot beef and grease. I took a big bite of burger and chewed slowly, eyes closed.

Sam told me a joke. It was pretty lame. Good thing he'd waited until I'd swallowed before delivering the punch line. It was so lame that its very lameness made me laugh.

He grinned.

A sharp rap on his half-open door. A deputy stuck his head in.

We turned smiling faces toward him.

"Sheriff, we got a problem at the jail. One of the prisoners just tried to off himself."

My smile collapsed as my heart jumped into my throat. *Alvarez?* But why would he give up hope now?

Another thought made my blood run cold. Had The Pillar gang figured out I was poking around, and they'd decided to shut him up and make it look like a suicide?

"Who? And how?" Sam demanded, his face pale under his tan.

"Plastic shiv." The grim-faced deputy mimicked slitting his wrists.

My stomach heaved. I'd gotten the *how* part right. Definitely looked like a suicide.

"Inmate's name is Patterson," the deputy said.

My throat closed. *But not the who...*

CHAPTER NINE

The coppery smell of blood smacked us in the face as Sam yanked open the double doors.

Even in the county jail, Patterson was kept out of the general population, housed in one of the holding cells toward the front of the building. The paramedics already had him on a gurney in front of his open cell door.

His eyes were closed, his skin as white as the sheet tucked under his chin and the thick towels elevating his gauze-wrapped wrists. An oxygen mask covered his nose and mouth.

"How is he?" I blurted out, my gaze sliding to the cell floor. *So much blood!* I swallowed hard and yanked my eyes away.

"Alive, but barely," the nearest paramedic said. The other held up an IV bag of clear liquid.

"I am, *was* his boss. I'll contact his family."

The nearest one gave a slight nod and they hustled the gurney down the hall, a corrections officer trailing after.

Dear God, let him make it, for his daughter's sake.

Sam rounded on another corrections officer standing nearby. "Finch, how the hell did he get his hands on a knife?"

The CO's blank expression didn't change. A grizzled, fiftyish man with leathery, tanned skin and big hands, he held up a plastic bag. "Found it on his bed, beside where he was lying on the floor."

It was a thin strip of red plastic, a shiv—probably filed down from a toothbrush or a plastic spoon.

Then I realized the plastic wasn't red...it was covered in blood. As was the bed, with splatter all over the back cement-block wall of the cell.

"He had a visitor," the CO, Finch continued. "He seemed kinda down when he was brought back to his cell, so I came in to check on him. Good thing, or he would've bled out before anyone found him."

Sam scowled at him, not joining in his self-congratulations. He took the baggie and turned to me, handing over his keys. "Would you mind getting an evidence bag out of my cruiser?"

I nodded and jogged toward the front doors, trying to rationalize away my guilt. I knew I was the visitor the guard had referred to. Had something I'd said pushed Patterson over the edge?

The ambulance was pulling out, lights flashing and siren wailing, when I got to the parking lot. I trotted to the cruiser Sam drove while on duty—*SHERIFF* printed on its side in big green letters—and clicked the trunk open to grab an evidence bag.

When I got back inside, the CO's face was no longer neutral. His lips were narrowed in a tight thin line, and something flashed in his eyes. *Anger?* Apparently Sam had given him an ass-chewing in my absence.

"Tell me what you saw," Sam said to him now.

The man swallowed hard, his Adam's apple rippling in his sinewy neck. "He was lying there." He pointed to the floor next to the cot, where there were swirls and smears in the blood. "Big gashes on both his wrists." The CO held up his own wrists.

"Was he conscious, did he say anything?" Sam asked.

The CO shook his head. "He was unconscious."

"And you've got no clue how he got the shiv?"

"Probably made it himself. Pilfered a plastic spoon from a meal tray, maybe. He's been pretty down since he's been here."

Sam frowned. "Jail isn't most people's idea of their happy place." His tone was snide.

I was starting to feel a little sorry for this guy, Finch.

Sam turned to me. "Can I borrow your crime scene guys?"

"I can spare at least one of them."

He nodded. To the CO, he said, "Seal this area off until the CSI techs are finished."

He turned on his heel and marched away. I followed.

The jail superintendent—tall, with a paunch and thinning hair, and wearing a cheap gray suit—caught up with us at the front doors. He paled when he saw me.

But I wasn't the one he needed to worry about.

"Where the hell have you been?" Sam snapped at him.

A brief hesitation. "Um, arranging for the clean-up company."

"Not until the crime scene techs are done with the cell," Sam said.

The superintendent nodded, his head jerking up and down like a bobble-head doll. "Yes, of course." He swallowed hard. "Look, I know I should've been there, but I faint at the sight of blood. It's a genetic thing."

Sam scowled, not answering him.

"I called 911 as soon as the CO reported it, and then called your office."

"The CO didn't call 911?" I asked. That would've sped things along some.

"No, he said he was trying to put pressure on the wounds, to slow the bleeding."

Hmm, just as easy to call 911 as to call you. I kept that thought to myself for now.

Scowling, Sam strode past the super, and I trailed him out into the February sunshine.

It wasn't the weak excuse for sunny I'd be getting if I were in Maryland right now. Down here the sun was intense year round. I welcomed the life-affirming warmth on my face.

We stood on the sidewalk, Sam silent beside me, as I made phone calls. The first was to Barnes. I succinctly filled her in and told her to get in touch with Patterson's ex-wife. Best for her to break it to their daughter that her dad was on death's door.

Then I called Bert Deming. "Can one or both of you come to the jail?" I said without preamble.

"Both of us, if it's important," he said.

"It's important." I brought him up to speed, adding, "Be sure to check for bloody rags or anything that could've been used to put pressure on the wounds."

"You got it, Chief." His voice was grim.

I disconnected, my heart heavy in my chest. This was going to hit the department hard. Even a disgraced ex-member of the force was too close to home, and Patterson had been with the Starling PD for a long time.

"So, you're smelling something as well?" Sam said.

"Smelling?" All I could smell was the cloying coppery stench of blood. It would be awhile before I could get it out of my nostrils. I debated if I had time to go home to shower and change, even though I didn't have any blood on me.

"Something fishy," Sam clarified. "Why did the CO call his boss first? And why wasn't he bloodier than he was? I only saw a few smears on his pants and hands."

"Yeah, me too."

"And what was that bullshit from the super about fainting at the sight of blood, and it being genetic?"

"That last part's actually true," I said. "My aunt's that way, and so was my grandfather. My aunt's doctor told her it was genetic."

And it dawned on me...could that be the reason I still got queasy and lightheaded at autopsies, no matter how many I'd witnessed? Had I inherited some of those genes?

Sam gave me a weak smile as we headed for his cruiser. "Well, the good news is we both kept our lunch down."

I snorted. "Barely."

———◆———

"This is crazy," I said from Sam's passenger seat. "It doesn't make sense."

"Suicide rarely does," he replied in a sad voice.

"Yes, but he's already served a third of his sentence, only eight months to go. And there's his daughter." I didn't tell Sam that I'd been beating myself up for the last ten minutes, wondering if I had somehow pushed an already unstable man over the edge.

But Patterson had to have already been contemplating suicide, or why would he have made the shiv?

We had reached the sheriff department's parking lot. Sam stopped the cruiser, cut the engine. "You wanna finish lunch?"

I grimaced. "I've kinda lost my appetite."

"Me too," Sam said. "Call you later." He leaned over, lips puckered.

I glanced out the windshield. Several deputies were wandering in and out of the building. "No PDAs, remember?"

Sam followed my line of vision. "Do you really care if they see a little peck?"

I shook my head slightly. "Things are too unstable right now in Starling, with the mayor in the hospital..."

"And someone's trying to kill him." Sam finished my sentence as he leaned back in his seat again. "Maybe his opponent in the upcoming election."

"I don't think it's Hayes."

"Why not?"

"Because he's not a stupid man. Would you shoot a rival with an antique gun, which half the city knows you own, and then just leave it lying under a bush?"

"Not unless I'd lost my mind."

I paused, trying to wrap my mind around this latest development with Patterson. "I'm thinking I need to talk to John Black. Some of this could link back to him, or maybe all of it does."

"Reprisal because the mayor forced him to retire and lose out on all those lucrative bribes?" Sam's tone was a bit skeptical.

"Maybe, and/or he paid someone to take Patterson out so he couldn't testify against him."

"The ASA isn't going to like it if you talk to Black, not with him formally under indictment now."

I pursed my lips. "I know, but it feels like there's a big piece of the picture missing, maybe several big pieces. I can't ignore a possible source of information. Not with the mayor's life on the line...and maybe Patterson's as well."

"That's a great argument to give her if she refuses to grant your request to see him."

"Oh, I'm not *requesting* anything. This is an ask-for-forgive-ness-not-permission situation if there ever was one."

Sam grinned, then his face sobered. "I think you need back-up though. I should go with you."

I scowled at him and opened my mouth.

He held up a hand. "I'm not being protective. But I think he'll be more respectful if we're both there, showing a united front. He'll be more likely to put on his public Mr. Nice Guy persona and at least pretend to be cooperative."

"He *has* a Mr. Nice Guy persona? I've never seen it."

"My point exactly," he said. "When it's only the two of you, he treats you with disdain, doesn't he?"

I let my frown acknowledge the truth of that. "Okay, when do you want to do it?"

"No time like the present. You wanna grab your car and follow me?"

"Who says you get to lead?" I said with a perfectly serious expression.

He gave me a startled look. "You can lead if you want?"

I punched his arm. "Gotcha!"

He threw his head back and laughed.

And something warm and gooey invaded my chest.

<hr>

John Black ushered us into a dark but spacious study. The walls were paneled in walnut, the furniture polished mahogany and black leather. A man cave if there ever was one.

He gestured toward two overstuffed leather armchairs and settled his large bulk on a matching loveseat. "What can I do for you, folks?" he asked, his tone fake jovial.

His face was broad and florid, and his hair a too-solid brown—no doubt a homegrown dye job. It was combed in such a way to disguise a receding hairline.

I leaned forward slightly. "Mr. Black–"

He held up a hand to interrupt. "Call me Chief, Judy. Everybody does. Is it okay if I call you Judy?"

I clenched my teeth behind a neutral expression. *No, everybody calls me Chief now. And nobody calls me Judy.*

"John, she goes by Judith," Sam said in a deceptively calm tone, then continued, "You probably haven't heard yet, but Jim Patterson–"

"Slit his wrists," Black said.

Doesn't this man ever let anybody finish their sentence?

"Yeah, I heard." Black shook his big head slowly. "Sad business. And with that little girl of his coming down the homestretch in high school. Bad time to lose her dad."

Sam and I exchanged a quick sideways glance. *He doesn't know that Patterson survived.*

If we got nothing else out of the man, the trip here was worth that tidbit.

"You ask me," Black was saying, "he took the coward's way out, abandoning his family that way. A man should always put his family first."

"That's a little harsh, John," Sam said, his voice gentle.

"Might be, but I tell it like it is. If he'd a hung on for a bit, I would've cleared us both."

"How so?" Sam said, sounding genuinely curious.

I should've been miffed at him for taking the lead. But then again, Black was responding to him. I kept still.

"The ASA doesn't have a very good case." Black made a scoffing noise. "A bunch of deleted first drafts of emails, dragged out of my cyber trash can and taken out of context. Harumph."

He leaned back and threw a thick arm over the back of the loveseat. "Once we'd gotten my case dismissed, I was gonna have my lawyer get Patterson's confession thrown out, on the grounds that he was coerced."

I opened my mouth to protest, since I was the one who'd interviewed Patterson, and I had *not* coerced him.

Sam shot me a look. I closed my mouth again, and almost laughed out loud. He was playing this guy like a fiddle.

Sam leaned forward, elbows on his knees. "You worked with Patterson for a long time. Anybody who'd have it in for him?"

"Why?" Black asked. "I thought it was suicide."

Sam shook his head slightly. "Gotta cover all the bases."

"Well, you don't work in law enforcement without makin' some enemies," Black said. "But I cain't think of anybody in particular who'd consider Jimmy worth killin'. Especially since he ain't police no more."

"Good point." Sam nodded. "Why kick a man when he's already down."

Black raised his eyebrows, also an unnaturally even brown, and his eyes bugged out some. "Ya know, I jest now thought of another possibility. Maybe Patterson somehow planted those emails, to implicate me. Maybe he was takin' bribes and figured he'd get off lighter if he could blame the whole scheme on me, if he was ever caught."

Sam's eyes had also gone wide. "He must've realized that would all come out during your trial, and his plea deal would be nullified. He'd go to prison for a long time, not only for the bribes but for trying to set up a police chief." His voice held a touch of wonder that Patterson would be so daring. "*That* would explain why he became suicidal."

Black was nodding vigorously. "That would explain a lot more than that, wouldn't it?"

Sam nodded again. "John, we also wanted to ask if you knew of anyone who might hate Mayor Daniels enough to want to take him out. You heard about the shootings, I'm assumin'."

"That's a bad business, for sure." Again, he shook his big head slowly. "Mayor Daniels has made some enemies, no doubt 'bout that. Lemme think."

The head shake, this time a little faster. "He's got some rivals, and folks who don't agree with his vision for the city, but..."

Would that be a vision of a safe city, free from police corruption? Of course, I kept that snide thought to myself.

"I cain't think of anything, though," Black continued, "that would rise to the level of motive for murder."

"Would you mind making me a list of those folks who disagreed with him?" I asked.

"Sure. I'll email it to ya tonight. And keep me in the loop about Patterson, would ya, Sheriff? I feel bad for that boy's family." He started to heave himself up off the loveseat.

"Chief," I quickly said, "there's another case I needed to discuss with you. We don't know if it's related to what happened to Patterson or not."

He settled back down, putting his big hands on his knees. "What's that..." he paused ever so slightly, then added, "Judith?"

"It's the Navarro homicide," I said, making my voice all innocent and sweet, "and the case for felony murder against Juan Alvarez. Patterson was the lead detective. Now that he's disgraced, Alvarez's lawyer might try to cast dispersions on the evidence against his client." I shook my head, hoping my expression was appropriately regretful. "And now Patterson's not going to be able to answer any of those questions."

Black nodded but didn't say anything.

"Are you confident," I continued, "that the case against Alvarez is rock solid?"

"As I recall, his two cohorts turned on him. Their testimonies are gonna make it hard to convince a jury that the kid wasn't involved."

I nodded. "Patterson told me he caught the case midway, and Sergeant Lewis had already identified Alvarez as a co-conspirator."

"That's right. That Lewis, now he's a smart one. You might want to encourage him to sit for the lieutenant's exam, and make him your Chief of Patrol."

Again, I wanted to laugh out loud. *Yeah, right!* I wasn't about to put Lewis—whom I'd already suspected of being buddies with Black—in charge of all my patrol officers.

Now that suspicion was full-blown, and I'd be taking a closer look at Lewis's record. My chest felt heavy. I hoped I didn't find anything out of line, not when it seemed like Lewis might actually be thawing a bit toward me.

"So there's nothing at all I should be worried about with that case?" I said. "It's about to go to trial."

Black pursed his thick lips. "Cain't think of anythin' that was hinky about that one. It was a straightforward drug deal gone wrong."

I glanced Sam's way, signaling that I was out of ideas to get any more information from Black.

Sam rose, offering the other man his hand. "Thanks for your time, John."

"No problem." Black beamed. "Always happy to help."

I did not offer my hand. He didn't seem to notice.

He ushered us out of the room and through his front door. "Thanks, y'all, for stoppin' by."

Once the door had thudded closed behind us, I said in a low voice, "I think Alvarez needs to be kept under guard. I can spare a couple of uniforms to help out. If these guys are willing to go after former police..."

Sam stepped off the porch. "Unfortunately, we can't be sure which of our people are in on all this."

I quirked my eyebrows at him as we walked to the street. "*Our* people?"

"Black's got somebody on the inside in my department. How else would he know so quickly about Patterson?"

"And my guess is that whoever called him was the one who tried to kill Patterson. But he, or she, didn't know they'd failed."

"They might know by now, though." Sam's expression was somber. "Patterson will need protection as well."

"You sound pretty convinced that he didn't try to commit suicide."

"We'll see what the docs have to say about it, but something definitely smells here."

"To high heaven," I agreed.

"The question is," Sam said, "was the attack because of the case you asked Patterson about this morning, or did Black try to have him eliminated so he couldn't testify against him?"

I grimaced. "It sure sounded like Black was building his case for blaming the whole bribery scheme on Patterson."

Then I grinned as I thought of something. "Black is gonna be so pissed when he finds out Patterson's still alive and we didn't tell him that."

Sam gave me a lopsided grin back. "Yeah, he is."

CHAPTER TEN

I was only halfway back to my office when my phone buzzed, Sam's name on my Bluetooth screen.

"The ER doc agrees with us," he said without preamble.

"Oh really?"

"As soon as they got Patterson cleaned up some, the doc examined the cuts more closely and texted me."

A beat of silence. "Well, don't keep me in suspense," I said.

"I was looking for the exact words in his text. Quote, 'The depth of the cuts are inconsistent with self-inflicted wounds.'"

"What exactly does that mean?"

"I don't know. I called him but got voicemail. I'll let you know as soon as I hear back from him."

"Okay. Thanks."

Back at the municipal building, I parked in my space and climbed out of my car. The February afternoon had warmed to seventy degrees, according to the sign above the bank across the street, and there was a soft, pleasant breeze. Spring was definitely in the air.

Smiling, I slipped out of my wool jacket, now too warm, and took a deep breath. This was great. It made up for the long, stinking hot summers—although I'd only endured the end of the last one, which had stretched well into October.

I glanced across the street again, and my smile faded.

There was Sam, walking beside some woman, and wearing his wannabe Stetson. It was part of his uniform, but he often left it in his vehicle.

How could this be? I just talked to him on the phone. Back at his office, or so I'd thought. But I didn't know that for a fact, only assumed that's where he was.

Heart racing, I ducked behind my car and watched them. I was going to get to the bottom of this.

They walked along, chatting, then stopped in front of a shop. A few more words were exchanged. "Sam" tipped his hat and walked on, and the woman went into the shop, a clothing boutique.

I jogged to the street. Horns blared as I almost got myself run over in my haste to get to the other side.

I looked up and down the sidewalk. No sign of Sam, or whoever the hell it was.

I went into the boutique. The woman was toward the back, rummaging through some dresses on a clearance rack.

I walked up to her. "Hi, could I ask you a few questions?"

She raised her head, a glint of suspicion in her eyes. "I guess."

"That man you were talking to outside. Do you know him?"

She frowned. "Good question. He said he recognized me, but I couldn't remember him."

"Did he say anything else?"

"Yes, he asked if I'd ever lived in or visited New York State."

My stomach clenched. That was where Sam was from. But it wouldn't be difficult to find that out.

"I told him," the woman said, "that I'd only been to New York City a couple of times, nowhere else in the state."

I nodded. "Did he give you a name?"

"Sam something?"

I pulled out my phone and scrolled for a good picture of Sam, without me in it. I found one of him standing next to a Clover County cruiser.

I turned it toward her. "Is this him?"

"Yes, but he didn't say he was a sheriff's deputy."

"He's not." Which was technically true. He was the sheriff, not a deputy—that is, if it was Sam.

I pulled out my badge. "But I *am* law enforcement. This is important. Was there–"

She waved a hand in the air. "I know who you are, Chief. That's why I'm answering your questions. I've seen you on TV."

I gave her a small smile. Those damn press conferences I hated did have one benefit.

"Did he say or do anything else?"

Her cheeks pinked. "Um, yes. He offered me fifty dollars to...well, if someone asked about him, to say that I didn't know what they were talking about."

"Did you take the money?"

She gave me an offended look. "No."

I wasn't sure I believed her, but if she'd taken the fifty, she'd reneged on the deal.

I was okay with that bit of dishonesty.

◆◦◆

Antsy, I wasn't in the mood to wait for Sam's call back. I got into my car again and drove to Shands-Starling Hospital.

In the ER, I asked around until I located the doctor who'd treated Patterson. He was thirtyish, with medium brown skin, a shaved head and kind eyes. I hoped the horrors he saw in his profession didn't someday stifle that kindness.

I introduced myself. "I'm following up on your message to Sheriff Pierson. Something about the cuts were off?"

The doc stared at me for a couple of seconds. "I'm not sure if I can talk to you about him. You're not family."

"Seriously?" I glared at him. "Then why did you contact the sheriff? And may I point out that if you are correct and this was *not* a suicide attempt, that makes it attempted murder. Are you going to obstruct a criminal investigation?"

The doc sighed, held up a hand and gestured for me to follow him. He led the way to the nurses' station, where he asked for a pad of paper and pulled a pen from the breast pocket of his white jacket.

"Do you know if he's right or left-handed?" he asked as he drew on the paper.

I closed my eyes, recalling Patterson holding his gun. "Left, I think."

"That fits," the doc said. "*Hypothetically*, these were the cuts on his right wrist."

I looked down. There were three lines on the paper. "All fresh?"

The doc nodded. "See that smaller one? That's a hesitation cut. He's got the knife in his dominant hand. He starts to cut, but can't quite make himself go very deep. Then he screws up his courage and slashes deeper, twice." He pointed at the longer, darker lines on the paper.

"You sound like you do think it's suicide."

The doc smirked. "Yes, all that's consistent with self-inflicted wounds. Now..."

He drew again on the pad. Two long, dark lines. "Whoever did this, they went for overkill, and that was a mistake. These cuts were as deep as the two longer ones on his right wrist."

"Okay?"

The doc held up his own hands, the right hovering over the wrist of the left, mimicking holding a knife "So, you've just cut your right wrist. Now you're holding the knife in that hand, which is weak because several muscles and tendons have been severed. There's blood all over the knife, making it slippery. And maybe you're getting lightheaded, and yet..." He mimicked slashing his left wrist. "You're still able to cut just as deep, and with your non-dominant hand."

"Shit," I blurted out.

The doc nodded slowly, his expression solemn. "I'm not saying for sure that these wounds *weren't* self-inflicted. But if I were a betting man, I'd bet in that direction."

"We found a plastic shiv next to him. Could something like that do all this?" I waved a hand at the pad.

Describe the shiv."

"About this long." I held my index fingers out, four inches apart. "Filed down to a sharp edge."

"Did it have a rough edge, like serrated?"

I closed my eyes, trying to remember the glimpse I'd gotten of the thing. "I don't think so."

The doc was shaking his head when I opened my eyes. "Cuts this deep and nasty, I'd say it's likely to have been a metal knife, and pretty sharp, maybe serrated. The cuts were a little ragged, but that could've been from hesitation."

I swallowed hard at the mental image of Patterson hesitantly slashing his wrists. I really couldn't believe he'd do that to himself.

Maybe the knife was pilfered from the jail's kitchen. Which a guard or a trustee could manage, but not Patterson. Unless someone passed it to him somehow.

"Thanks, Doctor." I gestured toward the pad. "And good catch."

He ducked his head and his cheeks turned bronze. "The wife and I are hooked on British mysteries. We've got Britbox *streamin' on the tele*." He said the last part in a fake British accent, with a small smile.

I smiled back. "How is Patterson doing? Is he gonna make it?"

The doc seemed to hesitate, his smile fading. Then he raised a hand and waffled it in the air, to indicate the answer was *maybe*. "He's in surgery at the moment. We've called in a specialist who's trying to repair the damage to the tendons and muscles. But he's lost a lot of blood."

I grimaced. "I know. I was at the scene."

He nodded, his expression now a bit bleak, and walked away.

Trying to imagine what it would be like to not have full use of my hands, I pulled out my phone to call Barnes. My eyes were stinging. I blinked hard to clear them.

"Hey, Chief. Where are you?" Barnes asked.

"At the hospital, checking on Patterson." Actually, I was headed for my car in the parking lot.

"Is he...?" Did Barnes's voice crack? I might have imagined it.

"He's still alive." I took a deep breath. "But it's touch and go. Did you get ahold of his ex-wife?"

"Yes." An exasperated sigh. "She said she wasn't going to upset her daughter at school. She'd tell her when she got home."

I shook my head. I knew their relationship was somewhere short of cordial, but still...the man could die. And his daughter had a right to see him before he did, to say her goodbyes if it came to that.

Not my business, I thought.

Out loud, I said, "Who's on watch right now?"

"The shift's changing now. Sergeant Armstrong is coming on duty, and Lewis is going off."

I knew the lack of a title in front of Lewis's name was intentional. Barnes tended to do that if she didn't like one of her fellow officers.

"Okay," I said as I unlocked my car. "Get Armstrong aside as soon as you can and tell him we need to put a uniform on Patterson's hospital room, and to make sure it's not someone who was chummy with the old chief."

"Oh?"

I knew she was questioning why the guard, not my reference to Black. She already knew he was as corrupt as they come.

"Yeah," I said, "it's looking like it wasn't suicide. Someone tried to kill Patterson."

I felt awkward making the next call, but I saw no way around it. I pointed my car toward the municipal building, then gave Bluetooth its instructions.

"Hey there." Sam's voice was cheerful.

"Um, I went to the hospital. I was too restless to wait for the doc to get back to you, so I came over..." Why was I explaining myself? My actions were perfectly normal.

"Anyway," I repeated to him what the doc had told me, finishing with, "I'm putting a uniform on his door as soon as he's out of surgery."

"At this rate," Sam muttered, "we'll have all our people doing guard duty."

I didn't say anything.

"Hey, sweetheart, are you okay?"

My eyes stung at the concern in his voice. "Yeah," I managed to get out.

"Is this getting to you? I mean, he was your detective, even if he did turn out to be corrupt."

"No. Well, maybe a little. But..." A lump in my throat, I struggled to think of something to say. "I'm mostly mad," I blurted out.

And realized the truth of it as I said it.

Yes, I was upset and confused about Sam, but under all that, I was *pissed*.

I had expected this job to be—not easy exactly, but a lot easier than it was turning out to be.

No one, not the mayor, not Mark Hayes, had warned me that I was being hired to clean up a corrupt department. If they had, I might have... What?

Would I have turned down the job? Probably not, but I would've come into it prepared, instead of getting blind-sided every time I turned around.

"Judith, are you there?"

"Yeah." And now I was doubting Sam. I longed to tell him what I was feeling.

Shit! For the first time in forever, I'd begun to trust a man, felt I could let him see me, truly see me. And then this.

Should I ask him if he was in town earlier?

No, the answer came back. Too quickly.

Was that my old distrust bubbling up? Or something else?

My mind flashed to my father coming home from work, and me, as a teenager, hiding in my room and listening for the timbre of his voice. Was he jovial or pissed at the world? And if I couldn't tell, should I go out there? What if I said something that would set him off?

Not that he'd ever gone after me.

"Judith?" Concern in Sam's voice still, but more strident.

My insides tensed. A flash of my father's arm high in the air, his hand fisted. My mother cowering...

I can't deal with this right now.

"Sorry, I'm kinda distracted. Traffic's heavy." A lie. "I need to go." I disconnected, my stomach churning.

By the time I pulled into the municipal parking lot, I'd managed to relax a little, my hands loosening some on the steering wheel.

My phone pinged. A text from Kate Huntington, the psychologist I knew from Maryland.

Just touching base. How are you doing?

I parked my car, then picked up the phone.

I'm okay, I tapped into it, knowing that was a lie. *In the middle of 3 cases at the moment. I'll call later if I can.*

No problem. Take care.

I smiled at the phone. Somehow hearing from Kate made me feel a bit better.

Is that because we're friends?

Gawd, I was so awful at friendship, I didn't even know what it was supposed to feel like.

CHAPTER ELEVEN

Contemplating those three cases—Alvarez/Navarro's, the mayor's shooting, and now the attack on Patterson—had me in a foul mood again by the time I reached the third floor.

Barnes jumped up from her desk as I strode across the bullpen. "Derek didn't get far tracing that call to your private line. It came from a disposable phone."

I grunted. "Figures."

"He's trying to find out where it was purchased, and with any luck the buyer used a credit card."

"Don't hold your breath." I walked past her and into my office.

Barnes followed me. "And nothing yet on that gang's financials, but he said he'd keep digging."

I turned toward her.

She had a worried look on her face. "You okay, Chief?"

I opened my mouth to snap at her, but caught myself. It wasn't fair to take my frustration out on her.

"Where's your brother?" I asked.

"Right here." Bradley's baritone from my doorway.

I turned and gestured for him to join us. "Close the door." Moving behind my desk, I added, "Let's hash all this through, see if we can make any sense of it."

Barnes dashed over to nab the comfy chair.

That almost made me smile. *Almost.*

I told them why I was at the jail—to ask Patterson about the Alvarez arrest—and what he had said. Then about our visit to Chief Black, and the doctor's assessment of Patterson's wounds.

"If someone tried to kill Patterson," Bradley said from his perch on the edge of his chair, "we've got two possibilities, related to two different cases. Either Black hired someone to take him out so he couldn't testify, or it has something to do with Alvarez and the Navarro homicide."

"Have somebody check for any ties between Black and the deputies or staff at the jail and the sheriff's department. Somebody had already contacted him by the time we got there. They were either reporting in that they'd done their job—they thought Patterson was dead—or they were keeping the old chief informed."

"I'll put Collins on it," Bradley said.

I pointed at him. "I want you to talk to Sergeant Lewis."

He shot me a look, like a kid who'd just been ordered by his mother to eat his peas.

I stifled a smile. Bradley and Lewis didn't get along all that well either, but if the sergeant had begun to thaw some toward me, I didn't want to undo that by dissecting his handling of the Navarro case.

"Get a blow-by-blow from him," I continued, "about how he came to identify Alvarez as being part of Navarro's murder."

Bradley nodded.

"Speaking of different cases," I said, "what's happening with the mayor's?"

Bradley said, "Bert and Ernie–"

His sister snickered.

He gave her a mock exasperated glare. "They finished up with the councilman's study. It was pretty clean but they found a few hairs and prints. They're getting samples and prints from the kids and the cleaning lady today, for elimination."

"And where's the mayor?"

"Still in the hospital in Jacksonville," Barnes said. "The doctors are running some tests to try to figure out why he reacted so intensely to the pain meds."

⚬

By four-thirty, Bradley had not reported back, and I was about to jump out of my skin. My mind kept bouncing from the Navarro/Alvarez case to the attempts on the mayor's life to Patterson, and on to Sam. All of those topics kept the adrenaline pumping and my heart rate up. I decided to tackle the issue that I could maybe do something about right now.

I closed my door, and then the copper blinds along the glass walls, turning my fish-bowl office into a cozy den. I wanted privacy for the phone call I was about to make.

I hesitated. Was I taking advantage of Kate, who'd consulted on several cases in Baltimore County...and had sometimes poked her nose in other cases uninvited? In all of those instances though, she'd had some kind of vested interest in the case. So I'd felt no guilt using her expertise to catch the bad guys.

But this would be the third time since my move down here that I was calling her for advice.

Then it dawned on me—I wasn't asking her about a case this time, but about Sam. Wasn't that one of the things friends did, talked about their love lives?

I texted first, from my personal phone. *Is this a good time to talk?*

By way of response, the cell phone rang. *Kate Huntington,* the screen read.

"Hey," I said. "Hope I'm not taking you away from something."

"No. Talking to an adult right now sounds like heaven to me."

I hesitated. "Why?" But did I really want to know?

"Oh, it's Billy. He's thirteen now, and he and some of his friends–" She broke off. A beat of silence. "But you didn't call to hear my woes."

"No, I... I want to hear them." That sounded pretty insincere to my own ears. Which it was. I'd rather eat sand, but I was pretty sure this was how friendships worked. You listened to each others' troubles.

And I was about to give her an earful.

"Billy and his friends," Kate was saying, "decided they are budding rock stars, so they recorded this song one of them wrote. The song is full of swear words. Billy recorded it on his phone and was playing it in the hallway in school for some of his other friends."

"Oh, dear." Did that strike the right note? It sounded like something my aunt would say. "Are they any good as singers, at least?" I asked, then thought, *Stupid question.*

"No! Their singing is atrocious."

I tried to stifle a snicker, but some of it snuck out.

A low chuckle in reply. "I guess this is one of those stories we'll tell our grandchildren so they can laugh at their father."

"What happened when he played it at school?" I could guess the answer.

"He got suspended."

Yup, guessed it.

"And Skip came up with the perfect punishment," Kate added.

Skip Canfield, her annoying PI husband.

"What's that?" I asked.

"Billy has to spend the day off from school writing a three-hundred-word essay on why it is inappropriate to swear in public, including what impact it has on other people. And it's gotta be good, and sincere, or he'll be grounded for a month."

I'd be grounding the kid anyway. But what did I know about parenting teenagers? And I had to admit, Skip's punishment was original and would probably be effective.

Was that warm spot in my chest for Skip Canfield?

What? No way!

An image of the man popped into my head. Tall and broad-shouldered, he was too muscle-bound for my tastes, but most women considered him drop dead gorgeous. He wasn't the least bit conceited, though. He didn't seem to realize he was handsome...

And thoughts of his broad shoulders reminded me of Sam.

Damn! Best get down to it.

"So, what's up in your world?" Kate asked, apparently agreeing with my unvoiced thought.

I took a deep breath. "Uh, I've got something weird going on with Sam."

"Oh?"

I told her about the sightings around town, always with a different woman, then the phone call suggesting I question him about "the woman," his response to that questioning, and finally my encounter with one of those women in the clothing boutique.

Kate listened patiently through all of it, making occasional I'm-still-here noises. One of the reasons, I guess, why she'd been a successful therapist—good listening skills.

"And I don't know what to think..." I trailed off.

"*And* all this is stirring up your trust issues."

I bristled. "Who says I have trust issues?"

A sound that could've been a soft snort. "Well, I've never known you to date before, and your only friends in Maryland were Dolph and his wife."

Dolph, my former partner in homicide, and my mentor as a newbie detective. I hadn't heard from him in ages.

Duh, maybe you should contact him.

"Okay, yeah, I'm struggling some with trust at the moment," I admitted.

"It is kind of a mess. But three things strike me. One, this guy you keep seeing around town, he's being pretty damn obvious."

Something I'd been telling myself all along.

"And two, Sam doesn't sound all that concerned. He thinks he's just got a look-alike. And–"

"But wouldn't he say that, all casual like, if he was trying to cover something up?" Did I really suspect it was him I was spotting and not some doppelganger? Or was I playing devil's advocate?

"Maybe," Kate said. "But a lot of men—dishonest men, that is—would gaslight you. Try to convince you that the guy only looked a little bit like them and you imagined more similarity than was really there."

I shook my head slightly. "I can't imagine Sam saying anything like that. It's..." I paused, realizing what I was about to say. I decided to say it anyway. "It's one of the things I lo..." No, I was not going to say *that* word. "I, um, like about him. He always takes me seriously."

And another niggling thought blossomed in the back of my brain. I tried to lasso it and yank it forward, but it stubbornly resisted. Damn these niggling thoughts.

"Third, the woman in the boutique," Kate was saying, "she sounded genuinely surprised that he was a sheriff, so he wasn't wearing his uniform. Can you imagine him wearing khaki when dressed casually. I'd think he'd be sick of that color, or feel like he was working when he wasn't."

"Hmm, it isn't a bad color on him. Goes well with his sandy hair. But, yes, when out of uniform, he leans toward blues and greens, like his eyes." I chuckled as a sense of relief washed through me, relaxing most of my muscles...mostly.

Then I remembered the baby.

"There's another piece," I said, "something else that anonymous caller said." I told her about Caroline's pregnancy.

"Oh, and that's another thing," Kate said. "If this really were Sam running around town, why would someone feel the need to call you about it?"

"Could be someone who's watching out for me?" Now I *was* playing devil's advocate.

Kate made another noise that definitely sounded like a snort. "Most people would mind their own business. And a friend, quote, 'looking out for you' would identify themselves."

"Good point. But I'm still..." I searched for the right word, "...annoyed that he didn't tell me back then about her pregnancy, when we were working those cases."

"Do you tell him everything about your cases?"

"Pretty much, at least the ones that have me stumped, or ones I think he'll find interesting. That's another great thing about our relationship. We're both law enforcement, so we get what the other one is dealing with."

"You've never kept something from him that you considered need-to-know or confidential?"

My mind flashed to a couple of such instances. "Yes," I admitted. "But I can't help wondering if he still had some kind of relationship with Caroline more recently. They'd dated a few years ago. Briefly, he'd said."

"You think something was still there?" Kate said. "Maybe casual, with bootie calls?"

"Could be. You know, friends with benefits. If the baby was his, it would've been conceived around the time that he and I met." *Not dating yet, though*, I added in my head.

But why didn't he tell me?

Kate sighed. "It's a possibility, but... I can't think of a positive reason why this person is calling, messing with your head, and trying to undermine your relationship with him."

That set off a whirl of emotions inside my chest. Apprehension, anger, and another I couldn't identify. "Good question. Why and *who* is doing this?"

A pause. "I have a wild idea," Kate said. "Why not ask Sam to join forces with you to try to find the answers to those questions? Either you will succeed, or he'll say or do something that gives it away that it really is him, playing games with you."

"That's a good idea," I said, at the same time thinking that I wasn't ready to implement it.

Kate would, though, if something weird was going on with Skip. She'd confront it head on. Of course, they'd been married fourteen years—a much stronger foundation of trust.

And more to lose. A part of me wanted to cut my losses now, just break up with Sam and be done with it.

That's crazy! More swirling emotions, and the thought that I was a coward when it came to relationships.

I shook my head to clear it. "Hey, another question. Do you ever get niggling feelings?"

"All the time," Kate said.

"I've gotten them before but they've been kinda bombarding me lately. What are they about, and should I trust them?" I was beginning to think that the stranger on the phone wasn't the only thing messing with me. My own brain seemed to be conspiring to push me over the edge.

"Actually, there is a neurological explanation for them," Kate said.

Ho boy! I never should've asked. I could sense she was about to go into professor mode.

"Lemme think how to put it," she continued. "See, there's this mechanism in our brains—an alert signal, if you will. I could tell you where it is but..."

Please don't!

"...you probably don't care about that. Anyway, it's activated when there's something in our environment that seems off, maybe something we didn't even consciously notice."

I thought about the niggling feelings I'd finally connected to the gang tattoo on Diaz's neck. "Like something triggering a memory but not enough to bring the memory into our conscious minds?"

"Good example. Anyway, that mechanism is very important to our survival. It can tell us when there's something unsafe around us that we haven't yet zeroed in on."

"Our instincts, then?"

"Exactly. As to your other question, can we trust them? Well, there's almost always a reason for them, but it may not be anything important.

Like a feeling that you've forgotten something, and it turns out to be something trivial."

"So it's okay to ignore them if I can't figure out what they're about?"

"That's the best course of action anyway, most of the time. Trying to force them into conscious awareness rarely works."

I snorted. "I noticed." Then I grinned to myself. "Speaking of noticing, have you always been a snorter and I just didn't notice it before?"

"Say what?"

"You snorted a few minutes ago."

She laughed. "Well, our relationship was a bit more professional before. But yes, I can snort with the best of them."

Snickering myself, I said, "Well, I'm honored that you now let me hear you snort."

We were both still chuckling as we said our goodbyes and disconnected.

But the light mood faded fast, replaced with worry and indecision and that other strange feeling I couldn't identify earlier.

A hollowness inside.

I thought about suggesting Kate's idea to Sam. That feeling intensified, along with a lump in my throat and butterflies in my chest. Was I *afraid* that Sam would say or do something that would tell me he was playing games?

The feelings intensified yet again, and my chest ached. "Yup," I said softly.

But was that outcome any worse than not knowing and living with this gnawing worry?

I wasn't sure.

I'd wait for now and see how things went.

CHAPTER TWELVE

I was staring into space, still processing the conversation with Kate, when my personal phone pinged on my desk.

A text from Sam. *What's up with your direct line?*

I picked up the phone and texted back. *Barnes got it changed.*

Duh, of course. Good idea. You free for dinner in a while?

Not sure yet. Waiting on a report from one of my people.

I could bring it to you?

My chest hurt and my eyes stung. This was such a normal conversation for us.

Give me a half hour. Let me see what's happening here.

Okay. I've got paperwork to catch up on.

Now my chest tightened with guilt. He was staying at his office, waiting on my decision about dinner.

And there was nothing at all stopping me from saying, *Sure, grab some carryout and come on over.*

Nothing except distrust, my old frenemy.

The phone was quiet, no more pings. Then the screen went dark.

A light knock on my door made me jump in my desk chair.

I snatched the phone off the desk and dropped it into a jacket pocket. "Come."

Bradley came in and closed the door behind him. He settled in the comfy visitor's chair. "Lewis was a little resistant at first, claimed he didn't remember the case all that well."

He gave me one of his half-smiles, one side of his mouth quirked up. "I reminded him that it was only last summer. 'I hope your memory's better than that when you take the stand in court,' I said."

Impatience surged but I tamped it down. Better to listen to Bradley's drawn-out story than to think about Sam.

"He replied with, 'I won't be testifying. Only detectives testify.'"

My mind wandered anyway, flashed to an image of Sam's smiling face. My stomach churned.

"At which point," Bradley was saying, "I reminded him that the detective on the case is in jail, so yes, he, Lewis, will be testifying."

Something he'd said yanked my attention back to the conversation. "Wait, did Lewis sound bitter when he made that comment about only detectives testifying?"

"Maybe. It's hard to tell with Lewis. He says pretty much everything with a sneer in his voice."

"Dear lord, I hope he's not planning on applying for one of our open detective billets."

"Would you promote him?"

"I might have to, if we don't have any other candidates who are better qualified. We haven't had many applicants."

Was that why Lewis was being friendlier? He wanted a promotion to detective?

"You'd think the climate here in Florida would be a draw," Bradley said.

"Yeah, but I can't help wondering if the word has gotten out that our department is corrupt."

"And/or that we're cleaning house." Bradley grimaced. "Who'd want to intentionally step into that mess?"

I sighed, waved a hand in the air. "Back to the case."

"Once Lewis's memory cleared some, he said the first-on-scene uniform reported that Navarro was still alive when he got there. He said, 'Alfie' just before he died. Lewis recognized the nickname, said he'd busted an 'Alfie' Taft for dealing once before. He tracked him to his girlfriend's house in Duval County."

Bradley paused for breath, then continued, "There were some smudged partials on a small bag of cocaine found in Navarro's pocket. Bert said they could be Taft's prints. Not enough points of similarity to hold up in court, but Lewis was able to use them as leverage to get Taft to confess and–"

I interrupted. "Why was Lewis doing the interrogation?"

"He said two detectives were out that day with Covid, so Chief Black told him to run with it."

"Do you remember any of this?"

"No, I was one of the ones out sick. The Delta variant, which was new at the time. I missed three weeks."

I shook my head. I'd still been with Baltimore County PD. We'd come dangerously close to being paralyzed by the absences due to Covid.

I pursed my lips. "Maybe Black was grooming Lewis for promotion to detective."

"Could be. Anyway, Lewis got Taft to confess and to finger Thompson. An eyewitness had said he saw three men running away, so Lewis pressed them both and they gave up Alvarez."

"Wait. I don't remember seeing any reference to an eyewitness in the file."

"Me neither." Bradley rubbed the back of his neck. "I was going to talk to the first-on-scene officer in the morning—he's on the seven to three shift. But I could track him down at home tonight if you want."

"No, you look as tired as I feel. Let's call it a day and start fresh in the morning."

Bradley pushed himself to his feet. "Sounds like a plan." He stopped by the door. "Oh, my sister asked if she could help out with the protection detail on the mayor's hospital room in the evenings. She could use the extra money."

I groaned internally at the thought of the overtime being shelled out right now. "What'd you tell her?"

"That she could take five to eleven, if it was okay with you. She's saving for first and last month's rent for a new place."

"Sure it's okay, but didn't she just move a few months ago?"

"Yes. She wants to get a place that allows pets, though." Bradley opened the door and left.

"Of course she does," I muttered. My assistant definitely had a soft spot for animals. She'd been the one to rescue Pipsqueak at a crime scene. But she couldn't keep her because of her lease's restrictions.

She's not getting the kitten back, I thought. Then shook my head at myself. When had I gotten so attached to that little ball of fur?

I began gathering my things to leave myself...and remembered Sam. I took a deep breath and texted, *Something's come up. No dinner tonight. Sorry.*

And now I understood the phrase, *heavy heart*. Mine felt like a lump of lead in my chest.

Even Paulie wouldn't be at the apartment this evening. He was on the three to eleven shift, training under the eagle eye of Jan Richards, the head dispatcher.

Telling myself to get a grip, I grabbed my laptop case and went home to my cat.

<hr />

By eleven the next morning, the word *frustration* had reached a whole new level of meaning for me. Cruthers and several uniforms were re-canvassing the neighborhoods around Holly Park. So far, no one had admitted to being told to avoid the park the morning of the shooting there.

Leaving Mark Hayes as our only suspect in the mayor's shooting, which I just couldn't buy. The case against him was too obvious, suggesting to me that someone was setting him up.

And Collins had found nothing that linked Chief Black to any of Sam's personnel. Whoever his informant at the jail/sheriff's department was, he or she was keeping a very low profile.

My direct line rang, *Bradley* on the caller ID screen.

I snatched up the receiver. "Tell me you've got something."

"Not much. The uniform we talked about," Bradley's mellow baritone filled my ear, "the first on the scene of the Navarro homicide—he didn't come in today. I called, got voicemail. No call back yet, so I'm headed to his house."

A soft rapping on the doorframe of my open door and Sam walked in.

"Okay, keep me posted," I said to Bradley, then disconnected.

"Hey there." Sam held up a white paper bag. "Brought sandwiches from the deli. Egg salad, in case you never had breakfast."

Good thing I'm a cop. I managed to keep my expression neutral. "Does an apple at five-thirty this morning count?"

He grinned. "Barely."

I gave him a fake smile. It felt more like a grimace.

Must've looked like one too, because he said, "Bad morning, huh?" He plopped down in the comfy visitor's chair.

He started pulling sandwiches and napkins out of the bag, and I couldn't think of any way to keep from sitting there and eating lunch with him. It was, after all, what we did almost every day.

"It's been a relatively useless morning," I said, while unwrapping my sandwich. I took a bite and chewed slowly. It was delicious. My stomach rumbled in appreciation.

Sam tore open a bag of chips and put it on the desk between us.

I took one and crunched it, then bit off another large chunk of sandwich. Eating was as good a way as any to avoid conversation.

Egg salad dribbled down my chin. Sam chuckled, as I grabbed a napkin.

Another chip, more sandwich.

Sam filled the void. "Looks like Patterson's gonna pull through. And by the way, I put that corrections officer, Gerry Finch, on leave. Paid, for now." He paused to take a bite of his own sandwich. "Your CS guys found some rags that Finch *might* have used to try to stop the bleeding. They had blood on them, but they weren't soaked in it."

I chewed and swallowed. "And they should've been, with all that blood." I took another bite, thinking that only law enforcement folks could talk about blood while eating.

Sam put down his sandwich and leaned forward. "Here's my suspicion. Either the CO was paid to take Patterson out, or to at least stand aside and let it happen. He calls the jail superintendent first, to delay the call to 911. Then dips those rags in blood to make it appear that he used them to try and help."

"That fits," I said. "He only had a few blood streaks on his pants' legs and hands."

Sam nodded.

"Hey," I said, as something occurred to me, "I wonder if this Finch fellow knew that the jail super faints at the sight of blood. By calling him and describing what happened, he pretty much guaranteed that his boss would steer clear of that area until after Patterson was removed."

While chewing, Sam nodded again, more vigorously. He swallowed. "I've got one of my best people looking into Finch's finances."

I took another bite of sandwich, and my phone rang again. I grabbed a napkin, wiped my fingers, and picked it up. "Bradley," I mumbled to Sam around egg salad. Then into the phone, "Whatdaya got?"

"Chief, this is weird. I was almost to the uniform's place—his name's Joseph Winters—and he calls me back. I told him I was coming to see him, and he begs me not to come to his house, said he'd meet me at this bar in Bennett. Asked me to make sure I didn't identify myself to anybody there as a cop."

The neighborhoods in the Bennett section of town ranged from solid working class to the working poor to the barely surviving. And most of the bars were in the latter two neighborhoods. "When are you meeting him?"

"In an hour. He said he needed to make sure no one was following him."

I grabbed up a pen. "Give me the address. I'm coming too. With all this cloak and dagger, this guy's gotta know something juicy. And you should have backup." I was also thinking that this was a good way to ditch Sam.

"What's going on?" he asked as soon as I'd disconnected.

I couldn't think of a reason not to, so I filled him in as I stood and pulled my Glock out of my desk drawer.

"Where's the bar?" Sam asked.

I read the address off of the sticky note I'd scribbled it on.

"That's a dive in one of the worst parts of town. Can I go with you?"

"What, to protect me?" I snapped.

He pursed his lips as he stood up. "Well, yes, in part. It's not a place a woman should go into alone, and you can't flash your badge to get the scumbags to back off. It sounds like this officer doesn't want to attract attention."

I opened my mouth.

He held up his hand. "And, if this turns out to be related to why Patterson was attacked, it's my case too."

I nodded, begrudgingly, and grabbed my jacket off the back of my desk chair. "You're a little overdressed though."

He glanced down at his uniform shirt. "I have a leather jacket in my cruiser, and I can take off some of the metal." He pulled his badge loose from his shirt and slipped it into his pants pocket.

My stomach tensed at how easily he had converted his uniform into just a khaki shirt.

I managed to keep my face and voice neutral. "My car, obviously."

The bar was indeed a dive, dark and smelly. The customers seemed to pull away from us as we passed through the narrow spaces between the tables. Was it because we were strangers, or had they made us as cops?

Toward the back of the long cavernous space, we sat at the bar. The bartender, a big black man with closely cropped hair and a goatee, approached. "What'll it be, folks?"

"Budweiser, in a bottle," Sam said.

"Coffee, please," I said, eyeing Sam. He normally drank Coors when he drank beer, which was rare. But maybe he figured that was too classy a brand for this place. We already stuck out, despite his battered brown bomber jacket over his now unadorned uniform shirt.

We were fifteen minutes early.

The barkeep brought our drinks.

"How are your burgers?" Sam asked.

"Juicy and cheap."

"Sounds good. I'll take one, well done. Honey?"

"I'm good thanks. Dieting." I wasn't about to eat anything cooked on the grimy grill behind the bar.

I suspected Sam didn't plan on eating much either, but the burger would give us an excuse to linger. He raised the beer bottle to his lips and tilted it up. But no Adam's apple movement. He wasn't actually drinking it.

I hid a smile and raised my coffee cup to my lips, but also didn't drink.

Five minutes ticked by. Bradley entered the bar, stopping by the door to give his eyes time to adjust to the dimness.

He walked through the tables and past our stools, without acknowledging us. He'd removed his suit jacket and tie and had rolled up his shirt sleeves, but he still looked out of place.

He settled at the table in the very back corner of the place.

Five minutes after that, a dark-haired man in jeans and a light green, long-sleeved tee-shirt entered. He also paused by the door, then spotted Bradley and made his way past the tables to the back.

I watched him out of the corner of my eye as he passed our stools. He was late thirties to early forties, fair skinned, and nervously looking around.

He didn't recognize me until Sam picked up his burger plate, and he and I followed him to Bradley's table.

"May we join you?" I said quietly and took a seat before he could respond.

He jolted, and his eyes went wide. They were a pale blue. "Oh my god. Chief? And Sheriff Pierson."

His head swiveled back and forth, checking to see if anybody was watching us.

I'd already done a scan of the bar before we'd moved. Everybody had their heads down, focused on their own glasses. This was the kind of place where people took their drinking seriously.

"What's going on, Winters?" Bradley said.

The man refocused on us. "I got a call last night, telling me to call out sick today, to say I have Covid and had to quarantine, so everyone would leave me alone." He paused, sucked in air. And nearly jumped out of his skin when the bartender stepped up behind him.

"Y'all need anything?" The big man loomed over the table. Winters shrank in his chair.

"No, we're good." I gave the barkeep a sunny smile.

I got a quick flash of white teeth in response and he went back to his post.

"Go on," I said softly to Officer Winters.

He shuffled in his chair. "I asked why and was told just to do it, if I knew what's good for my family."

"Your family?" I asked.

He nodded. "Wife and two kids, eleven and nine."

"Who was the caller?" Bradley asked.

"Number was blocked, but I think I recognized the voice."

"Who?" Bradley demanded.

Winters took another deep breath, straightened his shoulders. "It, um, might've been Chief Black." He glanced from my face to Bradley's. "Do y'all know why I'm supposed to make myself scarce?"

"Yes," Bradley and I said in unison.

"And when we're done here," I added, "You're to go home and pack up your family for a surprise vacation. Leave as fast as you can. I hear Disney World's not too crowded this time of year."

He nodded, some of the tension visibly leaving his body.

"You were first on the scene last May," Bradley said, "at the Navarro homicide."

"Yes?"

"We've been told there was a witness," I said, "but there's no mention of one in the case file."

"There was. We were back in the area the next day, doing a second canvas. Some guy came up to me and told me he saw three men running away. I wrote it up and turned it in as a supplemental report."

Bradley and I looked at each other and shook our heads. "Tell us all of it," I said, "everything you can remember."

"The guy was white, older than me—dark hair, kinda scraggly. He said he was across the street from the riverwalk and saw three guys take off running. Then he realized they'd left somebody bleeding on the boardwalk. He ran over, but some woman was already there, taking the guy's pulse, and she was on her phone. He assumed she was calling 911 so he chased after the men. But they'd veered off into the side streets and he lost track of them."

"Did he give you a description of them?" Sam asked.

"Two were white, one Hispanic, but he couldn't tell me much more than that. He said he never got close enough to see details."

"Hair color?" Bradley said. He was jotting notes in his pad.

"Dark for the Hispanic. He thought the white guys were blond or white-haired, but he wasn't sure."

"What was the witness's height and build?" Sam asked.

Winters closed his eyes, recalling. "He was about my size—five-eleven, medium build." He opened his eyes and shook his head. "I don't remember any other details. I included his name, description and contact info in my report."

"Which has since disappeared," Bradley muttered.

Winters's eyes went wide again, but he didn't say anything.

"The file said Navarro was still alive," I said, "when you got there."

"Yeah, barely."

"He said a name?"

Winters shuddered. "*That* name I remember, 'Alfie.' Then the kid just stopped breathing. The paramedics got there about then, but they couldn't revive him."

"Was the woman who called 911 still there?" Sam asked.

"Nope, but that's not surprising in that area of town. Nobody wants to get involved." Winters scratched his head. "I was actually kinda shocked that witness came forward the next day."

"Can you think of anything else?" I asked.

Winters sat still for a beat, before shaking his head again. "But I've got a throwaway phone, one that can't be traced readily. We bought it for my oldest son. Didn't want to spend a lot on a phone that he'd probably lose. If I think of anything, I'll call you..." He paused and gave us a small grin. "...from Disney World."

I took out one of my cards. It had the department's main number on it and my police-issue cell number. I scratched out the former—I didn't want his calls going through the switchboard—and added my new private line number. I slipped it to Winters. "I'll always be at one or the other of those numbers."

Bradley was tapping his pen point on his pad. "Who was the watch commander you turned your supplemental report in to the next day?"

"Sergeant Lewis," Winters said.

I stifled a snort. *Why am I not surprised?*

CHAPTER THIRTEEN

Back at the municipal lot, Sam and I climbed out of my car. I glanced across the street and thought I saw a flash of khaki. I blinked and it was gone.

Now I'm imagining khaki shirts everywhere!

"Next step?" Sam asked as we walked into the building.

"I'm going to call one of my psychological consultants."

On the third floor, Barnes was at her desk, doing paperwork. She lifted her head as we approached. "What's going on?" She'd kept her voice low.

I shook my head slightly. "Not sure yet. I'll fill you in later."

I would've preferred Kate but I knew she had back-to-back classes today at the university where she taught. Bill Walker would have to do, and he did have some expertise that Kate lacked.

He'd been our janitor for the last few months but had just completed a program that qualified him to do divorce mediation. And he was half a semester away from completing a master's program in social work.

A reformed batterer himself, he planned to specialize in cases involving domestic violence. But he was also a bit of an expert on Raiford prison, having spent a couple of years there for assault and battery, of his wife.

In my office, Sam settled into the visitor's chair and picked up his abandoned sandwich.

I dropped my jacket on the back of my chair and grabbed my desk phone's receiver before I even sat down. I called the watch desk first.

"Sergeant Armstrong."

"Hey Sarge," I said, "would you mind staying a few extra minutes this afternoon? I need to talk to Lewis before you hand things off to him."

"No problem, Chief. I'll send him over as soon as he comes in."

"Thanks."

I disconnected and made my next call. As the phone rang in my ear, I was hoping it was late enough that I wouldn't be waking Walker, since he worked nights.

He answered, and I settled behind my desk as we exchanged pleasantries. I told him the phone was on speaker and Sam was there, then said, "While you were at Raiford prison, did you have any interactions with a gang called The Pillar?"

"Yes. White supremacists. They tried to recruit me. I told them we weren't a good fit."

"And they accepted that?"

"Yeah. They made some nasty comments questioning my manhood, but they left me alone after that. I think the fact that I spent all my spare time in the prison library told them I wasn't good gang material."

"But they had some Latino members?"

"A few, and some blacks. They used them mostly for grunt work. Especially anything that was dangerous."

"Okay, see if this makes sense to you," I said. "We've got a white supremacist gang who recruits whites but doesn't pressure them. They also recruit black and brown people, and they *do* pressure them. I know of at least one Latino former resident of Raiford who was told join or die. He felt like the diversity was a joke. I'm thinking it's an attempt to disguise their white supremacist nature–"

"But everybody at Raiford knew what they were really about," Walker interrupted.

"So why the front?" I shook my head and mentally tabled that question. "We've also got a homicide of a Latino kid, supposedly a drug deal gone wrong. He named a member of The Pillar as his killer before he died. And he'd filed a complaint, later withdrawn, about a gang harassing him because he wouldn't join them." I paused for breath.

"The drug deal was probably a set up then," Walker said.

Sam had stopped eating his sandwich and was listening intently.

"Yes, probably," I agreed. "Within the next few days, the guy the victim named, along with a buddy of his, another member of The Pillar, are arrested, and they strike a deal with the ASA to turn on a third guy, in exchange for lighter sentences. This third guy is Latino. He says he'd also been approached and pressured by the gang, but he refused to join. And he swears he was nowhere near the place where the homicide occurred."

"Wait," Walker said. "That fits with something that happened in Raiford. They were pressuring my cell mate to join them, a black guy. He refused and was terrified they were going to beat him up, or worse. But a few days later, he's accused of stealing things from the laundry where he worked and he ends up in solitary. Plus he was about to come up for parole, and that was the end of that."

"So that's another way they seek retribution for those who refuse their invitation," I said.

"Yes," Walker added, "and it kills two birds with one stone. They get away with something because it's blamed on their resistant recruit."

"Or in this case, the gang members who killed the first resistant kid get lighter sentences by turning in the other resistant kid."

"That's a pretty slick setup," Walker said.

"Yeah, and these two bozos aren't smart enough to come up with that themselves. There's somebody else pulling the strings."

"Somebody smarter and farther up the food chain," he said. "I might be able to find out who that is."

"Okay, but be discreet." I was thinking about Patterson, whose attack might or might not be related to this case. "These guys don't play nice."

Walker snorted. "They sure don't. I'll let you know if I find out anything."

I thanked him and signed off.

Sam leaned forward in the visitor's chair. "At least some of the pieces are coming together."

"Yeah," I said, distracted by yet another niggling feeling. There was something I should've done, some lead I'd forgotten to follow up on...

"I'm beginning to think Alvarez may be innocent," Sam said.

"Me too." But it still nagged at me that he'd seemed to be lying, or at least not telling the whole truth, toward the end of my last discussion with him.

Sam opened his mouth again, as my phone rang, the private line. A phone number but no name came up on caller ID.

I risked it and snatched the receiver up. "Chief Anderson."

"Hey, Chief. Winters here. I did think of something else." he sounded downright cheerful.

"Where are you?" I asked, as I hit the button to put him on speaker.

Winters's voice filled my office. "On our way to Orlando. We only packed some basics. We'll buy anything else we need at the Walmart in Kissimmee."

"So, what did you remember?"

"The witness, he had a tattoo, on the side of his neck."

My heart kicked up several notches. "What did it look like?"

"Three rectangles, on end. One black, one brown, one a dark outline."

"With his white skin showing through," I said, a smile growing on my face.

"Yes. It was faded some, and his skin was kinda funny around it. Super white and dried out looking."

"Officer Winters, I'm putting a commendation in your file."

"Wow. Thanks, Chief."

"Stay safe."

"Will do. I made the hotel reservation in my wife's maiden name and I took enough cash out of the ATM back in Starling to pay for everything that way."

"Put in an expense voucher when you get back," I said.

"Really? Gee, thanks a lot, Chief."

I hung up the phone and turned to Sam. He was holding up a hand. With only the slightest of hesitations, I high-fived him.

"The witness lied," he said. "He was part of the gang's plan to set Alvarez up. But what's with the dry skin around the tattoo? It must've been pretty obvious for Winters to have noticed and remembered it."

"My first thought was that he was trying to get rid of the tattoo, with bleach maybe."

Sam nodded. "But why?"

"Excellent question," I said. "Got no answer."

Sam finally finished his sandwich and left. Once he was out the door, I tried to coax my latest niggling feeling out into the light.

That didn't work, so I began reviewing incident reports on my computer, hoping the distraction would lure it out. Sure enough, halfway through the third report the thought popped up, front and center. *Assistant State Attorney Newhouse.*

I'd mentally speculated, while talking to Patterson yesterday, that the ASA might be in cahoots with John Black. But the subsequent events had pushed all that aside.

I considered having one of our detectives check out Newhouse but decided that was a bad idea. Blatantly investigating an ASA was bound to come back to bite me.

Damn politics!

Then I thought of a better place to start. With Dot Wilder, interim Special Agent in Charge of the Florida Department of Law Enforcement's Jacksonville office. She'd been discreetly investigating the corruption in my department even before I'd caught on to it. And the evidence she had compiled had helped to make the case against Black.

I called her office, waded through automated menus, and charmed my way past her assistant. Dot finally came on the line. "Judith, how are things going?"

"Not that great. A lot's been happening lately."

"So I hear."

"Hey," I said, going for a semi-casual tone, "you wouldn't happen to be investigating an ASA by the name of Newhouse, would you?"

A pause, then "I can neither confirm nor deny..." She trailed off, a slight chuckle in her voice.

"Well, he might be connected to one of the cases I'm dealing with." I filled her in on the Navarro homicide and my efforts to determine if Alvarez was guilty or perhaps was being set up by The Pillar gang.

"The arresting detective mentioned that ASA Newhouse was overly eager to prosecute Alvarez, even though the detective thought the kid was telling the truth, that he wasn't even there." I added what Patterson had said about Newhouse in general, and concluded with the fact that said detective was attacked and almost killed shortly after I'd talked to him.

"Are you talking about Patterson?" Dot asked, her voice sharp.

"Yeah. You heard about that, huh?"

"Of course. He's my star witness in the case against Black. Have you heard anything new? Is he gonna pull through?"

"Nothing new today," I said. "He survived surgery yesterday. And I've got a guard on his hospital room door."

"I heard about that too," Dot said. "Thanks. You beat me to it."

"So, if this kid is being set up, what are the odds that Newhouse was in on it?"

The sound of air being blown out in a sigh. "Probably good, but I can't prove it. And please don't repeat that to another living soul."

"Would he be likely to set up a hit on Patterson because I was talking to him about that case?"

A short pause, then she said, "We thought Black tried to take Patterson out."

"That's the other possibility, but the timing is awfully suspicious. It was maybe an hour and a half between when I talked to him at the jail and the call that he'd supposedly tried to kill himself."

Another sigh. "I don't see Newhouse getting his hands dirty. We think Black set up most of the network of corruption, and the ASA was just one cog. But we've been monitoring Newhouse's finances. I'll see if he came into any significant money around the time Alvarez was indicted."

"Thanks, that would be a big help. Here's another question though—why would Newhouse transfer to another district if he had regular bribes coming in through Black?"

"Because your mayor asked the Attorney General herself to transfer him."

"Hoho, the same mayor that someone's been taking potshots at?"

"One and the same. Mayor Daniels."

"So the attacks on him could be reprisal for disrupting that part of their bribery network?"

"Maybe," Dot said. "But again, I can see Black hiring someone to go after Daniels. Newhouse, not so much. My guess is that he's keeping his nose clean and praying that nobody catches on to the bribes he's taken in the past."

"Okay, can you let me know if you turn up anything that might be helpful to my case, or should I say to any of my cases?"

"Absolutely. But Judith...check with me before you talk to Black again, and stay away from Newhouse. I don't want him suspicious that we're on to him."

I thought for a moment, trying to decide if I was willing to promise that. "For now," I said, "we'll work on it from the other end. See if any of our other persons of interest have ties to either of them."

"Good. I'll buy you lunch once all this is over."

My turn to sigh. "I'm not sure it's ever going to be over. Every time I think I've dug up all the corruption, I turn over another rock and something slithers out from under it."

"Hang in there," Dot said. "We'll get them all eventually."

"If you say so." We disconnected.

With another sigh, I turned back to my incident reports.

⸺◦⸺

At ten of three, Sergeant Lewis appeared in my doorway. "You wanted to see me, Chief?"

I motioned for him to come in while I called Bradley and told him to join us.

I gestured for Lewis to take the comfy chair. Normally it would be Bradley's as the higher ranking officer, but I was hoping to encourage the thawing process.

A few seconds later, the lieutenant came in and closed the door behind him. He eschewed the uncomfortable chairs and mimicked his sister's usual stance, leaning against the doorjamb.

"Sarge, we've got a discrepancy in the Navarro file," I said in a neutral voice. "You told the lieutenant there was a witness, but there's no mention of him in the file. We both double checked."

Lewis shrugged. "I added the officer's follow-up report to the file. Don't know what might have happened to it."

I suspected Chief Black had removed it for some reason, but I kept that thought to myself.

"You also told Bradley that Alfie Taft fingered the other guy, after you'd interrogated him for some time."

"The *lieuutenant...*" Lewis dragged out Bradley's title, a slight sneer in his voice, "must have misunderstood me. I'd busted Alfie before and knew he and Thompson were 'known associates.'" He made air quotes. "I brought him in and sweated him until he confessed and fingered Alvarez as the third guy."

"I'm surprised they didn't ask for lawyers," I said.

"I was too, but then these gang members, they don't care all that much whether they're in prison or not. They've got a pretty sweet set-up on the inside."

I cocked my head to one side. "Oh?"

Lewis shifted in his chair, suddenly a bit uncomfortable. "Yeah, I mean the gangs have a lot of power in there. And of course, drugs are rampant."

I wondered if he'd meant more than that. "So you knew Taft and Thompson were gang members...but you told me before that you didn't think The Pillar was active in Starling."

Lewis's eyes went wide. "Well, I figured they were in a gang, with all their tats, but I didn't know it was that particular gang."

"I see." I digested that for a beat. Okay, I'd buy it. The Pillar tattoos weren't all that noticeable, with all the other ink on their necks. And when you're interrogating a suspect, the side of their neck is the last thing you're looking for.

Then again, he couldn't have done a very thorough check into their records if he'd missed their gang affiliation. But he had been pinch-hitting—he wasn't trained as a detective.

Lewis rustled in his chair. His semi-permanent smirk was drooping.

I opted to move on. "Did you ever talk to the witness?"

"No. Detective Patterson took over the case before I got a chance to do that. I assumed he would follow up."

Uh, huh... But Patterson hadn't said anything to me about an eyewitness who saw three men running away. Which made me even more suspicious that Officer Winters's report had been removed *before* the case was turned over to the detective.

But the royal question is why?

"That'll be all, Sergeant," I said. "Thank you."

He rose and left my office, but his swagger seemed a little off.

I stood and grabbed my jacket from the back of my desk chair.

"Where are you going?" Bradley asked.

"To the assistant state attorney's office."

I asked Barnes to call the ASA's office and make sure she was in, but to not tell them I was on the way. I wanted the element of surprise.

I didn't hang around for an answer, though. Maybe it was having to be around Sam for so long—pretending everything was okay—followed by dealing with Lewis, but I felt a sudden urge to get the hell out of the building, to get some air. Once outside, I walked toward the courthouse in the next block, and the building beyond it that housed the ASA's office.

Barnes texted me. *She's in.*

Thx, I texted back and pocketed my phone.

As was my habit, I scanned the area around me. Twenty-some years in law enforcement tended to make one hypervigilant.

I spotted a sandy head, above a long-sleeved khaki shirt, a block ahead. Several people were between us on the sidewalk.

I picked up my pace, passed a few of those people.

The khaki-shirted guy had his arm around a woman's shoulders this time.

I started jogging toward them.

The man glanced over his shoulder, too quick for me to make a positive ID. But he was white, and the jaw line sure looked like Sam's.

He said something to the woman. She peeled away from him and crossed the street, jaywalking in the middle of the block.

He picked up speed, power-walking now.

I broke into a run. Another quick glance over his shoulder and he took off.

I had closed the gap some when he veered into a building.

I raced to its glass door. It was a laundromat. I jerked the door open and bolted inside.

Several people looked up, staring at me.

"Guy came in here," I huffed out. "Khaki shirt?"

One of the women pointed to the back of the long room of machines.

I ran for a gray metal door. It wasn't locked.

Pulling my Glock, I eased it open. Beyond it was an empty and rather messy office. I ran through it and out another heavier fire door.

I was in an alley, and I was alone.

———◦———

I was sweaty and disheveled by the time I got to the ASA's offices. As I approached her assistant's desk, I straightened my jacket and tucked in my shirt.

"Chief Anderson?" the young woman said. Then, "Wait! You can't go in there," as I kept walking past her.

I knocked once on her boss's door and opened it.

Assistant State Attorney Brenda Stone was African-American, short and on the stout side, and she had a reputation for being ambitious. We hadn't particularly hit it off the couple of times we'd interacted so far.

Now she jerked her head up. "Chief, what the hell–"

"Counselor, I wanted to warn you. I think we may have been had."

CHAPTER FOURTEEN

In retrospect, maybe barging in wasn't the best tactic.

But I wasn't sure the ASA would have met with me if I'd announced my intentions. Prosecutors rarely like it when you shoot holes in their cases, especially ones that are going to trial soon.

Brenda Stone had adamantly refused to delay the Alvarez trial, even before I'd finished spelling the whole mess out to her.

"So who's this mystery eyewitness?" she demanded.

"Wish I knew," I said. "All we have is a general description, no name or address. And he may have changed his appearance by now."

"Well, find him. He might strengthen our case."

"Haven't you heard a word I said? Alvarez may very well have been set up."

She folded her arms over her chest. "That's not what the evidence says."

"Evidence presented to you in a neat package, by a now discredited detective."

"I don't need Patterson," Stone said. "Sergeant Lewis and the officer first on the scene will be enough to establish why Taft and Thompson were arrested."

"And if the officer or Lewis mention the eyewitness that we can't produce and who isn't in the case file?"

"They won't because I won't ask them about him. And I'll instruct them to stick to what I do ask."

Up to this point, I'd kept my cool, more or less. But... "You don't care that he might be innocent." I raised my voice. "You don't care about justice?"

I expected her to throw me out of her office. But instead she stood up straighter behind her desk and said in a pompous voice, "Justice is served when we follow the evidence."

I snorted. "What evidence? The testimony of two heavily tattooed gang members with records as long as my arm."

"And we've got the hair," she said.

I froze. "Hair? What hair?"

"Hair found on the victim's track suit, straight and black. The lab tech said they were a match with Alvarez's hair."

Again, something that was missing from the case file. But I kept my mouth shut about that.

"Which lab tech?"

She waved a hand in the air. "I don't know. One of your Sesame Street cl–, uh, guys, I guess."

Grrr. Had she been about to call Bert and Ernie *clowns*?

With difficulty, I reined in my anger. "You're sure they're Alvarez's hair?"

"Still waiting on the DNA, but they were a microscopic match. And the FDLE lab promised to have the DNA results by next week. They're running behind."

"You do realize that the victim also had dark, straight hair?"

Stone gave me a defiant glare. But then she deflated some, her shoulders sagging. "Look, I inherited this case. The plea deals had already been made, the evidence gathered. And my instructions are to finish the job."

"But you could ask for a continuance. I need more time to investigate and get to the bottom of what's going on."

She blew out air. "I don't suppose it would do any good to tell you to stop investigating, would it?"

I stared at her for a beat. "I have a detective in jail for corruption. Of course I'm going to double-check his investigations. You don't want one of them blowing up in your face, do you?"

She heaved another sigh. "Find that witness. I'll make the decision about a continuance after I see what he has to say."

"*If* we can find him," I said, exiting her office.

Back at 3MB, I called Bradley into my office and told him our new priority was to find the witness.

"Unless Winters can remember more details," he said, "we don't have much to go on."

"Yeah, and what we do have—dark, unkempt hair and a faint tattoo—may be gone by now. A shampoo and a trim would take care of the hair."

"And," Bradley added, "he might've found a better way to remove the tattoo from his neck by now."

Something niggled at the back of my brain. Something about necks... *Damn these niggling feelings!*

"Have some of our people check out tattoo parlors in the area. Find out if any of them have been asked to remove a Pillar tattoo in the last seven months."

"Um," Bradley said, "I don't think tattoo parlors do removals."

"Who does do them?"

"Probably aesthetic centers."

"What the hell are those?" I demanded, residual anger at the ASA making me impatient.

"Places people go to make themselves more beautiful. They do Botox and chemical peels and stuff like that. It's a growing industry."

I ground my teeth, then decided it was time to let go of my anger before I gave myself a heart attack.

I took a deep breath. "Oh, is that where you go to keep your boyish good looks?" I teased.

His smooth cheeks turned pink. "No," he said emphatically, but then caught on and grinned. "I'm naturally gorgeous."

I snickered, and another niggling thought presented itself. One I *was* able to drag to the forefront of my brain. Juan Alvarez hesitated ever so slightly toward the end of my last interview with him. *Had he been totally honest, or was he holding something back?*

"Let's talk to Alvarez again," I said. "Make damn sure he's telling us the *whole* truth."

"You want me to go with you and double-team him?"

I thought for a moment. "No, let's bring him here. Head out to the sheriff's department. I'll call them and tell them we want to borrow the prisoner for a while."

"Got it, Chief," Bradley said and left my office.

I texted Sam. *Hey, need to borrow Alvarez for a few hours, put a little pressure on to make sure he's telling the truth. Bradley's on his way.*

The response was quick. *Tell him to text me when he's here. I'll bring the prisoner out the back.*

Will do, I texted back, then sent Sam's instructions on to Bradley.

My phone pinged. Another text from Sam. *I guess this means you're not free for dinner.*

Nope, not looking good.

I tried to stifle the guilt that surged in my chest.

While I waited, I had Barnes call Bert Deming to come to my office.

"Wha' cha need, Chief?" he asked, standing in my open doorway, a tablet tucked under his arm.

I gestured for him to come in.

Barnes began to follow, but I decided Bert might not be totally honest if we weren't alone. I shook my head slightly.

She nodded and pulled the door closed.

I waved toward the comfy visitor's chair and asked, "You remember the Navarro homicide from last May?"

"Vaguely." He settled in the chair, put the tablet on his lap. "Do you have the file handy?"

I ignored that question for now. "There were some hairs found on the victim's clothing. Did you do the microscopic analysis or did Ernie?"

"I did, then they were shipped off to the FDLE lab for DNA testing."

"Do you remember what you found?"

He shook his head and opened the cover on the tablet. "But I can find out." He tapped on the screen a few times. "The hairs matched the suspect's, Juan Alvarez. My report wasn't in the case file?"

"No, and I can't figure out why someone would've taken it out."

He grimaced. "It might not have made it in there. Record keeping wasn't the greatest under Chief Black. So I always sent copies of my reports to everybody involved in the case. His clerk...she never did make the transition all that well to electronic files."

The clerk who'd retired at the same time as Black, and whose position he'd stripped from the budget, along with a lot of other things.

"You sent a copy directly to the investigating detective, Patterson?"

Bert nodded.

Hmm... Why hadn't Patterson mentioned it?

"Wait a minute." Bert swiped the tablet screen a couple of times. "That's what I thought. I made a note that there was no sample from the victim to compare and rule out that they were his."

"How likely would that be?"

He shrugged. "Hair analysis, on its own, is not exact—most judges won't allow it as evidence in court—without DNA to back it up. And even two hairs from the same person are not exactly the same."

He looked down at his tablet again. "I noted that I hadn't ruled out the victim when I sent the hair to FDLE. They'd have access to his hair, from the samples taken during the autopsy."

"Contact them and see if they've done that comparison yet."

"Will do, Chief."

Bert left, and I rubbed the heel of my hand against my aching chest. *Damn.* I'd really wanted to believe Juan was innocent.

———◆———

Twenty minutes later, Bradley and I were sitting across the table from Juan Alvarez, in our larger interview room.

The recording equipment was running, and we'd reminded him of his rights. The latter had caused his beige skin tone to pale toward ghost white.

"Relax, son," Bradley said with a small smile. "We're on your side."

I wouldn't be too sure of that at this point, I thought, but I also smiled.

Alvarez gave us a tense smile back, then dropped his gaze to his hands folded in front of him on the table. We'd removed his handcuffs once in the room.

It was a slight risk, especially since there was no one in the observation booth—Barnes had gone on to her shift with the mayor's bodyguard detail. But we were two against one, and I didn't expect the kid to try anything.

Alvarez swallowed hard, his Adam's apple bobbing in his skinny neck. "I'm sorry." His voice quavered a little. "It just made me nervous, when the sheriff took me out the back and handed me over to someone I'd never seen before."

My heart rate kicked up a notch. *Did he know something about The Pillar possibly infiltrating the jail staff and/or the sheriff's department?*

"You don't feel safe at the jail?" I asked.

"Well, yeah, now I do," he said. "Because there's either a deputy or one of your officers in front of my cell now. But I figured if you had that extra security on me, then you weren't totally sure about the jail's guards."

"Do you know anything about any of them being on the take?"

He shook his head.

"Okay. If you hear anything or see anything suspicious, let the sheriff know."

He didn't respond.

I let that go for now and leaned forward. "Juan, we want to help you out. But first, we need to be absolutely sure that your story holds up." I eased back some. "Tell us again about your encounters with the gang, from the first time they approached you."

"It was the week after Easter," he said, his voice steadier. "These two guys, both white, fell into step with me as I was walking home from school. They asked if it wouldn't be cool to belong to a brotherhood, a club of sorts."

He went on to describe that and three more encounters with these two gang members. Bradley was taking notes but I half tuned the kid out, focusing on his body language. He was slightly tense, appropriate for the anxiety-provoking memories he was recalling. But there were no tell-tale signs that he was lying.

Alvarez paused after recounting the last encounter, when they had made veiled threats against his parents and grandmother.

"Describe the two guys," Bradley said. He opened the file folder in front of him and scanned it as the kid talked.

Again, relatively relaxed body language, all things considered.

When Alvarez stopped, Bradley looked at me and gave a small nod, indicating the descriptions matched what he'd told Patterson months ago. But not word for word. A made-up story would either be overly rehearsed and therefore exactly the same, or mistakes would be made as the memory of the earlier lies faded with time.

I leaned back in my chair, faking a relaxed casualness. "Tell us about the night Navarro died."

His body tensed, but then visibly relaxed. He shrugged. "Not much to tell. I was home studying for the SATs."

"How'd you do on the test?" I asked, my voice nonchalant.

"I, uh..." He paused, his eyes darting away from us and back again. "I flubbed it. I have to take it again, once...*if* I get out of jail."

"And you never went out that Friday night, not even for a breath of fresh air?" My voice was only slightly sharper than it had been, but the kid tensed.

He swallowed hard. "Um, I think I did go for a short walk, just to clear my head."

I fought to keep my own body from tensing, then nodded and kept quiet, inviting him to elaborate.

"Um, nobody saw me, unfortunately. I'd have a better alibi if they did."

I stayed silent.

He glanced from me to Bradley and back again, but also said nothing more.

"How long was your walk?" Bradley prompted, his tone neutral, his head tilted, eyes seemingly on his notepad. But I knew he was watching the kid out of his peripheral vision.

Yet again, the Adam's apple bobbed, and something flashed in the kid's eyes. "Not long. Maybe twenty minutes."

"Where'd you go?" Bradley asked.

Another shrug. There was definitely more tension in his shoulders now. "Around the neighborhood."

"And nobody saw you?" Bradley pressed. "Not even a car going by?"

His eyes went wide, but he shook his head.

I leaned forward, faking an angry expression. I slapped my hand on the table.

He jerked in his chair.

"You're lying," I yelled, and realized I wasn't faking. I *was* pissed at this kid. If he'd wasted our time...

His eyes turned shiny.

Shit, is he gonna cry?

His mouth fell open. "I, uh...no..." His voice shook.

"Look, kid," Bradley said in a soothing voice, "we want to go to bat for you, we really do. But you have to tell us the *whole truth*." He came down hard on the last two words.

Elbows on the table, Juan bowed his head and covered his face with his hands. "They, they grabbed me, from behind," he choked out.

Adrenaline zinged through me. *Now we're getting somewhere.*

"They who?" I said, intentionally softening my own voice.

"Those guys..." Muffled and still shaky.

"From the gang," I said.

He nodded his head, still buried in his hands. Then he looked up. His cheeks were wet.

My chest ached a little. He was only seventeen, truly just a kid.

Bradley nudged the box of tissues on one end of the table down to him.

He took a tissue, swiped at his eyes and nose. He sniffled. "They grabbed me and dragged me into a van of some kind. They were laughing at me, calling me names like 'spic' and 'Latrino.'" He made a disgusted face. "They hit me with something, on my head." He reached up and touched the back of his skull. "And everything went black."

The kid stared down at his hands, once again folded on the table, the tissue clutched between them. "When I woke up, I was lying on the riverwalk, next to this guy. I thought at first he was maybe a homeless guy, like, passed out drunk. But then I saw the knife."

He paused, gulped for air. "I wasn't thinkin' straight. I pulled the knife out...Maybe he was still alive and I could help him, ya know. But when I saw all the blood...I ran."

Navarro *had* still been alive at that point, barely. I didn't mention that. It was unlikely this kid could've done anything that would have helped. Indeed, pulling out the knife probably made things worse, but he didn't need to know that either.

"What happened to the knife?" Bradley asked, his voice neutral.

"I realized I was still holding it, so I threw it in the river. I ran all the way home and took a shower. The water..." He made a low gagging noise. "It turned pink, from the blood on my hands."

"And your clothes?" Bradley asked.

"I didn't see any blood on them. I just put them in the hamper. My mom's long since washed them."

"Describe what you were wearing," I said. We would send a uniform and one of the CSI guys to his house to retrieve the clothes. They might be able to find traces of blood.

He did so, and Bradley wrote it down.

"Did you see anyone around the riverwalk?" the lieutenant asked.

I held my breath, hoping the kid had seen the missing witness.

But he shook his head.

Damn! Then it dawned on me that their statements didn't jive. Winters remembered the witness saying he'd chased three men who'd run away from the victim, and that was around the same time that a woman had been checking for a pulse and calling 911.

At least one small part of that was true. The anonymous call to dispatch *was* from a female.

But Alvarez was saying he was alone when he ran from the scene.

"You're sure you didn't see anyone else around?" I asked.

"Positive."

Since we now knew that the mystery witness sported a Pillar tattoo, I was more inclined to believe Juan's version, that he was alone.

"Why didn't you tell all this to the police when you were first picked up?" I asked.

"I didn't remember it at first," Alvarez said. "I remembered leaving the house to take a walk, then taking a shower later, and my head was hurting. I didn't even realize there was a gap in there..." He trailed off.

Bradley was giving me a sideways skeptical glance.

I made a note to check with Kate on memory loss after a blow to the head. Would it last that long?

Or was this kid lying through his teeth about not remembering?

"The night after I was arrested," he said, "I had a dream about a bloody knife, and bits and pieces started coming back after that."

He stopped to suck in air. "But I'd already said I never left the house. I hadn't said anything about taking a walk. I figured that would make me look guilty, when it was perfectly innocent, or so I thought at the time."

He hung his head, shaking it. "If only I'd stayed in the house..."

"It wouldn't have mattered," I said. "They would've found a way to lure you out, or if they realized you were home alone, they would've broken in."

Bradley turned slightly toward me, his head tilted to one side. The unspoken question, *You believe him?*

I gave a small shrug, not at all sure what the answer to that question was.

The kid hiccuped, pulling our attention back to him.

"Anything else you haven't told us?" Now Bradley's voice was a little sharp.

He shook his head again.

"Lieutenant, get Mr. Alvarez to a cruiser, preferably without anyone seeing him." I glanced at the small window high on the wall. It was a square of graying sky. And the clock slightly below it read quarter of six.

I turned to the kid. "Thanks for coming clean with us, Juan."

He looked up at me, fear naked on his face. "Are you still going to help me?"

"If your story checks out." I gestured for Bradley to step into the hallway with me, where we could confer for a moment.

My voice low, I asked, "Any point in searching the river for the knife?" I already suspected what the answer would be.

"Probably not. It's either washed downstream by now or it's buried in silt."

I nodded, and the lieutenant stepped back into the interview room to collect the prisoner.

I texted Sam while walking to the bullpen, telling him that Alvarez was on his way back to him.

Definitely no to dinner then? he texted back, as I entered my office.

I sat down in my chair while texting, *Afraid not. Up to my eyeballs here.*

My stomach churned. I hated lying. And I especially hated lying to Sam.

But, I realized, the churning wasn't totally about that. I was a little seasick from the emotional roller coaster.

I'd wanted to believe Juan was innocent, but the hair had cast doubt on that. And now we knew he had been at the scene, and he'd lied about it.

But that could explain how his hair got on the victim, when he pulled the knife out.

And he seemed to be telling the truth about the men kidnapping him and waking up next to the body. It was hard to fake that much emotion.

But he could be a better liar than I'd given him credit for.

Then another thought hit me, and the churning morphed into a lump in the pit of my stomach.

Now I couldn't even trust the old case files. And not just because Black might've removed something incriminating, but because his clerk was a lousy record keeper.

A vise closed around my chest. I groaned, putting my elbows on my desk, and lowering my face into my hands. I'd wondered many times in the last few months why I'd taken this job.

But for the first time, the thought of quitting crossed my mind.

Screw this! I'm going home to my cat.

———— ◆ ————

A note was propped on the kitchen counter.

Lasagna in the fridge (Mom's recipe), and salad (I know you're not eating right!)

See ya later,

Paul(ie)

I smiled a little and tossed the note in my recycle bin. Even though I wasn't particularly hungry, I pulled out the lasagna to stick in the microwave.

While it heated, I texted Kate, asking about amnesia after a blow to the head.

She texted back. *Depending on how bad the concussion was, the last ten minutes to as much as a few hours, or even a whole day, might not have been processed. Some parts will come back but usually not the last minute or so before the blow.*

But he remembers being hit on the head? I typed into my phone, disappointed that she hadn't called instead of continuing to text. That meant she was in the middle of something and couldn't talk.

Unlikely, she responded. *His mind probably filled in that gap with a logical assumption. There isn't sufficient time for the memory of the last few seconds to be processed and stored, before the brain cells are scrambled.*

I nodded to myself. Made sense.

I texted, *How about after the concussion? He lost twenty to thirty minutes, but it came back later.*

Could be from the concussion, or psychological, if he's blocking out trauma.

Yeah, I thought, *I'd consider finding a dying man next to me as traumatic.*

Thanks, I texted. *Really helpful.*

Great. Talk soon!

Definitely.

I was feeling a bit lighter as the microwave dinged. My stomach rumbled, suddenly hungry.

I decided to wait up for Paulie, um, Paul. We'd hardly even crossed paths since he'd started working on Wednesday. But he was off tomorrow, Saturday, and even though I would go into the office, I could sleep in some first.

I found a bottle of white wine, his preference, in my wine rack. Someone had given it to me for Christmas, but I preferred red.

I put it in the fridge, then took a shower and donned some old sweats. Nice thing about a Friday night date with your cousin, you don't have to get dressed up.

I binge-watched some sitcom until eleven, when I put together a tray of cheese and crackers and fruit. Paulie...

Paul, Paul, I need to stop even thinking of him as Paulie.

Paul would be hungry after an eight-hour shift.

At eleven-twenty, the deadbolt snicked open and the door knob turned. I jumped up and spread my arms wide behind the display on my cardboard box coffee table.

My cousin's eyes went wide at the sight of wine bottles, tall-stemmed glasses and plates of food.

"Happy end of your first week of work," I sang out.

Paul snorted, but then smiled. "It wasn't even a full week and I'm exhausted."

I gestured toward my old black leather sofa. "Concentrating that hard has got to be a strain."

"It is." He sank onto one end of the sofa. "But I'll get used to it."

I sat on the other and curled my feet up under me. "So, any luck researching apartments?"

He shook his head as he leaned forward and poured wine into the two glasses. He handed the red one to me. "That anxious to be rid of me, huh?"

Not rid of you, I thought, *just out of my apartment.* "No," I said out loud.

But one of the reasons for wanting him out of my place was now moot. No more booty calls from Sam until I figured out what was going on there. I firmly pushed that thought, and its accompanying feelings, away.

Paul chatted for a while about the new job, while I listened and sipped wine, both of us nibbling on the food.

When he wound down some, I told him about my sightings of Sam, or his look-alike, around town, and summarized my conversation with Kate about it.

"Tentatively," Paul said, "I agree with your friend. Maybe not quite as sure of his fidelity as she is, but she has some good points. And here's another..." He leaned over to nab a cracker and slice of cheese. "Why would he keep letting you see him?"

He sat back, munched, then added, "This isn't *that* small a city. Surely he could find places to hang out with other women farther away from the municipal building, so you would be less likely to see him."

"That *is* another good point," I said. I sat quietly, thinking, for a moment. "Assuming someone else is doing this, popping up near the building in a khaki shirt, the question is, why? Why in the devil would anyone want to do that, to get me thinking that Sam was unfaithful?"

Paul shrugged. "Someone who wants him for themselves maybe?"

"I suppose I could ask him if anyone's been coming on to him lately." A small wave of relaxation washed through me, at the same time as my stomach clenched. A mix of relief—maybe I could stop holding Sam at arm's length—and anxiety that he might yet break my heart.

Break my heart? Am I that attached to him?

Yeah, I had to admit that I was. I blew out a long sigh.

"Or I could just break up with him and get it over with," I blurted out.

Where had that come from? A fist closed around my heart.

My cousin raised his eyebrows at me. "You know what that's called, don't you?"

"What?"

"Reject before you're rejected."

"Well," I said, "that idea has its merits."

"*Not* in this case," he said emphatically.

When I didn't respond, he added, "The odds are quite high that your guy has done nothing wrong. And the reject-before-rejected is a knee-jerk reaction that we all have at times. It's *not* rational."

"We all have?" I watched him from the corner of my eye. "Is that what happened with you and Blake?" Blake, the man my cousin had sworn was the love of his life, until he refused to talk about him six months ago.

Paul looked away, toward the apartment door. "Yes, only Blake did the rejecting." He took a deep breath. "I guess he sensed I was getting restless. But I'd made a vow. I wasn't going to cheat on him. I was even going to counseling..."

He suddenly rose from the sofa, pulled me to a stand, and wrapped his arms around me.

I stiffened initially, then leaned into the warmth of the hug.

It was good to have him here. *He's family.*

A phone rang.

Paul frowned. "That doesn't bode well at this hour."

We stepped apart, and I picked up the police-issue cell phone from my makeshift coffee table.

"We need to take you furniture shopping," Paul muttered.

I glanced at the name on the screen. "It's my assistant...Yeah, Bar–"

"Chief, oh my God..." Her voice sounded strange. Muffled noises in the background.

Was that somebody crying? Every muscle in my body clenched. "What's happened?" I demanded.

"It's the mayor..." Her words came out on a strangled sob. "They got him this time. He's dead."

CHAPTER FIFTEEN

Paul drove me to the scene. He'd insisted I was too upset to drive, which was nonsense and he knew it. He was just curious.

"You know what happened to the cat, right?" I asked from the passenger seat.

"Pipsqueak? What happened to her?" His voice was alarmed as he glanced my way.

"Not her. The *curious* cat."

He rolled his eyes and turned his gaze back to the road.

Once at the scene, I jumped out, then leaned my head back into the car. "Either go home or stay behind the tape. You are *not* police personnel."

He grimaced. "Spoil sport."

I didn't wait to see what he did. Jogging to the officer with the scene log, I held up my badge. Which was probably unnecessary, but since I was still in my sweats, it wouldn't hurt.

The tape cordoned off a large section of road, several hundred feet long, with two mashed-up cars, a fire engine and an ambulance inside it.

The officer held the tape up for me. "They've called for a second ambulance. The driver of the other car didn't make it."

"Where's–"

The person I'd been about to ask for had spotted me and ran over. "Oh Chief, I'm so sorry. He came out of nowhere."

"Small side street," the other officer offered.

"He's just a kid," Barnes sobbed out. "*Was* just a kid. Paramedics said the car smells like a distillery. I didn't...I couldn't go over there." She burst into tears.

I put an arm around her shoulders and turned her so her back was toward the mangled cars. "Wellbourne?" I asked.

"She's okay." Barnes sniffled and swiped her uniform sleeve across her face. "We were both on the driver's side of the car. But the mayor..."

"Was not," I finished for her.

She nodded, her face screwed up as if she were trying not to cry again. "I even made sure he had his vest on," she choked out.

I glanced past her at the mangled vehicles. Kevlar was nothing against a speeding car.

I brought my gaze back to Barnes. The fire engine's headlights shone on her wet cheeks. There were some small cuts and abrasions, and a nasty red patch below one temple.

I pointed to it. "That looks like a chemical burn, maybe from the air bag. Go get a paramedic to check it out."

Bradley ducked under the tape behind me, as Barnes walked away. "She okay?" he asked, anxiety in his voice.

"Banged up some, but I think so." I worried that she might have a head injury. She didn't usually acquiesce to medical examinations that readily. I shook my head to clear it. "As is Wellbourne," I continued. "The mayor and the other driver–"

"I heard. Both dead. I'm gonna go take a look at the cars."

I nodded and he strode off. He wore pressed jeans and a collared knit shirt. I shook my head slightly as I walked toward the ambulance and paramedics. No sweats for the lieutenant, even on a Friday night.

Sergeant Lewis fell into step beside me. "We'd just done the change of shift when we got the call. Johnson's on the watch desk now, but I had to come out."

I nodded.

"Mayor probably died instantly. Right side of the car's all bashed in." His voice sounded rough.

I glanced over but couldn't make out his facial expression in the shadow cast by his hat brim.

"This is *not* okay," he said.

"No, it isn't. And we're going to find whoever's responsible."

Lewis stopped and grabbed my arm, hauling me to a standstill as well. "You think it was intentional? The kid died too."

"Yes, I do. This would be way too much of a coincidence. Two attempts on the mayor's life and then this."

He tilted his head back, and I could now see he was pale and wide-eyed. He looked downright shocky. And there was something in his eyes. Fear maybe?

"Are you okay?" I asked.

Before he could answer, Bradley joined us. "Kid's air bag didn't deploy. And get this, he's wearing a football helmet and neck brace."

Lewis swayed on his feet. We both grabbed for him, but he went down.

I thought he'd fainted, but he landed on his butt and covered his face with his hands. "This has got to stop," he mumbled into them.

I stared down at him, then up at Bradley. "See if you can find out what he's blubbering about."

The lieutenant nodded and pulled the sergeant to a stand. Lewis's face was still covered with his hands.

"I've called in Collins and Cruthers," Bradley said, as he turned them both back toward the scene's perimeter. "The kid has no ID on him so I'll put them on finding out who he is."

"And on tracing the car?" A high-pitched female voice from behind me.

I twisted around.

Wellbourne looked a bit worse than Barnes, multiple scrapes and cuts and a bruise blossoming on her left cheek. Her skin tone was a blend of ashen and tan, her freckles a macabre mask of brown dots.

She fingered the bluish tones on her cheek. "Hit my head against the side window," she muttered and swayed on her feet.

I started to grab for her but she held out a hand in a stop gesture. "No way this was an accident."

"That seems to be the general consensus, Agent Wellbourne," I said. "Don't worry. Yes, we'll be tracing the car."

I waved a hand at a paramedic, gestured him over. He took charge of Wellbourne and led her away.

Paulie appeared at my elbow. "Can I drive you home?"

I scowled at him, but I didn't have the energy to yell at him for entering the scene. "I'll drop you off. I'm going into the office."

He nodded, then glanced at my legs. "You might want to change first."

I looked down at my sweats. *Damn, he's right.*

———◄O►———

For once, my cousin had the good sense to stay quiet. I parked in front of my building, and we went up in the elevator in silence.

But we were barely inside my door when he said, "You know–"

I held up my hand. "This is a rough night. A lot for my people to process. Just go to bed. I'll see you some time tomorrow."

"A lot for *you* to process," he said.

"Paulie...*Paul*, just go to bed and let me do my job."

He looked crestfallen, a little hurt maybe. "Okay. Call me if you need a shoulder."

I relented some. "Thanks." I tried for a smile but fell short—it was probably more of a pained expression—and went off to my bedroom to change my clothes.

It dawned on me, on the way to 3MB, that I should call Mark Hayes. According to the pecking order, he was the interim mayor.

Even though he's a suspect.

As it turned out, he'd already heard from his admin who'd gotten a call from her firefighter husband. "He was on the scene, said it was pretty messy." Hayes's voice, coming through my dashboard speaker, sounded upset.

"It was," I said. "The good news, grim as it is—the mayor most likely died instantly."

A pause. "I'm getting dressed now. I'll be in my office in twenty minutes if you need anything. I mean the mayor's office...this is so surreal."

"Yes, sir, it is."

"I'll be working on remarks for a press conference for first thing in the morning. I'd like a briefing before then on the accident."

If it was an accident. I kept that thought to myself for now. "You'll get it, Mr. Mayor."

"Um, I'm not sure I'm up for being called that just yet. Let's stick to Mark."

"Sure, sir. Uh, Mark."

We both knew I'd revert to Councilman Hayes, or rather Mayor Hayes now. The man had asked me to call him Mark a hundred times, but I couldn't bring myself to do it.

Bradley was waiting for me outside my office. "Collins ran the boy's prints. He's been arrested three times, once for shoplifting and twice for vandalism."

"So we have an ID then?"

"Daniel Christopher Jones, Jr., sixteen. He lives, lived rather, in the Bennett section. Two younger brothers, nine and six. Mom's from Honduras. Dad's African-American, a wounded vet. In a VA rehab place in Jacksonville."

I winced.

"Yeah," Bradley said, his expression solemn. "No vehicles registered in their names. I was about to go make the notification. Wanna come?"

"No, I don't *want* to, but I will. We need as much info as we can get from this family, and–"

"A woman's touch might be helpful," he finished my sentence.

The Joneses lived in a rather rundown apartment building near Holly Park. Definitely not the best neighborhood in town. But the mom didn't work outside the home, and all they had was the dad's military disability pay.

I let Bradley take the lead. He knocked, waited a minute, and knocked again. Another couple of minutes ticked by. He was raising his hand again when the door opened slightly, on a safety chain.

He held his badge to the crack.

The door nudged closed, then opened farther, without the chain. A short, plump woman—with tan skin and long, sleek black hair—clutched the collar of a purple robe tight under her chin.

"*No hablo ingles,*" she said, but her brown eyes were already wide with fear. Police officers on your doorstep in the middle of the night never meant good news.

"May we come in, ma'am?" Bradley asked, gesturing to the living room behind the woman.

She hesitated, took a step backward, and tripped over her own slippers. Bradley grabbed her nearest arm to steady her. "It's about your son."

She began shaking her head, more and more vigorously, and pulled her arm loose. "No, no. No. Nooo." She wailed, whirled around, ran toward a hallway, which probably led to bedrooms.

We stepped inside, closed the door behind us, and waited.

A few moments later, a boy came out of the hallway, leading his mom by the hand. "What's happened to my brother?" His face was a light brown mask, but there was a tremor in his voice.

"I'm afraid he's dead, son," Bradley said.

The boy took a deep breath, set his mouth in a tight line, and turned to his mom.

Interesting. He's not surprised.

He let out some rapid-fire Spanish.

The mother wailed and fell to the floor, yanking her hair around to cover her face.

Her sobs felt like claws in my chest. My eyes stung.

The boy tugged on his mom's arm, said something else, probably encouraging her to get up.

Bradley took a step forward, holding out a hand to help. The boy shot him a hard look, and he stopped.

The boy managed to get her onto a shabby loveseat. He sat down beside her and wrapped his arms around her.

She continued sobbing, but let out tiny bursts of Spanish.

"Chris was a wild one," the boy translated, "but I prayed to *Jesu*..." He pronounced it the Spanish way, *hey-sus.*

Another spurt from his mother. "We thought he would grow out of it," the boy continued.

She sat up, wiped her wet cheeks with her fingers, and said something else.

The boy went wide-eyed, looking more like the nine-year-old that he was, instead of trying to be the man of the house. "She wants to call my...d-dad." He choked some on the words.

"Perhaps it would be better to tell him in person," I said, in a soft voice. "I can have an officer drive you all over to be with him." The boy translated my words for his mom.

Bradley shot me a sideways glance. Chauffeuring was not a service we normally provided.

But hey, I'm the police chief.

I stooped down in front of them, resting my butt lightly on a wooden coffee table.

The room was crowded with furniture, but immaculately clean. Did they have to downsize from someplace larger? *Maybe...* After the dad was wounded and had to go on disability.

"First," I said gently, "we need to ask you some questions."

The boy translated, and the mom nodded.

"Has Chris been in trouble before?" I asked, starting off slow. And it didn't hurt to ask a question that you already knew the answer to—to judge the interviewee's honesty.

The boy translated and the mother answered with a short spat of Spanish.

"Yes," the kid said, "but he got in with some wrong ones."

"Wrong ones?"

"A bad crowd," the brother said without consulting his mother.

"Do you know who was in this bad crowd?" I asked him directly.

He shook his head. His mother said something.

"Older kids, white," he translated.

On a hunch, I asked, "Were these older kids part of a gang, by any chance?"

The boy stiffened. He spoke to his mother. My high school Spanish was rusty but I was pretty sure he asked her the last time she'd seen Chris.

I couldn't catch her answer—it was too rapid.

"No," he said, his jaw clenched and his eyes narrowed. "She said, 'Chris is a good boy, deep down.'"

His mother might have said that at other times, maybe many other times. But that wasn't what she'd just said. I let that go for now. "Did he have his driver's license?"

"His learner's permit," the boy said, without consulting his mother. "He was taking driver's ed classes. They're free at the Y for military kids."

The kid sat up straighter and his face relaxed some. "Is that how he died, in a car wreck?"

"Yes," Bradley said from behind me, "but there's more to it."

The kid stiffened again.

The mother had lowered her face into her hands and was crying softly.

"Why don't you take your mom to her room?" I suggested. "Let her lie down for a while. But then we need to ask you a couple more things. Ask her if that's okay."

The boy's eyes took on a wary look, but he nodded. He helped his mother up from the loveseat and steered her down the hallway.

When he came back, he said, "She said I should offer you something to drink."

We both shook our heads. "We're fine," I said.

"She also asked me if I was involved in whatever Chris was up to."

"Were you?" Bradley said in a soft voice.

"No." The boy sat down again, this time in a recliner that had seen better days.

Bradley and I took the loveseat, across from him. "But you know something about it," I said. "What he was up to, that is."

"She said I should tell you whatever I know, as long as it won't get me in trouble."

I nodded slightly. "It won't."

The boy was only nine. Unless he'd been actively involved in plotting the mayor's death, I couldn't imagine anything we could or would charge him with.

"Chris was really excited lately. He said he was going to make a ton of money, and we could move to someplace nicer, in Jacksonville...close to Dad. He'd even have enough for a secondhand car, he said, so he could drive Mom around."

"What did he have to do to make that money?" Bradley asked.

"He had to drive a car into somebody else's, but he said no one would be seriously hurt, because of the air bags. He was told it was to warn the other guy off. That the other guy was trying to infringe on 'their turf.'" The kid made air quotes.

"Did he say who wanted him to do all that?" I asked.

His eyes shiny now, he said, "No. After he hit the other guy's car, he was supposed to get out and run away."

"The people who had him doing this," Bradley said, "they gave him the car?"

The boy nodded.

"But you have no idea who they were?" I asked again.

The boy shook his head.

I opened my mouth to thank him as I began to push up off the loveseat, but Bradley leaned forward. "Frederico—"

I dropped back down again, assuming he'd thought of another question.

"I go by Jaime, my middle name." The kid used the English pronunciation, Jamie. "Chris was named after our father, and I was named after my granddad, my mom's father." His face clouded. "He was killed getting his family out of Honduras."

Bradley nodded, cleared his throat. "You thought what Chris was doing was kinda cool, didn't you?"

The boy pursed his lips. "Yeah, I guess. When he first told me about it, and I was imagining not being poor anymore. But not now, not if that's what got him...killed."

Bradley nodded again. "It's natural to look up to your big brother, but you're the big brother now. You need to be a better role model. Can you do that?"

Jaime thought about that for a beat, then squared his shoulders. "Yes, I will be."

"Good," Bradley said.

And I made a mental note to praise Bradley for bringing that up, and to see what additional assistance this family could get, from *somebody*.

As Bradley drove past the municipal building to the parking lot entrance, I spotted Bert Deming, standing under a streetlight in front of the building. The senior member of my CSI duo was shifting from one foot to the other, like a little boy who needs to go to the bathroom.

"Good lord," I muttered, "now they're accosting me before I can even get inside."

Bradley chuckled softly as he pulled into his official parking space. I climbed out of his car and trotted around to the front of the building.

"Oh, there you are, Chief." Bert's relief was palpable. "I was afraid you'd go home without coming upstairs."

I started to question why he'd have that concern—after all, the mayor of our city had just been murdered. Then I remembered. He was used to my predecessor, who'd been the definition of lazy. Chief Black would have indeed gone home, especially if the killer had already been identified. He would've assumed the obvious. A drunk driver caused the accident. End of story.

"We found some stuff out about the car." Bert fell in step with me as I entered the building and strode to the elevator. "The VIN was filed off on the top of the dash, but not on the engine itself."

I nodded. A lot of people didn't know that a vehicle's identification number, or VIN, was stamped in two places.

The elevator arrived as Bradley joined us. We all climbed aboard.

"Derek traced it through DHSMV records to a junk yard in Jacksonville," Bert said.

"DHSMV?" I asked.

"Department of Highway Safety and Motor Vehicles," Bradley said.

"That's a mouthful," I commented.

He gave me one of his half-smiles. "Even the initials are a mouthful."

"The junk yard sold it," Bert continued, "to a Max Layes."

I snorted softly. "As in the potato chips?"

"Yes," Bert said, "only with an *e*. L-a-y-e-s."

Like Hayes. Bradley and I shot each other a glance.

And now I couldn't help wondering if the VIN on the engine was intentionally overlooked. They wanted us to find this bogus buyer.

Only who the hell is "they?"

Bert's expression turned grim. "The buyer had to produce a driver's license to the junk yard owner, who then signed off on the title and handed it over. But he made a copy of the license for his records. It's a forgery. A good one, but nonetheless, a forgery. They would've caught it at DHSMV, but the transfer of the title hasn't been processed yet. The car was bought on Thursday."

After the shooting in Holly Park that only winged the mayor but didn't kill him.

As the elevator bell dinged announcing our arrival on the third floor, Bert added, "And it wasn't that the air bag didn't go off. It wasn't there."

I'd raised my foot to step out into the hallway, but whirled around instead. "Say what?"

"In the kid's car," Bert said, "the space where it's supposed to be. It was empty. And his seatbelt may have been tampered with as well. The windshield's shattered, and there's blood on some of the shards on top of the dashboard. Did his head hit the windshield?"

I stared at him.

"Yeah," Bradley said. "That's what the first-on-scene officer reported. The kid was wearing a football helmet, but his face had some cuts on it." The elevator doors began to close. He reached out and held the open-door button.

"We just found out from the boy's brother," I said to Bert, "that somebody else gave him the car, and they were paying him to cause the collision."

Bert's already fair skin paled. He swallowed hard. "And they didn't want him to survive to talk about it."

I nodded, my chest tight. "Send me the copy of that driver's license." I assumed Bert hadn't recognized the person in the photo, but I wanted to see for myself. "And go over that car again, with a fine-tooth comb. See if anything else has been tampered with."

We stepped off the elevator, but Bert stayed on it, headed back down to the fenced-off yard behind the building where cars involved in crimes were processed.

———— ◄O► ————

At five-twenty a.m., I gave the interim mayor his briefing. I informed him that we had strong evidence indicating the crash was not an accident. I left out the part about the car being bought in a bogus name suspiciously like his own and with a forged driver's license.

Bert had forwarded the copy to me. The blurry photo could've been any of several hundred white men in Starling with expensive haircuts.

"But," I added, "I suggest we *not* tell the public, just yet, that it wasn't an accident."

Hayes scrubbed a hand over his face. "I agree."

At six-thirty, I stood in a line of city officials behind him as he gave a press conference, relaying the news to the residents of Starling that their mayor had been tragically killed in a "collision" while coming home from the hospital. He promised more details would be made available later in the day.

At eight-ten, I was sitting at my desk, waiting for an update from Bradley on the car, when my private line rang. Caller ID read *Mayor*.

I picked it up. "Yes, Mayor Hayes, what can–"

"Chief, it's Carol." Raised voices in the background. "You'd better get up here. Mr. McAllister and the councilma...um, mayor are about to come to blows."

CHAPTER SIXTEEN

The panic in Hayes's assistant's voice had said there was no time for the elevator. I took the stairs, two at a time.

I could hear them as soon as I shoved open the fire door. I ran toward the noise.

Carol gave me a relieved look from behind the desk of the mayor's assistant. I spared a half second to wonder what would happen to Bonnie, Mayor Daniels's assistant.

Carol gestured for me to go through the slightly ajar door behind her desk. I didn't bother to knock.

Hayes sat behind the expansive mahogany desk. His dark hair, normally well coifed, stood up in places. He had a nervous habit of running his hands through it. His face was blotchy and his eyes red-rimmed. He'd removed his suit jacket and tie and had rolled up his sleeves.

McAllister, still in full businessman armor, leaned forward over the desk, his palms planted on the polished wood. The overhead light glinted off of gold cufflinks, peeking out below the ends of his suit jacket's sleeves.

Red-faced, he roared, "Get out of that chair!"

I closed the door firmly behind me. He glanced my way.

"You know," I said, my tone conversational, "you can be heard all over the fifth floor."

"I don't care," McAllister yelled. "Get this interloper out of the mayor's office."

"I told you," Hayes said, "the City Charter—"

I held up my hand. "He *is* the interim mayor."

"But he's a suspect," McAllister spluttered, "in the mayor's murder."

"And how do you know he was murdered?" I kept my voice calm, but I was doing a slow burn inside. City Hall leaked like a sieve, but Mark Hayes was usually more discreet.

"Well…" McAllister spluttered, then threw his hands up in the air. "After two attempts on his life, it would be a huge coincidence that he's randomly hit by a drunk driver."

"Yes, it would be. And why do you say Mr. Hayes is a suspect?"

"Because of the gun, of course." His voice was still raised. "It's his."

"Which we suspect was a plant. It's way too obvious." Maintaining eye contact with McAllister, I tilted my head toward Hayes. "And he's not a stupid man."

"So he's *not* a suspect?" McAllister's shrill tone was incredulous.

I gave a slight shrug and made sure my own voice remained neutral. "He's a person of interest in the attempts against the mayor, but he's not a serious suspect at this time."

"Well, if there's any suspicion at all, he shouldn't be sitting in that chair."

"I'm following the City Charter," Hayes piped up.

I ignored him, hoping he'd forgive the disrespect. I was keenly aware that we were talking about him as if he weren't there.

But my gaze remained on McAllister. There was some dynamic going on here between him and me, and I didn't want to seem, not even for a second, like I was backing down.

McAllister's red face went a shade darker still. I was becoming concerned that he'd give himself a stroke.

"Who do you think should be sitting there?" I asked, again in a neutral tone.

"Me. Mayor Daniels designated me as interim mayor." His voice came down a couple notches in volume. "I should be handling the city's business, until the City Council can convene and either confirm me or appoint someone else."

Hayes rose from behind the desk. "McAllister, I will happily convene the City Council." His tone was sharp—he'd apparently had enough. "And have them vote on whether or not *I* should continue as interim mayor. But you and I both know that you were really Daniels's campaign manager. You're not qualified to run this city." He scoffed. "You're not even a resident here."

"I am so. I rent a place, and I'm, er, searching for something to buy."

Hayes waved a hand in the air, dismissing that issue even though he'd introduced it.

I said to McAllister, "I think it's time for you to leave–"

Before I could continue, he took a step toward me, his posture menacing. "Ah, so you're taking sides, even though your position is supposedly apolitical."

I gave him a look that stopped his forward momentum. "My position *is* apolitical," I said, slowly and firmly, "but as Mr. Hayes has pointed out, he's following the City Charter."

McAllister pursed his lips. "Respectfully, this is none of your business, Chief. Your job is to investigate the mayor's murder."

I don't need you to tell me my job! I managed to swallow those words and said instead, "Every man and woman in my department is doing just that."

McAllister rocked back on his heels, crossed his arms over his broad chest. "Good, then you won't be wasting any more time reinvestigating closed cases."

I narrowed my eyes at him. "What do you mean?"

His expression had turned smug. "The ASA called Mayor Daniels, complaining that you were looking into the Navarro homicide and might very well give the defense ammunition that would undermine the state's case."

I tried not to react externally, as I cussed Brenda Stone out in my head.

McAllister turned back toward Hayes. "*Mister* Mayor," he exaggerated the title, "please tell your Chief of Police to stick to current, active cases."

I glanced quickly at Hayes, then brought my gaze back to McAllister, managing to maintain my best stone-faced expression.

But that one glance had been enough. I'd never seen Hayes so furious—jaw clenched, eyes blazing.

"I think we're done here, *Mister* McAllister," he said, in a dangerously quiet voice. "The city thanks you, but your services are no longer needed. Chief, please see that Mr. McAllister is escorted from the building after he's removed his personal belongings from his office."

I apprised the watch commander of what was going on. Sergeant Armstrong reassured me he'd personally escort the late mayor's former special assistant from the building. He'd come down hard on both *former* and *special.*

I caught myself giving him a small grin. His tone and expression said he didn't think much of McAllister. The sarge had little respect for authority, unless one had earned that respect. I shared that attitude, but still, I shouldn't be encouraging him.

Okay, maybe I am taking sides, I thought, as I walked toward my office. But was I being unfair to McAllister, letting my general dislike of politicians taint my view of him?

He hadn't actually done anything wrong or offensive. And he had a point about Hayes being a suspect, no matter how questionable the evidence was.

Should Hayes be recusing himself from sitting in the mayor's chair? Was I being too lenient with him because I believed he was the exception to the rule, an honest and dedicated politician?

I snorted. Those words sounded so *wrong* strung together in the same phrase.

I'd made an enemy, though, and that was not good. But with Mayor Daniels gone, did it really matter? McAllister no longer had any power.

Once again, the thought flitted across my mind that I should quit this lousy job.

Bradley and Bert Deming were huddled by my door. And Barnes was at her desk, in a fresh uniform, with a couple of butterfly bandages on the worst of the cuts on her face and a gauze pad taped to her temple. The other minor cuts were scabbed over, and a bruise had formed on her cheek from her close encounter with her air bag.

I thought about trying to send her home but decided not to waste my breath. She wouldn't go.

"We have some more info on the car," Bradley said as I approached.

I motioned everyone into my office. Bradley made a gesture, offering Bert the comfy visitor's chair.

He gave the lieutenant a quick smile but perched on the edge of one of the others.

Somehow, that didn't surprise me. Bert was so serious, a bit of a nervous-type personality, and his expression said he had more grim news. Not the time to be relaxing in a comfy chair.

Then Bradley looked at Barnes and gestured toward that chair. She defiantly glared at him and leaned her butt against the closed door, notepad in hand.

He rolled his eyes and sat down.

Normally, I would be chuckling at their antics, but I just shook my head and turned to Bert. "What have you got?"

"One additional thing about the car itself. The tires are in pretty decent condition. There's no significant warping of the tread that would indicate sudden braking."

"And there were no skid marks at the crash site," Bradley added.

"Two objects inside," Bert continued. "One, a broken pint bottle of whiskey. It fell down between the driver's seat and his door. Got two partials off of the largest piece of glass. Not enough to get any hits when I ran them. But when we have a suspect, they might help with confirmation."

"I take it they're not the kid's," I said, noting Bert's confidence, perhaps misplaced, that we would eventually have a suspect.

He shook his head.

"Nor do they belong to our person of interest." Bradley meant Mark Hayes.

"The other thing," Bert said, "was a cell phone, smashed to smithereens under the passenger seat, which was rammed up against the dashboard by the impact."

"So, maybe it was on the passenger seat and flew off?" I made a swooshing gesture with my hand. "Then got smashed by the seat."

Bert nodded. "The seat came off the sliders, and the metal side frame landed right on the phone. Derek has it, but he's not hopeful."

"Armed with what Bert found," Bradley said, "and what he didn't find—the air bags—I went to talk to the salvage yard owner who sold the car." He flipped through some pages in his notepad. "Black guy. Name's Jerome Evans. I checked him out. He's clean."

The lieutenant blew out a short sigh. "He said he'd taken the air bags out to inspect and resell them—they're apparently worth a few hundred dollars, even secondhand. He was about to remove the tires, since they had some decent tread left, when this Layes fella came along. He said he had a car just like it that he was fixing up with his son, for the boy to drive. He figured the junker would have some of the engine parts they needed, as well as the decent tires. Offered good money for it so Evans agreed."

"Could Evans identify Mr. Potato Chip?" I asked.

Bert snorted softly.

"I showed him a photo array that included our person of interest." One side of Bradley's mouth quirked up in that half-smile of his. "Evans said all white people look the same to him."

A short chuckle escaped my lips, despite the gravity of the situation. "That's probably valid," I said. "I asked my frien...um, my psychological consultant about that once. She said it was true that people have trouble telling others apart, if those others aren't part of their own group, regardless of what defines that group—race, age, gender. Of course, she had a psychobabble name for it, out-group something or other."

I stifled a smile at the memory of that conversation. Kate had admitted that she sometimes had trouble telling her students apart, because they were so much younger than her.

Bradley nodded. "Evans also said that he'd tried to convince the guy not to drive the car, since it had no air bags. But Layes wasn't willing to pay the two-hundred dollars for the driver's side bag, even though Evans offered to reinstall it for free. Nor did he want to pay to have the car towed. He said he'd rented a garage near there, even mentioned an address—Evans only remembered the street name—where he and his son were working on their car. Said it was only a short drive."

"And lemme guess," I said, "that street doesn't exist."

"Nope," Bradley said. "By the way, the number on that forged driver's license, it isn't exactly that of our person of interest. But with only two of the numbers altered, it's his."

Bert already knew who that POI was, but I was glad for Bradley's discretion. If we started bandying Hayes's name around as a suspect, eventually someone was bound to overhear us.

I turned to Bert. "Anything else left for you to check out on the car or at the scene?"

He shook his head.

"Thanks. Good work," I said.

He rose. Barnes opened the door to let him out.

Then she closed it again and perched on the edge of the chair he'd vacated. "Are you thinking the bogus driver's license is a plant, to set up our person of interest?"

I wanted to say yes, to believe Hayes was innocent, but... "Not sure," I said instead. "But if it is a set-up, the person orchestrating it is being a little obvious."

Not as obvious as the gun in the park, though. It was conceivable that someone like Mark Hayes, who was *not* a seasoned criminal, would think he'd changed things enough on his fake license to hide his identity.

But that amateur belief didn't jive with the fact that the fake license had apparently been produced by a skilled forger. Did the person setting Hayes up *want* the trail to lead back to him, but maybe not right away?

I turned to Bradley. "You got anything else?"

He shook his head, and he and Barnes rose to leave.

"Hey, Chief," Barnes said. "Did you ever get breakfast? I could go to the deli."

"No thanks. Christopher Jones's autopsy is in a couple of hours. An event best approached with an empty stomach."

"I could cover that," Bradley offered, with a sympathetic look.

I felt my face heat up. How embarrassing that he was inured to the impact of an autopsy while I wasn't, even though I had a decade more experience as a cop than he did.

"No," I said. "Thanks though. I, um, want to bear witness, I guess, for the sake of those boys and their mother."

Bradley nodded. "I get that."

CHAPTER SEVENTEEN

I arrived a little before ten-thirty at the austere white building in Jacksonville that housed the District Four Medical Examiner's Office. Sam was waiting out front, which took me by surprise.

What's your interest in this?" I asked as we fell into step. My tone was sharper than I'd intended.

He shrugged, grabbing the door handle and holding it open for me. "Call it a gut hunch that this might be related to the attack on Patterson, in *my* jail."

Was that a note of defensiveness in his tone?

I walked past him into the building. It was somewhat of a stretch to think there was a relationship between the mayor's death and the Patterson attack. Was this a ruse to see me, maybe corner me into having a talk about *our* relationship?

We entered the autopsy room together. It was cold, of course. These rooms always were.

We stopped, side by side, and Sam sidled over, bumping my shoulder with his. I knew he was playing and normally I'd respond in kind. But not today.

The pathologist was not in the room yet, and the diener was busy preparing the body. It was the same guy as the last time I'd been here. "It's Howard, isn't it?" I said.

"Yes, ma'am." He didn't look up from what he was doing.

I was trying hard *not* to think about what he was doing. "Is that your first or last name?"

Sam was watching me, a curious expression on his face.

"First," the diener said, then glanced up. "Oh, hi, Sheriff." And the man actually smiled.

A jolt of resentment tightened my chest, startling me. I checked on Sam's reaction out of the corner of my eye. Did he notice me stiffen?

He was smiling back at the morgue attendant. Was the latter a sexist? Either that or he was one of those locals who resented new transplants from up north.

Sam was a transplant as well, but he'd been down here for years now. Had he made it into the old boy network?

Or Howard just doesn't like me.

I realized I was focusing on the diener's imagined prejudices to avoid thinking about the current status of things with Sam, *or* about what was coming next.

The ME himself, a short, dapper man with gray hair, entered the room. He was swathed in a disposable gown. After greeting us, he said, "Your boy here wasn't drunk. His blood alcohol level was only .07, but his clothes reeked of the stuff."

I nodded. "We found a broken pint bottle of whiskey. He probably took a few swigs for courage and then put it in his pocket or on his lap. It broke in the accident, soaked his clothes."

The ME gave me a brisk nod back. He snapped on gloves, turned on his recorder, and began his description of the body. "...African-American male, in seemingly good health, sixteen years of age..."

Those four words—sixteen years of age—hit me like a fist to my solar plexus. I may have even gasped a little.

Sam reached over and gave me a quick pat on the shoulder.

I looked his way, and realized my eyes were watery. His face wasn't very clear.

Suck it up, Anderson. I literally did just that, sucking in air through my mouth as I straightened my shoulders.

Sam offered a small smile of support.

I responded with a slight nod, managing, I hoped, to maintain a neutral expression. But my heart ached, and not only for the dead boy.

A hollowness had opened up inside of me, a longing for the ease I'd felt before in Sam's presence. I could only hope he assumed my awkwardness was due to the discomfort of attending an autopsy.

"This is interesting," the ME said. He was holding the boy's head turned to one side and pointing to something on the kid's neck.

"What's interesting, Doc?" Sam asked.

The ME gestured for us to approach. Since no incisions had been made yet, I figured it was safe to comply.

Sam and I stood on either side of the older man. I looked down.

Three tall rectangles on the boy's neck, the one in the middle the tallest. One of the shorter ones had been filled in with black. The other two were only dark outlines.

Hmm, doesn't work as well on brown skin.

"I'd say that's *not* an actual tattoo, but indelible ink on the surface." The ME shot the diener a sharp look, which I interpreted as a nonverbal scolding for not catching the markings when he washed the body. If it hadn't been *indelible* ink...

I glanced up and met Sam's eyes.

"My gut was right about possible connections." His voice was tense, but also sad. "The kid was a Pillar wannabe."

———— ❦ ————

We sat in the diner off of Route 301, between Jacksonville and Starling. Having placed our orders for breakfast at lunchtime, we both clutched cups of coffee. An awkward silence stretched out.

Or at least it felt awkward to me. I'd tried to get out of coming here with Sam, a fear growing inside me that he was going to confront me about my aloofness lately, and that would somehow lead to us breaking up.

But, as he'd pointed out, we were both running on empty. Neither of us had eaten since last night. A good idea before an autopsy, but not if one wants to be able to think straight.

Plus, I'd now been up for thirty-two hours straight. I needed fuel.

"So I'm–" I started, as he said, "Should we–"

We both stopped, let out nervous chuckles. Sam made a you-first gesture.

I took a deep breath. "I'm thinking the Navarro case is somehow related to the mayor's, via that gang tattoo on the kid's neck. And, if Patterson was attacked because I came to the jail to ask him about that case, then that's related as well."

I was stating the obvious, but the cases were the safest topic of conversation.

Sam nodded, sipped more coffee. "Have you talked to Foster in the Jax Sheriff's Office about this gang?"

"Not yet," I said. "At first I assumed I was cleaning up a shoddy investigation by Patterson and the former chief, or at worst, money had changed hands to make sure the investigation remained shoddy. I didn't particularly want to air that dirty laundry with the JSO."

"Makes sense, but now might be the time to read him in."

"Yeah. I'll make that call from my car, though, not in a crowded restaurant."

Sam nodded again, as our food arrived.

My stomach rumbled loudly. He chuckled.

I tucked into my veggie omelet and extra crispy bacon, not just to appease my hunger, but to avoid making further conversation.

"Are those green things I see in your eggs?" Sam asked.

"Tryin' to eat healthier," I mumbled around a mouthful.

"Good." He smiled. "I'd like you to stick around for a good long time."

I pretended I hadn't heard the comment, but my cheeks heated as I stuffed more bacon into my mouth.

Sam worked on his stack of blueberry pancakes for a while. The waitress came around and freshened our coffees.

Sam took a sip and smacked his lips. "Damn, they make good coffee here."

"And omelets," I muttered.

"So, what's next?"

I sat back and heaved a small sigh. "I had planned to talk to Navarro's sister today, before..." I waved my fork in the air, "...last night."

I stabbed a small chunk of green pepper on my plate. "My people are working the mayor's case, so I think I'm going to continue with that plan, once I talk to Foster."

"Any progress on the mayor's case?"

I made a face. "The car is leading us nowhere, except down a probably fake trail back to Hayes. My CS team found nothing useful in his study. Only random fingerprints, all of which belonged to members of his household or the city council and staffers. He said they had to hold a council meeting there a couple of weeks ago...Remember, when the building was being fumigated?"

We'd had an invasion of palmetto bugs the end of January, after a particularly wet month drove the creepy things inside. They were members of the roach family, but twice the size of their Maryland cousins, and they had wings. I shuddered at the memory of one landing on my desk chair, as I'd been about to sit down.

I pushed away the remnants of my omelet and the one remaining strip of bacon. "The lock on the French doors leading out to Hayes's patio is a joke. Someone could've picked it when no one was home and helped themselves to the rifle."

"But that someone had to have known the rifle was there. If it had been a random theft, they would've taken other things as well, like the computer." Sam paused. "And it's *lanai*."

I blinked, confused. "Who's Len Nigh?"

Sam gave me a smirky smile. "Lanai, not patio. Down here, they call it a lanai."

I rolled my eyes. "Yeah, it had to have been somebody who'd been in the house. But it could've been one of the kids' friends, who then gave or lent the gun to someone else."

"Or got nervous they would get caught and threw it away somewhere, and someone else found it."

I shook my head. "Unlikely, since the ammo for it was taken as well. That's pretty methodical. I think it's more likely someone intentionally took it, and the ammo for it, to set Hayes up. So it's someone he knows."

"That's a very long list. He's a politician."

"Exactly," I said. "The gun's not much help right now."

But I made a mental note to talk to Hayes again about possible enemies who might set him up this way. And to broach the delicate subject of interviewing his kids regarding anyone they might have had over to the house recently. It was conceivable that someone had asked, or even hired, one of their friends to steal the gun.

"What are you going to do next with your case?" I asked Sam, hoping to keep us talking shop so the conversation was at least close to normal levels of relaxed.

"Have a long chat with that corrections officer who found Patterson and supposedly attempted to stop the bleeding. After having cooled his heels on leave for a couple of days, I'm hoping he'll be more forthcoming.

If someone on my jail's staff helped with that attack..." He trailed off, his lips clamped into a tight line.

I nodded sympathetically, but then couldn't resist playing devil's advocate. "He could've just disliked Patterson, a bent cop, so when he found him, he didn't try that hard to save him."

Sam nodded, his expression still sour, as he raised a hand to signal for the check.

I was a little uncomfortable with letting him pay, considering how I was feeling about him right now. But that was one thing he was old-fashioned about. "In all else," he'd said one time, "we're equals, but I hold open doors and pay restaurant tabs. Otherwise, I have to deal with my father's voice in my head, yelling, 'I raised you better than that, boy.'"

Out by my car in the parking lot, Sam leaned in for a kiss.

I knew it would be a chaste one in this setting, but I couldn't... I turned my head to the side. "I, uh, think I'm coming down with something. And I haven't had a Covid booster recently."

His gaze lingered on my face for a few seconds, before he gave me a small smile. "Okay, I'll call you later."

"I'll let you know if Foster has anything interesting for us."

He nodded and jogged off toward his vehicle.

And I felt like a heel, for several reasons—one being that the expected ambush about our relationship had never happened.

Detective Foster, a veteran with the Jacksonville Sheriff's Office, did indeed have some interesting things to tell me.

"Yes, I'm familiar with that gang." His voice, coming from my dashboard speaker, sounded a bit gravelly. "Have you seen their tattoo?"

"Yeah. Do you know what it means?" I pulled off of Route 301 onto the road leading to Starling.

"I do. The taller white rectangle is the main pillar of society. In other words, white people hold our society up."

"And it's taller because whites are superior?"

"That's what it used to mean. But that's not what they're selling to their newer, more diverse recruits."

"I know of a couple of cases here in Starling where they've recruited Latino and Black kids, or tried to."

"They're telling them," Foster said, "that the other pillars are also important to our society. They're smaller only because there happen to be fewer black and brown people."

"Uh huh, but I've heard that they use the minority recruits to do the more dangerous jobs."

"Like run down your mayor."

"Oh," I said, "you *are* well informed."

"I've got a buddy in the gang unit. He got a copy of the ME's preliminary report, because of the inked-on tattoo."

"The ME's office is really on the ball then," I said. "I just left that autopsy a little over an hour ago."

"They are when it comes to this gang. They've been more active lately, and the sheriff here is concerned."

"More active how?" I asked.

"Recruiting more, and as already mentioned, more diversely. And my unit's got a recent hit-and-run homicide that we think is linked to them. Kinda similar to your mayor's accident, only the victim was walking down the sidewalk. Driver got away, and we later found the car, but no sign of him. Car was stolen, of course."

"Of course. What makes you think it's linked to this gang?"

"The victim was a prominent Black businessman, who also funded a charity aimed at connecting with at-risk kids and convincing them to stay in school and out of the gangs."

"Oh."

"Yeah," Foster said.

"I'll send you copies of the reports on our cases that we think may be connected to this gang. Or in one case, we know they're connected to it."

"The Navarro case?" Foster asked.

"Yup, that's the one," I said, as I pulled into the municipal building's parking lot. "But it's a lot more complicated than that."

"Sounds like I have my afternoon reading all lined up. I'll send you the file on the businessman."

"Thanks."

Foster disconnected.

I turned off my engine and sat back in the driver's seat. Heaving a sigh, I called Barnes. "You got current contact info on Navarro's sister?" I asked.

"She works at a daycare center, and they are open on Saturdays. She gets off at five-fifteen. Want me to text you the center's and her home addresses, and her phone number?"

"Yes. I'll catch up with her after work. Anything else going on I need to be involved in?"

"Nope. Everybody's out in the field. Cruthers and Collins are at Christopher Jones's school, talking to his friends. I'm not sure where my brother is."

I asked her to forward the relevant case files to Foster, including a note about the missing witness in the Navarro case. "And get a copy of Bert's report on the hairs added to that file before you send it over."

"What hairs?"

That's right...I hadn't filled her in on that yet, nor on Alvarez's lie that he hadn't been at the crime scene, when he actually had been there.

Suddenly exhausted, I said, "Ask Bert to tell you about it. I'm gonna go home and catch a couple of hours sleep."

"Sweet dreams, Chief." She disconnected.

"Yeah, right," I muttered to myself.

<hr />

I held my breath as I opened my apartment door.

My prayers were answered. Paulie, um Paul—*Damn, that's taking some getting used to*—was not home. A note on the breakfast bar said he was apartment shopping.

I stumbled into the bedroom. Pipsqueak followed, rubbing against my ankles. I picked her up and held her nose to nose. "Sorry little girl, but I really need to sleep."

I closed her in the study, now Paul's—yay, I remembered that time—room.

Back in my own room, I stripped off my jacket and kicked off my shoes. Otherwise still fully dressed, I flopped onto the bed and fell asleep, literally as my head hit the pillow.

A persistent ringing slowly pulled me back from oblivion.

I opened one eye. No cell phone on my nightstand. Where was it?

More ringing. It was coming from the pocket of my jacket, on the floor next to my bed. I reached down for it.

The ringing had stopped.

"Thank you, lord," I muttered and closed my eyes.

Brringg, brringg.

"Aw, shit."

I sat up on the side of the bed, looked at my alarm clock, and groaned. I'd been asleep an hour and ten minutes.

Berringg, brringg. Was it my imagination or was the ringing more insistent?

I picked up the jacket, fumbled the phone out of its pocket, and answered it. "This better be good."

"Chief, it's Peter McAllister. Please, don't hang up. I owe you an apology. And I have something important to tell you."

CHAPTER EIGHTEEN

"What?" I said, my voice abrupt. I decided I was okay with that.

"Um, I'd rather not get into it over the phone," McAllister said. "And I do sincerely apologize for the scene this morning. I was...Well, you were just doing your job."

"I can meet you later, around six." I tried to modulate my tone. After all, it was mid-afternoon. The guy didn't know he'd awakened me from a sound sleep. And he was apologetic, as he should be.

"Um, I think what I have to tell you is kind of important. And after you hear it, you'll maybe understand better why I was so upset this morning."

I glanced at my bedside clock again—three-twenty. "Meet me at four, in my office."

"Might be better at the deli down the street. I'm not sure I'm allowed into the building now."

"Good point. At the deli." I disconnected, hoping none of my cops would be hanging around there that late in the afternoon. If word got back to Hayes that I'd met with McAllister...

Damn, I hate politics!

McAllister was at a back booth, nursing a cup of coffee.

I'd no sooner sat down than the deli owner's teeny-bopper grand-daughter appeared at my elbow, with a steaming pot.

"High test, right, Chief? Black."

"Good memory," I said.

She smiled, flashing a mouthful of metal braces. "Gramps says I can take over this place, when he retires, if I show that I'm a good worker and treat customers, quote, 'like the queens and kings that they are.' What can I get y'all?"

"I'd watch who you call *queens*," McAllister muttered under his breath.

Ah, a little homophobic, are we?

I gave the girl a smile back. "Nothing else. Thanks for the coffee."

She grinned and practically skipped back up the narrow aisle between the booths and the glass-front display cases of meats, cheeses and a multitude of salads.

"Again," McAllister said, "let me apologize–"

I held up a hand, cutting him off. "Apology accepted. We're all a bit on edge right now."

"More than a bit in my case, it turns out. Mayor Daniels was a friend. I didn't realize how much his death had affected me until I saw Hayes sitting in his chair."

"So, what did you need to tell me?"

"That call I said I made to Hayes, it never happened."

My jaw dropped despite myself. "What do you mean?"

"He called me, sounding kinda panicky, said he'd been in the park for other reasons and heard the shots. He ran over and saw the mayor on the ground. The mayor choked out, 'There you are, Hayes,' as if they were supposed to meet there. So Hayes went along with that, then called me."

McAllister paused, took a sip of coffee. "He said he was meeting a lady friend there, in the park, but it was in the early stages. He didn't want his kids finding out and getting upset, when the relationship might not go anywhere. I said, 'And the press.' He conceded that he didn't want them finding out either, but again because a big deal on the news about his new girlfriend would upset his kids. Especially the youngest, he said, who was really struggling with his mother's death."

McAllister slowly shook his head. "All that sounded reasonable at the time. Until later, when I found out about the note on Danny's desk. But by that point, Hayes had already told the police that I'd called him. I decided to go along for a while and see what happened. I was about to speak up when that rifle y'all had found turned out to belong to Hayes. But then you said that was too obvious a set-up. So I stayed quiet. Something I'm now regretting."

Indeed, you told more lies to cover for the first one.

He blinked several times. His eyes were watery. "Maybe if I'd told you the truth sooner, Danny would still be alive."

I'd never heard anyone call Mayor Daniels *Danny* before. Maybe this guy was a close friend. I wouldn't have put it past Daniels to indulge in some nepotism and give a friend a made-up job in the city government.

"So what about the note on his desk?" I asked.

"Oh, that was bogus. It wasn't from me. But it wouldn't have been hard for Hayes to find something I'd written and mimic my printing. You see, I always print things like that. My handwriting is atrocious. Nobody can read it." He gave a wan smile. "Sometimes I can't read it myself."

"And also easy for Hayes to take back the note after the mayor had seen it," I said. Their offices were near each other, and the staff wouldn't have thought it strange to see Hayes go into the mayor's office, even when he wasn't there.

Something occurred to my sleep-deprived brain. Why would Hayes meet a girlfriend in Holly Park, which was on the edge of the red-light district?

Was he really meeting a prostitute? I opted to keep that thought to myself. But it made more sense than a girlfriend. Hayes's wife had been dead less than six months.

And meeting a pro for sex would definitely be something he would not want anyone, especially the press or his kids to find out.

"Anything else you need to tell me?" I asked.

"Nope, that's it." McAllister flashed one of his charming smiles, which had seemed kind of smarmy before. But now I was warming up to the guy, despite his homophobic crack. Maybe he'd been trying to be funny.

I gave him a small smile back, and rose from the bench, dropping a ten-dollar bill on the table. "Thanks for coming clean about the call. And I'm sorry for your loss."

"Thanks." He picked up the bill and tried to hand it back to me. "I've got this."

"Leave it for the girl."

He muttered a couple words under his breath, but then smiled again. "She's a cutie, isn't she?"

"Yes, she is."

"Oh, by the way..." McAllister stood, looking past me at the empty booth next door. "Um, can you be a bit discreet about all this?" he asked in a low voice. "As you know I'm job-hunting now, and being used as a pawn by a murderer wouldn't exactly be good for my reputation."

"We don't know yet," I said, also in a low voice, "that he *is* a murderer, but I will certainly check this out. And yes, I'll be discreet."

At five-fifteen, I was waiting in my car outside the daycare center where Navarro's sister worked.

I'd called Bradley, filled him in on what McAllister had told me, and sworn him to secrecy. "For now," I'd added.

"Locate Hayes and ask him if you can see his phone and the number of the caller Wednesday morning, whom he's saying was McAllister. And note what other calls he made or received that morning. If he won't show you his phone or he's deleted recent calls, then thank him politely and get started on a warrant application for his phone records."

The briefest of pauses, before Bradley had said, "You got it, Chief."

Now, I was trying to decide how I felt about Mark Hayes. Even if the more innocent explanation turned out to be true, he was either sneaking around on the sly with some woman or he was using prostitutes. Having a secret girlfriend wouldn't be that bad, but I was leaning more toward the prostitute angle, considering the location of his planned tryst.

I shoved those thoughts aside and sat up straighter in my seat, as several moms and one dad, all with small children in tow, exited the building and headed for vehicles scattered around the parking lot.

A few minutes later, a petite Latina, roughly mid-twenties, came out the door.

I jumped out of my car and approached her. "Maria Navarro?"

She tensed and gave me a wary look. "Who wants to know?"

I pulled my badge from my pocket and showed it to her.

She examined it for a couple of seconds, relaxed some, then her eyebrows went up. "*Chief* of Police?"

"Yes. I'm following up on your brother's case."

"About time. You gonna see that those scumbags get longer sentences?"

"Well..." I was about to say that wasn't possible at this point. They'd already been given plea deals.

But, if I find proof that they'd lied...

"Possibly," I said instead. "Is there somewhere we can talk?"

She glanced around. "We can sit in my car."

"That's fine."

She led the way to a small blue compact, even smaller than mine. A Mini Cooper convertible, older model.

She was a good four inches shorter than me and slid behind the driver's seat with ease. It took me a moment to figure out how to fold my five-seven frame into the passenger seat.

She lowered her window halfway. I followed suit. Even in February, the car was warm inside from sitting in the sun all day.

She turned in her seat to face me. "I guess you want to hear about the rape." Her tone was jarringly abrupt.

A defense mechanism, I surmised.

"Did you recognize the men?" The file had been sketchy on details. *Two white males* was all it had said.

"No, they had white hoods over their heads, and wore black leather jackets."

"Hoods? Like the KKK?"

She nodded.

Why wasn't that *in the file on the SA? And what the hell else was missing?*

The rape kit report *had* been in there, at least. It said no semen, but traces of latex. They'd worn condoms. Once again, we'd had almost nothing to go on.

But now we had hoods and leather jackets, although I wasn't sure how that helped.

"They grabbed my arms from behind," Maria was saying. "I was putting groceries in my backseat, and when I backed out of the car, they were there..." She closed her eyes, her face pinched. "They were on me in a second and dragging me into a van."

After a pause, she opened her eyes but remained silent, now staring out the windshield.

"Is there anything else you can tell me" I said gently, "that might help us to identify them?"

"Wait, the one that was holding me down first, he had letters tattooed on his knuckles. They spelled *love*. I thought at the time that these bastards had an odd way of showing it."

Prison tattoos! L-O-V-E on one hand and H-A-T-E on the other.

"Did you tell the officer about that at the time?"

"No, I just now thought of it."

I nodded. "Anything else on his hands? Or on the other guy's?" I was praying for a swastika, like the one on Alfie Taft's hand.

She thought for a moment, then shook her head. "I only saw his one hand. And the other guy... I don't know. I mean, he wasn't wearing gloves, but I never really got a good look at his hands."

Damn, I thought, but said, "Thanks. That bit about the tattoos will help."

"Miguel was really torn up about it. He was sure they were from some gang that had been trying to recruit him, and none too gently. He'd filed a harassment complaint against them, but that night they found him and beat him up, bad. Said if he didn't withdraw it, they'd kill him."

Her eyes filled with tears. "So he did, and a week later, I was raped. And the night after that, he was dead."

"Did he say which gang?"

She shook her head again. "It didn't matter. Miguel had no interest in that lifestyle. He was planning on going to art school, once he'd saved up enough money." A tear broke loose and trickled down her cheek. "He was very talented."

She turned toward me again, shoulders back, face defiant. "And no way was he using drugs. He was a health nut. Your body is a temple and all that jazz. That crap about it being a drug deal that went bad is total BS."

This certainly all fit with the scenario I'd been using as my working theory. The gang members had approached Miguel again, maybe to threaten more bad things would happen to his family. But he still refused to join up. So they killed him and planted the cocaine to make it look like a drug deal gone bad.

And that would explain the amount of the cocaine. Why waste an entire eightball when a smaller amount would do?

"I'm sorry for making you relive all this," I said.

She deflated, then sighed. "No biggie. I relive it every night, when I go to bed and close my eyes."

———◆———

My phone rang halfway back to the municipal building.

"Caught up with our interim mayor," Bradley said when I answered. "His phone only shows one call that morning, before the shooting. An incoming call from a number he's saying he doesn't recognize. But he's swearing that call was from McAllister, telling him to meet the mayor in the park."

"He didn't make any calls?" I asked.

"Not from his cell phone," Bradley said.

"So if he called McAllister to ask him to lie for him *after* the shots were fired, where the hell did he call from?"

"Maybe he called from his house after you left. Was that before you talked to McAllister?"

"Yes, it was. Okay, go ahead with a search warrant request for his home phone and cell records. Time to take off the kid gloves. And get Derek working on the origin of that unknown number on Hayes's cell from that morning."

"You got it, Chief."

Dusk was descending on the city as I parked my car in the municipal lot. The sun had just slipped behind the buildings, casting long shadows.

I decided to take a walk. Maybe some brisk exercise would help the blood flow to my tired brain.

I suddenly felt someone fall into step beside me. I whirled around.

Peter McAllister stood there, a tad too close.

Resisting the urge to step back, I patted my chest and willed my jittery heart to slow down. "You startled me."

He gave me a weird half smile. "Sorry, Chief." We started walking again. "Um, there's something else I wanted to tell you—another reason why I'm not at my best right now....I'm, uh, going through a divorce, and it's getting messy."

I stifled a sigh. Being a good listener was essential for a police detective, but sometimes it backfired and led to the interviewee believing you were a confidante, a friend even.

"No kids, thank God," he said. "That would be even messier."

Why is he telling me this? I wasn't *that* good a listener. Or was he setting things up to make me feel sorry for him?

Or was he about to ask me out? *Aw, shit!* My heart picked up speed again.

"I have a boyfriend." Oops, I was more tired than I thought. Those words were supposed to stay inside my brain, not pop out of my mouth.

McAllister looked chagrined for a second, but then he flashed the charming smile. "I'm sorry. I didn't mean to make you think I was hitting on you."

Weren't you? my inner skeptic commented. Thankfully the words stayed inside my head this time.

I felt my cheeks heating. To rescue us both from the awkwardness, I quickly said, "I know someone who's about to become a divorce mediator. Have you thought of trying that?"

McAllister stopped a few feet from the nearest street corner. "That might be a good idea. Do you have this person's card?"

"Um, no, he hasn't actually finished his training yet. But he could explain to you how it works, and help you connect with someone who's good at it."

"That would be great."

"I'll text you his number. Look, I need to follow up about that phone–"

As if my words had conjured him up, I spotted Bill Walker stepping off the curb at the opposite corner.

And I was extremely grateful for that distraction, as it dawned on me that I shouldn't say anything just yet to McAllister about who called who—not until we'd checked all of Mark Hayes's phone records.

"Hey, Bill." I waved.

Walker paused in mid-step, looked my way, and smiled. His face was partially in shadow, but there was no mistaking those pearly whites—the product of expensive orthodontics during his silver-spoon upbringing, which had sadly also exposed him to domestic violence. DV cut across all socio-economic strata.

A large, rectangular shadow loomed between us. A woman screamed, and a white truck raced through the intersection.

When it was gone, Bill Walker was lying on the asphalt.

Heart in my throat, I bolted into the street, waving my badge, praying that was enough to stop any oncoming traffic.

A flash of khaki ahead. The tilt of a man's head.

I froze for a second in the middle of the intersection. "Sam?" I yelled.

He glanced up, looked around, but not at me. Then he was absorbed by the crowd of bystanders.

"I called for an ambulance." McAllister's voice from behind me.

It brought me out of my confused stupor. I raced forward, pushing people aside. And there was Walker on the ground, groaning and clutching his right leg.

The wave of relief was so strong, it made my knees wobble.

He's alive.

CHAPTER NINETEEN

So many things that could've happened differently!

I couldn't seem to stop that thought from looping through my brain.

If I hadn't called out, causing Bill to pause? If the woman who'd screamed hadn't looked up to see the white van? If her companion hadn't reached out and grabbed Bill's shoulder, yanking him backward?

The van had raced forward and clipped his right side, sending him spinning to the ground. But if it hadn't been for all those other things... I paused, making myself stop to breathe. If it hadn't been for all that, he would be dead, instead of strapped to a gurney and on his way to the hospital.

I stood still, willing my heart to slow down. Then I looked around. Where the hell had McAllister gone? I didn't see him anywhere.

Whatever. He wasn't the problem right now. I needed to get my people organized. Get them to interviewing all these pedestrians, before they scattered to the winds.

Suddenly, Barnes was by my side, and her brother. "Stop these people from leaving," I gasped out.

They moved off holding their arms out, herding people, telling them to stay calm, to remain on the scene.

I slumped to the curb, fighting tears. "Why am I reacting like this?" I mumbled.

"Because it was too much all at once."

I jerked around. Sam was sitting beside me on the curb.

"Where the hell did you come from?" I demanded, my voice not at all friendly.

He had the audacity to smile. "I was in the deli, having coffee...with someone." He pushed his wannabe Stetson to the back of his head. "Did you get any sleep at all today?"

I snorted softly, beginning to get my bearings. "A little over an hour."

He shook his head. "I don't know about you, Anderson, but I'm getting too old for these kinda hours."

He'd said it with a chuckle in his voice, trying to lighten the mood, but I wasn't totally sure I was willing to take it that way.

"Seriously," Sam said, "things are happening too fast here. Every time we pursue a lead, something happens..." he trailed off.

"Oh, my God. Maria!" I fumbled my phone out of my pocket and called the watch desk.

"Hey, Chief." Sergeant Armstrong's voice.

"Sarge, send a uniform to do a wellness check on Maria Navarro, sister of a murder victim, Miguel Navarro. Her address is in his case file. And then put a protection unit on her, two cruisers, front and back of her place."

"You got it, Chief."

Sam put his arm around my shoulders. I realized I was shaking.

"I've got a really bad feeling about all this," I said.

"So do I." Sam's voice was grim.

"I guess Saturday night steaks on the deck aren't happening tonight," Sam said as he stood in my office doorway, hat in hand.

I shook my head, hoping my rueful expression was convincing. And part of me was disappointed, on many levels. I looked forward to our standing Saturday-night dates. Some weeks, it was my only chance to truly relax.

"If we somehow, miraculously, solve this case by this evening," I said, "I plan to go home and crash."

He nodded. "Watch your back, Chief."

"And you yours, Sheriff." Another mini-tradition we'd developed when one or the other of us or both were working a tough case.

He went out the door as Bradley entered the bullpen, his sister in tow. I waved them over to my office. "What have we got?"

Bradley sprawled in the comfy visitor's chair. "Conflicting reports from the bystanders. Why are eyewitnesses so unreliable?"

"Because they're human," I said.

He nodded, his expression glum. "General consensus, though, is that it was a white panel truck, no markings. One fella got a partial plate."

"KRP," Barnes said, consulting her notepad. She was in her usual spot, leaning against the doorjamb of the open doorway. "No white panel trucks registered with those three letters in their plate numbers in a four-county radius."

"However," Bradley held up an index finger, "a plate, with those three letters on the end, was reported stolen by the owner of a 2021 pickup in Duval County."

"Stolen when?" I asked.

"Last March," he replied. "Almost a year ago."

Something occurred to me. "Hang on a sec." I called up the Navarro sexual assault report. "Yup. Maria Navarro described the vehicle she was dragged into as a white van."

I picked up my cell, found her contact info, and punched her home number into my desk phone.

"Hello?"

"Hi Maria, Chief Anderson here. Quick question. The van, that evening, could it have been a commercial panel truck?"

"Um, I guess. It was, like, more heavy duty—sturdier than a minivan a mom would drive. The back was empty, except for black rubber mats on the floor."

"Thanks. That's very helpful–"

"Hey, why is there a cop car in front of my aunt's house?"

"Your aunt's house?" I asked, momentarily confused.

"Well, my house too, I guess. I live with her."

"Um, there's one in the back as well. Just a precaution. Were you planning on going out tonight or tomorrow?"

"Not tonight, but I was going to take my aunt to church in the morning. She doesn't drive."

"Okay, I'll instruct my people to use an unmarked car in the morning, and to be discreet."

"But why? Am I in danger?"

"Probably not, but ever since I began looking into your brother's homicide again, well, some things have been happening. If you notice anything strange, the least bit off, call 911 and give them your name, you'll be connected to the officers in those cars outside, okay?"

"Yeah, I guess. The neighbors are gonna think I'm in some kind of trouble with the law."

"I'm sorry about that, but the cruisers are also a deterrent."

"Okay. How long will I be under siege?"

"Hopefully not beyond the weekend."

I disconnected and looked at Bradley, who was watching me intently. "Yes," I said, "it could've been a panel truck. No seats in the back, only black floor mats."

"So you're thinking Walker's accident wasn't one?"

I nodded.

"No fresh skid marks in the intersection," he said.

I nodded again. "If anything, it seemed like the driver sped up. Barnes–"

"Check on his condition." She headed for her desk.

"You thinking what I'm thinking?" Bradley asked. "That all this is related."

"Yes, and it all seems to revolve around gangs. Maria didn't know what gang was trying to recruit her brother, but my money is on The Pillar, since their men later killed him."

Bradley nodded. "I've been reading up on gangs in general. One article was particularly interesting."

He leaned forward in his chair. "The gangs that have connections to those in Central America, they started moving in a new direction about twenty years ago. There were no-tolerance crackdowns in a lot of those countries, beginning in the late nineties. Anybody with gang tats and/or hanging out in large groups came under the scrutiny of government forces, who often shot first and asked questions later. As a result, some of the gangs shifted gears. Rather than trying to intimidate the citizenry and rival gangs, they went more undercover. And they began recruiting preppy types who could blend in, and who were attracted to the kind of money that gangs rake in from drugs and extortion."

"Say what?" I said.

"Yeah, and that trend drifted northward, into the U.S." Bradley shook his head. "There are still plenty of old-style members—like the two who went after Navarro. Covered in ink and blatant about their gang affiliation, and more violent. But a fair number of gang members now, they're going for the subtle approach, and they're living longer."

"What do you mean?" Barnes asked, having resumed her position in the doorway.

Her brother looked at her. "It's still a violent lifestyle, but with less emphasis on gang rivalry and more on making money, the average lifespan of gang members has risen to forty. It used to be thirty."

"Oh, wow," she said, her eyes wide. Then she turned to me. "Mr. Walker was treated and released. They wouldn't tell me about his injuries."

I blew out a sigh of relief. "They couldn't be that bad though, if they didn't keep him."

Bradley nodded, his face relaxing some. "Checking further into the two gang members whom we know were involved in Navarro's death, I found some more details. In addition to the reduced charges, the three-strikes rule was waived."

He ran a hand through his dark hair, leaving it sticking up in places. Circles under his eyes said he'd gotten about the same amount of sleep in the last thirty-some hours as I had. "And their fines were paid in cash sent via a courier."

"Paid by the gang," I inserted.

"Very likely." Bradley gestured toward my computer. "You might not have seen Derek's report yet. He wasn't able to find much on the gang's finances *per se*. Apparently they don't have bank accounts and such. Or if they do, they're well hidden behind dummy corporation names. But both Taft and Thompson have off-shore bank accounts, and their commissary accounts in prison have been kept full."

He leaned even farther forward, elbows propped on his knees. "Here's something else that's interesting. The Gang Unit in Jax says two members of The Pillar's upper echelon haven't been seen or heard from in months."

"What do they think that means?" I asked.

Bradley shrugged. "There could've been an internal power struggle, and they're both in shallow graves somewhere. Or they may have decided to get out of the life, and they have new identities now."

He pushed himself to a stand, a soft moan escaping his lips.

"Find out one other thing for me," I said, "and then go home and grab some sleep."

"What's that, Chief?"

"Find out if either Thompson or Taft have love-hate tattoos on their knuckles. Maria Navarro recalled that detail today." If I remembered correctly, Taft had H-A-T-E on the same hand with the swastika. Odds were good he had L-O-V-E on the other one. And Thompson—he'd had those weird blurry spots on his scarred knuckles. Had there been tattoos there that he'd had removed, maybe after he realized Maria might have seen them?

Bradley nodded and left, Barnes trailing after him.

I was staring into space, trying to decide what to do next—go home and try to get some rest, or order something in for dinner—when Bill Walker appeared in my doorway, on crutches.

"Hey there," I said. "Am I glad to see you."

"Hey." He maneuvered over to a visitor's chair. "Figured I'd touch base, and thank you for saving my life."

"Wasn't me. The couple behind you pulled you back."

"But if you hadn't called my name, I would've taken another step, right into that truck's path."

"How bad is it?" I gestured toward his crutches, now propped against the front of my desk.

"Broken leg, a couple of cracked ribs." He held up a hand, the wrist wrapped in an elastic bandage. "And a mild sprain. Landed wrong on it. But it could've been a lot worse."

He shook his head slightly. "And the irony is, I was coming to tell you I'd put out feelers to some guys I know from prison, but I'd gotten nothing back."

"Why do you say irony?"

"Because they wasted a perfectly good hit-and-run on me, since I had nada to report anyway."

I sat up straighter in my desk chair. "You think it was intentional then?"

Bill nodded. "I got a glimpse of the driver, just before he hit me. He was looking right at me, and smiling." He mimicked a broad grin.

"Confirms what we'd already suspected. Could you identify him?"

The grin faded. "Probably not. He had a baseball cap pulled down over his upper face. Not even sure of his race. Latino, or maybe a white guy with a tan."

"Could you work with Derek and try for a sketch?"

"Sure, but *try* is the operative word there."

"I'm so sorry you got hurt."

He shrugged. "Comes with the territory, I guess, when you work for the police." He gave me a half smile. "Even as a janitor."

"Yeah, but that job's not *supposed* to be dangerous. Is there any way to cancel those 'feelers?'" I made air quotes.

"No, and trying to might make things worse."

"How'd you get here anyway, with your right leg out of commission?"

"Uber, which is what I should've done earlier, but I thought it was a nice evening for a walk. My car's on the fritz."

"Okay, I'm sending you home with a uniform." I reached for my desk phone. "He'll bunk on your sofa 'til this is over."

He held up a hand. "I don't have a sofa. I live in a rooming house. How about if I bunk here, in my supply closet? I've got a cot in there. I use it to catch a couple hours of sleep between the end of my shift and my first morning class. Helps me focus better."

"Sure. I was about to call out for something for dinner. You want anything?"

A low grumble came from his stomach.

We both chuckled. "Italian sound good?" I asked.

"Sounds great. My treat, for the part you played in saving my ass."

I reached for my phone, but Bradley appeared in my doorway. He broke out a full smile at the sight of Walker. "Hey, Bill, glad to see you up and about so quick."

Then Bradley turned to me. "They both have those tattoos on their hands."

"Both?" I questioned, my eyebrows raised.

"Well, that's what their intake records from Raiford say."

Aha, so Thompson did *get his love-hate tats removed.*

"Before you leave," I said, "get someone to pull Maria's rape kit and take it to the FDLE lab, to check for their touch DNA on her clothes. I'd love to add some years to those bastards' sentences for sexual assault."

"You got it." Bradley disappeared.

Bill Walker gave me a curious look, but he was too discreet to ask questions.

I offered a somewhat general answer anyway. "We're starting to connect some dots, including to a sexual assault from May. Might've been the same truck used."

Walker's lips pressed into a grim line. "Let me know if there's anything else I can do to help."

⸻◆⸻

After dinner at my desk with Bill Walker, I opted to go home and get some rest. My people would call me if there were any new developments.

But sleep was not in my immediate future. Paul was home.

He sat at the breakfast bar, a cold beer in front of him, and examined an eight-by-ten package, wrapped in brown paper.

We exchanged greetings and he held up the package. "This came in the mail. Looks like it might have been damaged. Wrapping's torn."

I took it from him and laid it back on the counter, then walked past him into the kitchen. "It doesn't matter."

I poured myself a glass of wine, telling myself to savor it. I wouldn't be able to have more than one, since the odds were high I'd have to go back to work later.

"Who's Camille Maxwell?" Paul asked.

"She was Camille Anderson for a decade." I sipped wine and resisted the urge to smack my lips.

Paul's eyebrows were halfway up his forehead. "Your stepmother?"

"Yeah. She sends me a birthday gift every year."

Paul poked a finger through the hole in one corner. "It's soft, whatever it is."

"Probably cashmere. She loves it."

"Well, aren't you going to open it?"

I shrugged. "I always give whatever it is to Goodwill."

"Still wrapped up?"

"No, I unwrap it. There's a note, which I toss, but I can't bring myself to throw away perfectly good clothing." I turned toward the refrigerator. "Hey, did you eat? There's lunchmeat in the fridge."

"I had something already." Paper rustling.

I turned back around, and snatched at the note in his hand. "Hey, what are you doing?"

He jerked away from me. "Just curious. And why is this so late coming? Your birthday was two weeks ago."

I checked the wrapping he'd left on the counter. "I was hoping by moving out of state, I'd duck her. But she sent it first class and it was forwarded."

He was perusing the note that had been inside. "You've never acknowledged the gifts?"

I shook my head. "I lived with her for less than a year, and our last conversation was a guilt trip from her for, quote, 'going behind their backs' to file for emancipation."

After my mother had died... I stopped myself, forced my mind to acknowledge reality. After my mother had committed suicide, I'd had two options, live with my father and his new wife or go into foster care.

Of course, for the latter to happen, I would've had to lie to prove my father unfit. And although he'd been abusive to my mother and I blamed him for her death, he'd never laid a hand on me.

Still, it had been a tough choice, and rough going. Dad and I had eventually achieved an uneasy truce by ignoring each other. But my stepmother kept trying to fix things.

When I'd turned seventeen, after being accepted for early admission to the University of Maryland, I'd filed for emancipation.

Now, with thirty-years distance, I could feel kind of sorry for Camille. She had done her best to parent me, had even insisted I get counseling. Which turned out to be a good thing, although I'd never have admitted it back then.

I was an angry teenager, whose mother had abandoned her. And Camille was barely thirty, sixteen years my father's junior. She'd never stood a chance in that household.

But she still clung to the myth that we had some kind of relationship, even though she'd been divorced from my father for twenty years and he'd been dead for ten. I shook my head again.

"Judith." Paul's voice pulled me out of my reverie. He sounded odd, a bit strangled.

I glanced his way.

The note still in his hands, he was staring at me, his eyes wide. "She's dying."

CHAPTER TWENTY

It was cashmere. A soft, light beige sweater.

The note began with: *I know you prefer to wear black and white, but this shade I think would look really good on you.*

She was probably right. It was about the same shade as the satiny lounging outfit Sam had given me for Christmas.

But it's so typical of her, ignoring what I want and imposing what she thinks is best.

Okay, that voice in my head sounded like a whiny teenager.

With Paul watching, I had little choice but to keep reading.

If you don't like it, though, there's a gift slip. It's from Nordstrom's. I'm sure they have one of those near you, in Jacksonville maybe.

It was a gorgeous sweater, but who wants to wear something that constantly reminds one of their dead mother, their abusive father and his rather pathetic second wife.

Okay, I'm stalling. It's really hard to write this next part. You see, I've been told, by my doctors, that I only have 5 or 6 months to live.

My eyes suddenly felt gritty. I resisted the urge to rub them. Paul might get the wrong idea.

I know I've said in previous notes that I might have saved my marriage to your father if I'd been able to do a better job of mothering you. That maybe then he wouldn't have been so angry with me.

Say what? That was some sick, twisted logic.

But I've come to realize that was wrong thinking, maybe even total BS. Your father was an angry man long before I met him, and no doubt long before your mother met him.

I don't know why it's taken me this long to acknowledge that, to myself and to you. But I felt it was important that I do that, before I have to go.

You don't need to write back or anything. I know you're a very busy person, a chief of police now, no less! I'm very proud of you.

I just wanted you to know I'm thinking of you, and I've finally faced the truth. Maybe now I can go in peace.

Love, Camille.

Somewhere along the way, the hand not holding the note had gone to my neck, where a large lump had formed in my throat.

I swallowed hard and said, "I can't believe she wrote *BS*. I never heard a cuss word cross her lips."

Her euphemistic use of *go* instead of *die* was more her style. Even as a thirty-year-old, she'd been a bit of a prude. But at least another thirty years had opened her eyes to a few realities.

"Are you going to write her back?" Paul asked.

"I don't know." I grabbed up the brown wrapping paper and sweater and threw them, along with the note, onto a pile of boxes along one wall of the living room.

Someday, I might actually have time to unpack those boxes.

"I'll think about that later. Right now, I need some sleep."

The woman was lying on the kitchen floor, the pill bottle beside her. She slowly rose and turned toward me. "You really should be nicer to her."

"Sheez, Mom, not you too." The voice was that of a peevish teen. "That's what Dad's always saying."

"She's doing the best she can."

"But she's the one who took Dad away from us."

"Not you, darling." Tears pooled in my mother's eyes. "Only me."

An annoying buzzing sound interrupted my thoughts. I'd been about to say something to my mother. What was it?

The buzz came again, followed by a ping.

I opened one eye. My cop-issue cell phone was dancing around on my nightstand, vibrating and pinging.

I sat up and rubbed my eyes, then glanced at the bedside clock...10:05. My bedroom curtains were drawn closed, but I assumed that was p.m.

I picked up the phone and read the text. It was from Bradley.

We might have the truck.

Did you get any rest?

A couple hours. I'm fine.

Okay, I'll be in soon.

I took a quick shower and donned a fresh black pantsuit and white shirt.

As I started to shove my personal phone into my briefcase with my laptop, I realized I had an unread message. It was from Kate, sent at eight-ten. *Hey Judith, got time to chat this evening?*

I sighed. The thought of a chat with Kate was setting off mixed feelings for a change. Normally, it was great to be able to let my hair down with someone safe. But right now... I wasn't ready to talk about my stepmother, nor did I want to rehash the Sam situation.

I texted back, knowing she was probably still up. *Sorry. On my way back to the office. This case keeps getting bigger and bigger.*

Okay, maybe tomorrow some time. Text me whenever you can.

Will do.

I immediately felt guilty. Did she want to talk to me about something going on in *her* life? Why did I always assume she was checking on me, wanting to hear my troubles?

I sighed again and shelved that concern for another time.

Outside my apartment building, the night air was cool but dripping with humidity. A stiff breeze ruffled my hair. Thunder rumbled in the distance.

A thunderstorm in February? I shrugged. I was learning that anything was possible with Florida weather.

A raindrop hit my hand as I reached for my door handle. Another plopped onto my head. I scrambled into the car, just in time. The sky opened up.

I checked in my mirror, finger-combed my short hair back into place, and headed for 3MB. Halfway there—it was taking longer than the usual twelve minutes because of the downpour—my phone rang.

I glanced quickly at the dashboard screen. *Bradley* it read.

"Accept call."

"Chief, I may have given us false hope," he said without preamble. "We have the truck, but the driver torched it before he took off."

"Damn!"

"Yeah," he said. "I used a stronger word than that. A patrol officer, Peters, she spotted it, driving down a side street. She followed at a distance, called for back-up. But it took off through a red light, and almost got T-boned. By the time she got clear of the intersection, the truck was gone. Then the call went out for a suspicious fire about six blocks from where she was. Turns out it was the truck."

"Are Bert and Ernie going over it anyway?" A burned-out vehicle probably wouldn't produce anything useful, but you never knew.

"Yes, and I've got officers canvassing to see if anybody saw the driver running away, or another vehicle in the area. And Bert said they might have some luck. This deluge helped put out the fire quickly."

"Tell them to pull out the rubber mats in the back, if they're not completely melted, and take them back to their lab for a thorough analysis."

"How do you know there are rubber mats back there?"

"If it's the same truck, there will be. Tell them to look for traces of semen and/or blood. Where are you?"

"On my way back in. And I have some other stuff to tell you about The Pillar gang."

"Wait until we're both in the office. Driving in this rain..." I trailed off, not willing to admit even to Bradley that, despite a few hours of sleep, I was having trouble getting my eyes to focus.

As I entered the bullpen, a little damp, Bradley popped out of his office. I gestured for him to follow me to my own.

And I was not surprised to find Barnes at her desk. Despite the cuts and bruises, she looked slightly better than her brother did.

Usually the height of sartorial splendor, he was a bit rumpled tonight. I suspected the sleep he'd gotten was on the cot in his office. And his face was pale and sagging.

Barnes followed us into my office and glanced my way. I nodded and she closed the door behind her. She took up her usual position leaning against it, and Bradley settled in the comfy visitor's chair.

"You were right," he said. "There were mats in the back, and relatively intact. Bert's hopeful they might get some hairs too. The fire didn't burn long enough to totally trash the inside. The outside was doused with gasoline though. No hope of getting anything there that might tie it to Walker's hit-and-run."

"Were those stolen tags still on it?"

"Yes, so we can tie in there, with the witness who gave us the partial plate number." He paused, scrubbed a hand over his stubbled face.

"On another note, the two gang leaders who disappeared. I've got more background on them, and descriptions."

"No mug shots?"

"They've never been arrested," Bradley said. "They—"

"Wait," Barnes interrupted. "How do you get to be a leader of an outlaw gang without having any run-ins with the law?"

"It's your new and improved gang," her brother said. "And believe it or not, one of them is in his early fifties. He's a more typical gang member—tough and hairy, came up through the ranks, but somehow he's managed to avoid arrest. Probably because he gets his underlings to do the dirty work, while he manipulates things in the background."

He pulled out his pad. "Name's Colin McPherson. Medium height and build. Brown and brown. Lots of tats, but not on his face. Big beard. The other guy is Jared Brandish. Forty-three, slightly taller than average, medium build. Also brown and brown. He was recruited by the gang while still in college, a pre-law major, business minor. Been with them over twenty years now, and worked his way to the top by helping to make the gang's business dealings, legit and otherwise, more lucrative."

"And these were the main leadership of the gang?" I asked.

"Yes and no. They were two of the three lieutenants who answered to the leader, one John 'Shank' Hillsborough. A far more typical gang member, he's been in and out of prison. Most recently, he was convicted of murdering a business owner who wouldn't pay his protection money. But prison hasn't slowed him down much. He's been building up The Pillar gang's presence and power at Raiford. Then, four months ago, he lived up to his nickname by shanking another prisoner in a brawl, and he seriously injured a guard who tried to break it up. He's been in solitary ever since with no visitors."

"The third lieutenant?" I asked.

"Joshua Phelps. Not much on him. He's also avoided getting caught at anything illegal. Another preppy type recruited in college, and younger, early thirties. He's now the sole, unincarcerated leader."

"And we have *no* recent photos of these guys?" Frustration was making my stomach clench.

"We do have one of Jared Brandish," Bradley said, "dining *al fresco* with some business types. It's only a couple years old. I emailed it to you, but it's not great."

I turned to my computer and found the email from Bradley, opened the attached photo. The guy looked vaguely familiar, lounging in a business suit at an outdoor cafe. Sunlight glinted off red highlights in his dark hair and off the aviator sunglasses that hid his eyes.

No, not vaguely familiar—*quite* familiar. I'd crossed paths with this guy at some point, but his name rang no bells.

I shook my head slowly. "What would attract promising, middle-class college kids to a gang?"

"Money and ideology," Bradley said. "A few years out of college, these guys would be making six figures working for a legitimate business. Sounds good, right? But in the gang, they were millionaires within five years, and that's only the money the Jax gang unit can trace. They all have off-shore bank accounts."

"And in the gang," Barnes said, her voice disgusted, "they can spew their bigotry around without concern for what's politically correct."

Bradley nodded. "Exactly, and not just spew it, but get it validated by the others."

"That might even be a more powerful draw than the money," I said.

"Oh, one other thing," Bradley said. "McPherson's wife is divorcing him *in absentia*."

"How does that work?" I asked. "Don't you have to get the missing spouse declared dead?" That was an area of the law I wasn't familiar with.

Bradley shook his head. "You put notices in the paper, I think. I went to talk to her this evening. She was pretty cagey."

"How so?" I asked.

"When I asked if she knew where her soon-to-be-ex was, she ducked the question. A couple of times, she opened her mouth as if to say something, but then closed it."

He shook his head again. "When I asked why she was divorcing him, she said that even before he, quote, 'took off,' he'd gotten all uppity and thought he was better than her now. She has a nice condo, and she's not employed. I kinda suspect the gang is paying her off to keep her mouth shut."

I hung around the office for a while, waiting for new developments. Bert and Ernie were focusing on the mats and other trace evidence from the floor of the truck. I was praying they'd come up with something.

I tried to take care of some of my own perpetual paperwork, but it was hard to concentrate.

Finally, shortly after midnight, Bert Deming texted me. *You in, Chief?*
Yes.
I'll be right over.

He was in my office ninety seconds later, a sealed cardboard box in his hands.

Barnes appeared behind him in the doorway. She was bleary-eyed and her disheveled bun suggested she'd been sleeping with her head on her desk.

Bert was practically bouncing up and down. "We've got hair shafts that match Thompson and Taft, plus a little dried semen. And blood that's the same type as Maria Navarro's. But we need to confirm with DNA results."

"Bradley," I yelled, not bothering with the phone. Nobody was in the bullpen at this hour anyway.

"I'll get him," Barnes said. But he was already halfway across the floor. They both crowded into the doorway.

I pointed to the box in Bert's hands. "Get somebody to take this evidence over to the FDLE lab for DNA testing."

Bert shook his head. "I was going to take it myself."

I gave him a skeptical look. "Who's gotten the most sleep in the last forty-eight hours?" I asked all of them.

Barnes and Bradley opened their mouths, but Bert quickly said, "I went home this afternoon, got five hours in."

I grinned at him. "Tag, you're it. But drive carefully. We do *not* want anything happening to that evidence."

He grinned back. "Yes, ma'am."

The others made way and he trotted between them and across the bullpen.

I said to them, "I suggest we all go home now and get some proper sleep. Not much more we can do until tomorrow."

"Are you going to take this to the ASA?" Bradley asked.

"First thing in the morning."

But the next morning didn't go as planned.

Despite having gone to bed after midnight, I woke at my usual time before dawn, and couldn't get back to sleep. I did a light workout—some push-ups and crunches—took a shower and got dressed.

Some bran muffins had mysteriously appeared on the kitchen counter.

"Did you buy these?" I asked Pipsqueak with a chuckle. I unwrapped one and offered her a small piece. She turned her nose up and sashayed away. I took a bite. "I see what you mean," I told her, spraying crumbs.

But it was sustenance. I gulped it down and headed for 3MB.

I stopped by my office, before going to see the ASA to let her know she might have new charges against Thompson and Taft, and perhaps she should reconsider their plea deals. I was smiling as I crossed the bullpen, contemplating that conversation.

I had to be careful though, I reminded myself, and not gloat too obviously.

Barnes was already at her desk. My smile faltered at her stormy expression.

She shoved the Sunday newspaper across the desk at me.

Front page, above the fold, was a photo of Peter McAllister. Under the headline, *MAYOR'S FORMER AIDE DECLARES HE'S RUNNING.*

Next line down, in smaller letters, *On Law and Order Platform, Blasts Starling PD.*

The byline was Stuart Frost's, of course.

CHAPTER TWENTY-ONE

In my office, I skimmed the newspaper article, then went back and read it more carefully.

Actually, McAllister had not directly criticized Starling PD. He'd phrased it as questions. Why hadn't we arrested, or at least seriously interrogated Mark Hayes? And if we were convinced he hadn't killed the mayor, than why hadn't we developed any other good leads?

Grrrrr. We are 'developing' leads, asshole, but they keep hitting brick walls.

Okay, visiting the ASA could wait. She couldn't file any new charges yet anyway, not until the DNA results were back. Still, I needed to talk to her soon, try again to get her to seek a continuance in Alvarez's trial until we could finish investigating.

Maybe the risk to her own reputation should her star witnesses turn out to be liars and rapists might convince her.

Or maybe I'll end up looking like an ass if Alvarez is really guilty.

I rubbed my forehead. My thoughts were like ping pong balls bouncing around inside my head. I shook it to clear it.

First things first. I needed some straight answers from Mark Hayes. I headed for the fifth floor.

I stepped off the elevator and marched to the mayor's admin's desk. I was surprised to find Carol there, on a Sunday.

But I was equally surprised that Hayes was *not* there. He was usually dedicated to a fault, and the city government was in chaos right now.

"Um, he called me about an hour ago." Carol's tone was tentative. "Said his youngest son was really upset by the mayor's murder. He had nightmares last night. So Council...I mean, Mayor Hayes decided to take his kids on an impromptu camping trip, to get their minds off of all that's been happening."

"What?" I managed to keep my jaw from dropping. "Okay, I'll call his cell, I guess." Although I would've much preferred being able to see his face when I asked him if he was a liar. I had also planned to ask him again about enemies who might have set him up.

But now I was wondering if I should ask that question. I wasn't as sure as I had been that it *was* a set-up. This little camping trip was awfully convenient.

Carol was shaking her head. "He said they'd be off the grid."

"Shit!" I said.

She nodded slightly, as if she agreed with the sentiment but was too polite, or too loyal to her boss, to say so out loud.

"Did he ask you to come in?"

"No," Carol said, "but I figured there should be *someone* in the mayor's office today."

"Where's Bonnie?"

"At the mayor's house...Mayor Daniels, that is. In addition to being his admin, she's a family friend."

"Okay, let me know immediately if you hear from Hayes." I didn't take the time to put a title in front of his name. I was furious with him.

Too agitated to wait for the elevator, I took the fire stairs. Pulling my phone from my jacket pocket, I called the watch desk. "Sarge, put out a BOLO on Mark Hayes."

"The mayor?" Armstrong's voice squeaked a little.

"Yeah, the mayor."

"To arrest him?"

"No, no." I realized too late that others would have read this morning's paper. "I have some questions for him, that's all. He is to be treated with respect. Pass that on."

No point in pissing off my boss any more than I have to.

A half beat of silence. "Okay, Chief."

"And take a look at a map and see if you can determine where someone would go camping to be, quote, 'off the grid.'"

"Sure, Chief."

I didn't bother to explain further. Whether he agreed with my actions or not, Armstrong would do his job, and so would our people.

Once on the third floor, I took a deep breath and tried to figure out what to do next.

Stop it, Anderson!

I wasn't in the habit of letting politicians, or would-be politicians, run my police department. I'd fought against that kind of interference with my homicide unit in Baltimore County, and I wasn't going to allow it to intrude here.

I took another deep breath and mentally shoved aside the words in that newspaper article. I had an investigation to run.

Okay, what next? I might as well go on to the ASA's office.

⸺ ◆ ⸺

I stood in front of the ASA's desk. I had been sitting in her visitor's chair a second ago. But somehow this moment demanded that I stand. "You're refusing to even consider filing these extra charges against Thompson and Taft?"

"You don't have enough concrete evidence." She also rose from her chair behind her desk. "So no, not until after the Alvarez trial. I don't want to jeopardize their willingness to testify."

"But that's the point," I said. "I'm not at all sure they're telling the truth about his involvement. They're lying to get off with easier sentences. They're in all of this up to their necks!"

Necks adorned with their lovely little fascist tattoos!

The ASA stood up straighter, although she still had to look up some to meet my gaze. "Well, they certainly couldn't have been responsible for recent activities. They've been in prison."

I shook my head, not at all sure what we were talking about at this point.

"Okay," I said, "But I'll be back when we get the DNA results."

"That's fine. That'll be after the Alvarez trial."

My stomach heaved. Did this woman only care about convictions, not justice?

I tried one more time. "If you give me more time *now* to investigate all this, I can either give you more evidence against Alvarez, if he is guilty, and make your case stronger. Or clear him and give you evidence against the real killer or killers."

"You've got two weeks. Come up with some actual evidence, not just speculation, and I'll ask for a continuance." Was that a pleading look in her eyes?

I froze for a second. Was she under some kind of pressure regarding this case? She'd said something last time, about inheriting the case and having to see it through.

I stared at her. She met my gaze and her eyes hardened. We had a staring contest for what felt like a full minute, although it was probably more like twenty seconds.

Finally, she said, "I assume you can find your way out, Chief. I have work to do."

I turned and left, feeling a little guilty, but only a little, that I hadn't told her about Alvarez's confession—that he had been at the crime scene, although he claimed it was against his will.

I hadn't gotten that far in my summary of recent developments when she'd begun to shake her head. I hate it when people don't hear me out.

There, that appeases the guilt nicely.

If she'd been listening—truly listening—I would've told her all of it.

———— ◆ ————

Carol's comment about Bonnie being at the Daniels's house had reminded me. As Chief of Police, I should put in an appearance and offer the widow condolences, on behalf of the department.

But first I stopped at 3MB to check in with Barnes. "Have we heard anything on Wellbourne? Last I heard, she was okay, but still in the hospital."

My assistant leaned forward and whispered, "She's in your office."

I tilted my head. "Oh?"

She cocked her own head toward my slightly ajar door but said nothing.

Okay, guess I'd find out directly from the Special Agent herself.

I nudged my door open. Wellbourne was slumped in the comfy visitor's chair, staring into space.

She turned her face toward me as I closed my door. Her light brown complexion still had an ashen undertone. The freckles sprinkled across her nose stood out, and her corkscrew curls were a bit limp.

The haunted look in her eyes made my chest tense.

She jumped to her feet. "I'm so sorry, Chief. I messed up."

I walked to my desk chair. "How so?"

Her expression stunned, she said, "I, uh, didn't protect the mayor."

I shook my head. "You were looking for gunmen, maybe guys with knives. Not a speeding car running a stop sign."

I looked her over, trying to decide what to do with her, send her home or put her to work. "Did the doctors release you?"

She began to nod, then shook her head instead. "I'm okay physically, just a few bumps and scrapes. But the doc wants me to see a counselor before he'll sign off for me to return to duty."

"Not a bad idea. I was about to go offer the widow my condolences. Want to ride along? I'd like to pick your brain some more, and Barnes's too, about Friday night."

She turned a shade paler, but nodded her head.

Maybe this is a bad idea, having her confront the widow of the guy she thinks she got killed.

But I didn't change the plan. I gestured for Barnes to join us as we passed her desk.

Outside the building, I held up my car keys. "You up to driving, Barnes?"

"Yeah, I got five solid hours of sleep last night. I'm good."

No hesitation. Good. At least one of them was ready to get back on the horse.

Wellbourne gingerly climbed into the back of my small compact.

Barnes looked up at the rearview mirror. "No clown car jokes," she warned in a mock stern voice.

I caught Wellbourne's weak smile in my peripheral vision.

My chest ached some but I kept my expression neutral as I turned slightly in the passenger seat. "Tell me what happened at the hospital that precipitated the mayor leaving. When did his wife leave? Begin there."

"They brought his dinner about five-twenty," Wellbourne said, "and he insisted his wife go home and sleep in her own bed. She'd stayed the night before, on one of those chairs that folds out flat. But he said there was no point in her staying, since they were only running tests the next day. He sounded kinda disgusted when he said that last part, like he was already fed up with the whole place."

She stopped, rubbed her forehead.

Barnes glanced up into the mirror. "Mr. McAllister arrived a couple of hours after she left," she prompted.

"Oh, yeah."

"Where were you two?" I asked.

"Agent Wellbourne and I took turns," Barnes said, "one in the room, the other in the hall. If either of us started losing focus, we changed it up."

"Good thinking," I said, then nodded for Wellbourne to continue.

"I was in the room at that point," she said. "The mayor and McAllister chatted for a few minutes about office stuff. I tried to tune them out, in case anything was confidential. Then the mayor said they were keeping him another day or two for more tests. And McAllister made this scoffing noise and said, 'More like they're stretching things out to milk your health insurance.' He'd apparently worked as an orderly for a while in college. He told the mayor that the hospital where he worked did that all the time, kept people over the weekend when nothing routine like testing was going to happen until Monday morning."

She stopped, took a breath. "The mayor got really pissed. He jumped out of bed and began to get dressed. I looked away, of course. He demanded we take him home, and McAllister said he'd see him at the office on Monday and he left."

She fell silent.

"But it took almost three hours," Barnes added, "to get out of there. We had to wait for them to find a doctor to write a prescription for his painkillers. The mayor was so angry, I was afraid he'd have a heart attack, but he was also wincing in pain from the gunshot wound. So I guess he decided he needed to wait for the script."

Wellbourne picked up the story. "They finally gave it to him but said there was more paperwork they needed to do. He just walked past them at that point. A nurse scrambled after him, insisting he wait for a wheelchair but he was having none of that."

I nodded. "If he left AMA not that many people would even know he was leaving."

Wellbourne shook her head. "He made such a fuss, everybody on that floor of the hospital heard what was going on. And he was still spluttering about it as we were going out the main doors to his car."

Shit, I thought but kept that to myself. Wellbourne might take it as criticism of her handling of the mayor, that she didn't keep him quiet about his intention to leave. But I knew from personal experience, there was no 'handling' Mayor Daniels when he was pissed.

"You took the most direct route to his house?" I asked Barnes.

"Yeah, there wasn't much traffic so I was able to watch pretty readily for a tail. We didn't have one." She said it with confidence.

"But we had to go by an all-night pharmacy to get his prescription filled," Wellbourne pointed out.

Barnes nodded. "We went through the drive-thru, but the pharmacist on duty wanted him to come inside, since it was a controlled substance and he needed to confirm the mayor's identity. The mayor jumped out of his side of the car and yelled at him, 'Look at me, you asshole, don't you recognize me?'"

Wellbourne chuckled softly from the backseat, then said, "Sorry. I guess it isn't really funny."

"No, I get it," I said. "He could get downright comical when he was on one of his rants."

But he had rarely let the general public see that side of him. He had to have been very worked up to go off on that pharmacist.

A wave of sadness washed over me. For him to go out like that when he was so furious. If there was such a thing as reincarnation and karma, he'd have a lot of work to do in his next lifetime.

"So," I said out loud, "what time was it when you left the pharmacy?"

"Dashboard clock said eleven-thirty," Barnes said. "We were seven minutes from his house."

"And five minutes later..." Wellbourne trailed off.

"Did either of you see or hear anything right before the crash?" I asked.

Barnes began to shake her head, then stopped. "I noticed the streetlight was out at that corner, so I slowed down some." She turned slightly toward me. "And come to think of it, I never saw any headlights coming out of that street. They should have shone across the dark road in front of me."

"I had my window cracked a little," Wellbourne said, "for some fresh air. Trying to get that hospital smell out of my nose. I might have heard tires squealing."

Or you might be imagining that. Out loud, I said, "As in someone accelerating, or trying to stop?"

She shrugged.

Good, she's not going to guess.

Barnes pulled into the Daniels' driveway. There were multiple vehicles lining each side of it.

I left Barnes in the car with instructions to call Bradley and tell him to check out anyone who was on duty on that floor of the hospital Friday night.

The mayor's departure hadn't been planned for that night, so there had to be someone planted there, to keep an eye on things and let The Pillar gang know when he was leaving.

And the whole thing had to have been carefully thought out ahead of time, the car procured, the boy given his instructions. It was an elaborate plan. They wouldn't have left anything to chance.

I rang the doorbell.

A young woman, perhaps the mayor's daughter, opened the door. I introduced myself to her. Wordlessly, she stepped aside.

Wellbourne and I paused in the doorway, taking in the scene. It was the informal wake that I'd expected when I saw the crowded driveway.

The young woman introduced me to those in the room. Most were relatives, some family friends. The only ones I recognized were the widow—a tall, thin, white-haired woman in a straight-backed chair—and the mayor's admin Bonnie, sitting next to her. They both nodded. The others murmured, "How do you do?" and went back to their own subdued conversations.

I intentionally did not introduce Wellbourne, just in case someone decided to aim their grief at her in the form of misguided anger.

We approached the widow's chair. Bonnie held Mrs. Daniels's hand. Neither needed an intro to Wellbourne, since the young agent had been the mayor's shadow for several days.

"Sit, please." The widow gestured toward the one empty chair near her in the circle.

But Bonnie jumped up and offered me her chair. Wellbourne took the other, across from us.

"On behalf of the Starling PD, our deepest sympathies, Mrs. Daniels."

"Thank you," she said.

I leaned slightly toward her. "Could we talk in private, if you're up to it?"

She froze for a half beat, then nodded. Rising, she led the way to a sunroom on the side of the house. Potted plants were lined up in front of jalousie windows.

The widow and I settled on a white wicker loveseat, Wellbourne on a wicker chair angled next to it.

"Did you notice anything suspicious at the hospital Friday night?" I asked, my voice gentle. "Maybe someone paying unusual attention to your husband's room?"

She thought for a moment, before shaking her head.

"What kind of tests were they running on him?" I could get that from the hospital records, with her permission, and I wasn't even sure they were relevant, but I wanted to get her talking.

"They started with routine bloodwork. Then they did some tests on his heart. They wanted to do a CAT scan as well, of his brain..." She trailed off.

I nodded. "Mr. McAllister thought the hospital was trying to milk your insurance by keeping him over the weekend. Do you think there was any validity to that?"

"Quite possibly. I felt at first that they were being overly thorough. After all, he's in good..." She paused, closed her eyes. After a beat, she opened them again. "He *was* in good health. Only a little high blood pressure, which got worse when he was mad."

Which was often. I kept that thought to myself.

"But if I'd been there when Mac brought that up, I would've argued for him to stay."

"Why's that, ma'am?" Wellbourne asked, her voice also gentle.

"He somehow seemed weaker than usual, but I wasn't sure if it was just because of the inactivity of being in the hospital, and the awful food. He wasn't eating very much."

She paused, looked away from us. "I'd thought about making him something here and taking it back over to him, you know, that night."

She turned back to us, her eyes shiny. "Maybe if I had...maybe if I'd been there, I could've talked him into staying in the hospital...or at least..." Her voice broke.

My throat tightened.

"At least our arguing about it would've delayed him some. And he wouldn't have been in that car in that intersection at that moment." She lowered her face into her hands and sobbed.

"Ma'am," Wellbourne said. "It wasn't–"

I cut her off with a sharp look, then took the widow's hand. I gave it a squeeze and let go, hoping it was the right gesture. I was really no good at the mushy stuff.

"If you think of anything, let me know." I pulled a card out of my pocket.

She shook her head. "I have your number on speed-dial. I thought it would be a good idea, you know, in case anything happened, I could call you directly right away. Not that it did any good."

I patted her hand and rose. "We do what we can," I said softly, "but the universe doesn't always cooperate."

She pulled a tissue from her sleeve and dabbed at her eyes and nose. "Thank you for coming, Chief."

"We can see ourselves out." I gestured for Wellbourne to follow.

Out in the driveway, Wellbourne and I blew out air in unison. "Does that ever get any easier?" she asked.

"Nope."

"I'm glad she doesn't blame me."

I wanted to say *get a grip*, but I didn't. As my friend Kate likes to remind me, you gotta let the emotions out—even the irrational guilty ones—in order to let them go.

Instead, I said, perhaps a bit more brusquely than was ideal, "Look, you and Barnes did your jobs. It wasn't your fault."

I paused, then added, in a softer, sadder tone, "Sometimes, the bad guys win."

"And that sucks," Wellbourne said.

CHAPTER TWENTY-TWO

Speaking of Kate—and trying to do better with the friendship stuff—I texted her as Barnes drove us back across town.

Hey, sorry I'm so tied up with this case right now. Was there something specific you wanted to talk about? I may be able to call later.

Nothing that can't wait. On my way to class.

Okay. I'll call as soon as I can.

With that obligation fulfilled, I turned my brain power to the cases, or rather the Case, with a capital C. I was more and more convinced it was one big case, with someone—or maybe several someones, most likely connected to that gang—pulling the strings.

What else could we be doing?

Bradley had texted me, while we were with the widow, saying that our people were checking out anyone at the hospital who might have overheard Mayor Daniels's rant. But that was like sifting through sand for gold. It might take awhile for a nugget to surface.

Wait, maybe I could get the FDLE lab to rush the results on Thompson's and Taft's clothing. If we could put them in that truck with Maria, the threat of sexual assault charges might get them to open up about their gang's other activities.

Because otherwise all we had to connect them to the mayor's death was a wannabe gang tattoo that the kid, Chris Jones probably inked on his own neck.

I typed a text into my phone, to Dot Wilder. *We brought in some evidence last night to the lab. Anyway to get that bumped up? It may be related to the mayor's murder.*

I read that back to myself, then went to the beginning and added, *Hope you are well and sorry to bother you on a Sunday.*

"Damn social niceties," I muttered as I hit *Send*.

"Did you say something, Chief?" Barnes asked from the driver's seat. I shook my head.

My phone pinged. A text message from Derek the Geek.

Chief, the number on Mayor Hayes's phone from the morning of the shooting in the park, it's a burner. Trying to trace its origins now.

Shit, I thought, *yet another dead end.*

I gritted my teeth and tried to concentrate on what we did have.

But something Mrs. Daniels said was floating at the edge of my brain.

Here we go with the niggling feelings again.

Was it a name? I went back over the introductions to her friends and family, but none of their names meant anything to me.

Mac? Yes, it was Mac!

She'd called McAllister *Mac.* Where else had I heard that name recently?

Mac was a common enough nickname, especially among those with Scottish or Irish ancestry. I even knew a Mac in Maryland—Kate's friend, Mac Reilly.

I picked up my phone from my lap and called the Daniels's home number.

Someone other than the widow answered. I introduced myself and asked for her.

It took a couple of minutes for her to come to the phone. "Hello?" Her voice was tentative.

"Mrs. Daniels, Chief Anderson here. Sorry to bother you. I have a quick question, to satisfy my curiosity. Mr. McAllister said he and your husband were friends."

"Yes, they knew each other from college. I think they were in the same fraternity."

"And where was that?"

"UNF. Mac was a couple years behind Danny." Her voice had turned mildly impatient.

Hmm, McAllister had called the mayor Danny.

"What does this have to do with anything?" she demanded.

"Probably nothing, but this is how an investigation works. We gather information, all kinds of information, and see how things fit together. Eventually the puzzle pieces fall into place."

"Okay, I guess that makes sense. But what investigation? Wasn't the crash an accident?"

"Um, we're just checking on some things, to make sure of that. Again, sorry to bother you, ma'am."

I quickly disconnected before she could ask more questions.

I called Bradley. "You got time to check something out?"

"Depends on what it is," he replied in an amiable voice.

I told him about the connection between Daniels and McAllister at the University of North Florida. "They were friends there, and they might have been frat brothers. Maybe it means nothing, but I've got a funny feeling."

"'Trust your instincts, but seek the truth,' that's what my partner when I was a newbie detective used to say."

"I wouldn't even say this is my instincts talking, more an annoying thought, but *my* mentor, when I was a newbie detective, used to say, 'Follow all leads.'"

"Hey, at this point," Bradley said, "I'm willing to chase after anything."

"When you have time."

"Got it, Chief. You heading in?"

"Yes. ETA five minutes."

I checked my messages and found a reply from Dot Wilder. *I'll see what I can do, but they are pretty backed up.*

Yet another niggling feeling...something about college, and gangs recruiting there. *Shit!* Could Mayor Daniels have been a gang member, and a rival gang took him out?

Okay, that's plain ole crazy. The mental image of Daniels covered in gang tats almost made me laugh out loud. A small snort escaped.

"Chief?" Barnes said, glancing my way as she swung into the municipal lot.

"Nothing." I shook my head to clear it. *What next?* I asked myself again.

The problem with believing that all these cases were related was that the whole thing then became a convoluted mess.

"Come on," I said to Barnes and Wellbourne, as we climbed out of the car. "I want to set up a new board."

"In addition to the murder board for the mayor's case?" Wellbourne asked.

I nodded. "For all of it."

———————————❦———————————

In the smaller of our conference rooms, I stared at the clutter we'd created on the white board. Barnes had moved magnets around, consolidating the photos and notes about the mayor's death, making room for the crime scene pics of Navarro's murder, the report on his sister's rape, and other relevant pics and mug shots, including Patterson's.

I didn't have the info on that case, so I texted Sam. *Hey, can I get a copy of your case file on Patterson's attack?*

Sure, what's up?

Just trying to put some pieces together.

I'll send it right over. Dinner tonight?

My heart ached in my chest, as I walked toward my office. I texted back, *Maybe. Too early to predict.*

I called up the email from Sam and opened the attached files. I printed out a couple of the crime scene photos and his latest report on the progress made. He suspected the corrections officer was involved but couldn't prove it.

Carrying all that back to the conference room, I contemplated what to do about Sam.

The answer came back, *Nothing right now.* When the dust settled from all this, we would need to talk.

Barnes had some difficulty getting the additional pics and the report onto the board. I grabbed a marker and wrote at the very bottom, under the report, *CO involved?* Then I erased the question mark. I was sure he was involved, but he couldn't have been Patterson's actual attacker.

I added, *not attacker, not enuf blood.*

Wellbourne had been watching our activity from a seat at the conference table. Bradley walked in as we were finishing up. He joined us in studying the huge array of information.

It was more than a little overwhelming, but having it all laid out in one place *was* helpful.

We had three Latinos who'd been pressured to join The Pillar gang, ostensibly to make it seem more diverse. Ricardo Diaz while in prison. He'd gone along with it, and they'd pretty much left him alone.

Then Alvarez and Navarro had both been pressured by the gang. Neither complied, so Navarro's sister was raped, probably by Thompson and Taft, and Navarro was killed by them. And Alvarez was set-up—we were assuming—to be blamed for that murder, and to get the gang members lighter sentences if they were caught.

When I went to the county jail to talk to Patterson about the Navarro homicide, he was attacked, although that could be unrelated, instigated by the former chief.

We also had three attempts on the mayor's life, the last one successful. It had seemed like a separate case, until the ME found that inked-on tattoo on the dead teenage driver. Chris Jones was apparently an initiate of The Pillar gang, who had most likely provided him with the car.

And either Mark Hayes had something to do with the attacks on the mayor, or he was being framed. And his excuse for why he was in that park had blown up in his face. Plus, he was now in the wind, supposedly camping with his kids and "off the grid."

I stifled a sigh. It was getting harder and harder to believe he was innocent, especially with the evidence all laid out on the board.

And then Bill Walker put out feelers with people he knew from prison, asking about The Pillar. And someone tried to kill him in a hit-and-run.

A knock on the conference room door interrupted my train of thought. "Come," I barked.

Derek the Geek stepped into the room. "Thought you'd want to know, Chief. The cell phone in the car that hit the mayor, it's a burner. And it's from the same batch as the other one, both sold from an electronics store in Jacksonville last spring. No luck tracking the buyer. He or she paid cash."

"Same batch as what other one?" I asked, distracted.

"As the one that called Mayor Hayes's phone the morning of the shooting in the park."

Interesting. "Thanks," I said, intending it as a dismissal, and picked up a marker to add that info.

"And I finally got a chance," Derek continued, a touch of excitement in his voice, "to take a look at that other phone and—"

"What other phone?" I asked, searching for the right spot on the board. Ah, there it was, *Holly Park shooting*.

"The one you gave to the sarge. Turns out it's the one that called Hayes's phone that morning."

I whirled around. "What?"

"Where did that phone come from?" he asked.

I thought for a beat, deciding whether to tell him that Hayes himself had turned it in. "Someone found it." I left it at that.

"Well, it's the number that was on Hayes's phone, and his number is the only one in its outgoing calls. Apparently, it was used just that one time. The only prints on it were Hayes's, yours, and the sarge."

My stomach clenched. "And it's from the same batch as the one in the kid's car?"

He nodded. "There were ten phones total, bought by the same person. And the only call on the kid's phone was an incoming from another of the phones in that batch."

"Thanks," I said.

Derek left the room.

"What phone is he talking about?" Bradley asked. His sister, standing behind him, had her eyebrows halfway to her hairline.

I told them about Mark Hayes finding a phone, supposedly, on the hood of his car, including his theory that someone had put it down while doing something else and had forgotten it.

"But who wipes their phone clean of fingerprints," Barnes asked, "*before* putting it down to tie their shoe?" Her tone was incredulous.

I pointed to the board. "Let's look at what we have against Mark Hayes again."

"Nothing from the first shooting," Bradley said, "other than the cartridge that wasn't completely mangled. It was the same type as the ones for his antique rifle, but Bert wasn't able to definitively match it to that gun."

"The bullet from the shooting in the park," Barnes added, "*was* a ballistics match with that rifle. And then there's the possible connection between him and the car used to..." She trailed off, her face pinched.

"Again," I said, "so obvious—Mark Hayes, Max Layes—that it screams of a set-up. And we now know that the call Hayes received the morning of the park shooting, that supposedly lured him to the park, was not from McAllister. But it was from a burner phone from the same batch as the one in the kid's car."

"The phone that he subsequently turned in," Bradley said, "with only his prints on it, which makes no sense."

Exactly, I thought but didn't say. Every time we added up what we had on Hayes, two and two equaled three or five.

"Why use a burner phone," Bradley was saying, "to set up a bogus meeting where you're going to shoot someone, and then turn that phone into the lost-and-found at the police station? The logical thing to do at that point is to toss the phone."

Yet another damned niggling thought was buzzing around the edges of my brain.

"That's what most people would do," Barnes said, "if they *found* a disposable phone. Well, maybe after they used up the minutes on it."

And the niggly thought coalesced. "That's it! That's what whoever left the phone on Hayes's hood expected. That he'd pick it up, putting his prints on it, and either keep it to use himself or toss it."

"Maybe they were watching him," Barnes said, "to retrieve it if he tossed it, and turn it in themselves?"

"They didn't know him well enough to realize he's a goody-two shoes," I said.

Barnes snickered at my choice of words.

"Yeah, it probably wouldn't occur to them," Bradley said, "that he'd be all worried about the poor schmuck who lost their phone and he would turn it in to us."

"Are we letting him off too easy?" Barnes asked.

I shook my head. "We're not dropping him from the suspect list, but if he's being set up..."

"So assuming that, who *did* call Hayes to lure him to the park?" Wellbourne asked. "Were they pretending to be McAllister? And did they then call McAllister, pretending to be Hayes, and ask him to lie?"

I whirled around. I'd forgotten she was there, sitting at the other end of the table and taking it all in. "That is kind of a convoluted mess, isn't it?" I said.

"Here's another crazy, convoluted possibility." Bradley waved a hand at the board. "Maybe Hayes is pulling some kind of double-dealing twist on us, leaving intentionally obvious clues that it's him so that we'll think he's being set up."

"He does have the strongest motive," Barnes said.

"That we know of." I tapped a finger against my lips, staring at the board. "But what's the connection to the gang? I never told him anything about them."

"He could have someone on the force," Bradley said, "who's reporting our movements to him."

Oh great, maybe there's yet another person I've been trusting who's up to no good behind my back.

"He could've pretended he was from the gang," Bradley added, "when he recruited Chris Jones to run into the mayor's car. Maybe to give us another false lead to chase."

I was having trouble believing Mark Hayes was capable of that much duplicity, but the goody-two-shoes persona could be an act. Sometimes, he really did seem to be too good to be true.

We all stared at the board again.

"Is it time to start re-interviewing people?" Bradley asked.

I sighed. "Yes." It's what cops do when new leads run low, and it was preferable to sitting around speculating.

"But let's mix it up some," I added. "Bradley, you take Ricardo Diaz. He works at a convenience store called Uncle Joe's. Home address is in the file. Now that we know more about this gang, ask him some pointed questions about how it operates inside Raiford. Who's in charge there, since the head honcho's in solitary? And what does Diaz know about the leadership outside the prison?"

I held up a hand. "But try not to jam him up with his boss. It looks like he's truly trying to turn his life around."

Bradley nodded.

"Who else is free to talk to people?" I asked him.

"I've got Collins and Cruthers working on finding the people from the hospital Friday night."

"Okay, leave Collins on that, but have Cruthers officially interview Mark Hayes. See what he can shake loose." I trusted the seasoned detective to be diplomatic but also thorough.

"*If* we can find Hayes," Bradley said.

I frowned. "Maybe Cruthers should talk to McAllister first. Find out what exactly Hayes said to him in that call Wednesday morning, what time it was, and did he get any indication where he was calling from. Oh, and did we get the warrant for Hayes's phones yet?"

"The judge signed it, but we can't get the info until Tuesday. Phone company's closed tomorrow for Presidents' Day."

"Don't we have an emergency contact?" I asked.

"Yes, but I didn't think it was pressing enough to drag him into his office on a Sunday...Until now, that is. I'll call him."

"Good. Barnes and I will talk to Patterson, if he's up to it." I turned to Wellbourne. "I know you haven't been officially cleared for duty yet, but a little computer research shouldn't hurt. You game?"

She nodded, her face brightening.

"Dig in and see if the corrections officer who supposedly tried to help Patterson has any connections with this gang, or with any of our other victims or suspects."

"Won't Sheriff Pierson be doing that?" Bradley asked.

Barnes shot him a look. I frowned at her.

"Yes," I said, "but it doesn't hurt to come at it from two perspectives."

"That leaves Walker's hit-and-run," Bradley said, "and Maria Navarro's SA."

I shook my head. "Walker doesn't know anything. He'd only put out feelers, and that was all it took for them to come after him. So let's not draw attention to him just now. And I'd rather not bother Maria yet either." I hated that talking to victims about crimes that happened months or years ago stirred the trauma up for them again.

"How about Alvarez?" he asked.

"We'll come back to him later as well."

"Okay," Bradley said, "off to drag my buddy at the phone company away from the Sunday game. And then to chat up Diaz." He left the room.

I leaned toward Wellbourne, who was pushing herself to a stand. "Also, check for connections between Mark Hayes and anyone else involved in any of these cases."

She frowned and her eyes clouded, but she nodded. "Got it."

Once outside the building, I stopped walking and turned to Barnes. "What was that look you shot your brother when the sheriff's name was mentioned?"

She feigned wide-eyed innocence. "I don't know what you mean."

"You are the world's worst liar."

Her eyes went even wider, and I almost laughed. "Apparently you've figured out that things are not totally wonderful between the sheriff and me right now."

She began to shake her head.

"Cut it out." I paused, blew out air. "Sometimes you're too astute. Just keep it to yourself, okay?"

"I, uh, wasn't planning on telling anybody."

"Yeah, but no strange looks either." My voice was firm. "Your brother's also a very astute person, or he wouldn't be Chief of Detectives. I absolutely do *not* want my love life discussed in the bull pen, or anywhere else for that matter."

She'd straightened to a parade rest stance. "Yes, Chief." And then she took it a little too far. She saluted.

I rolled my eyes. "Oh, for cryin' out loud." I stomped off toward my car.

CHAPTER
TWENTY-THREE

Barnes suggested we stop at the gift shop and get some flowers, or something. I wasn't sure how I felt about that. Patterson was still a dirty cop who'd sullied the name of my department.

But I knew he wasn't intrinsically a bad guy. And it's hard to stay clean when your boss, the Chief of Police no less, is the one handing you the bribe money.

We settled on a small plant. I made Barnes carry it up to his room.

"From the department," she said, setting it down on his bedside table. "We hope you're doing better soon."

It sounded lame to my ears, but Patterson gave us a wan smile from the raised head of his bed.

"I have a few questions," I said, "if you're up to it."

He nodded.

"I know you've been over this with Sheriff Pierson, but tell me what happened."

"Not much to tell." His voice was a bit weak, his face pale. "The CO brought me my lunch. I ate it and laid down on my bunk to read. I felt drowsy, and the next thing I knew I was waking up here, in the hospital. It was two days later, and the doc was asking me if I'd tried to kill myself."

He paused, audibly sucked in air. "I didn't, by the way. I'd never do that to my daughter."

"Nobody's said anything to you," I asked, "before or since, that might've been a warning to keep your mouth shut?"

He shook his head slightly. "This wasn't a warning. They wanted me dead. The doctor says he thinks the food was drugged. It must've been. Even if I'd fallen asleep naturally, I would've woken up when someone started carving on me."

He paused for breath. "They're retesting the blood sample they took when they brought me in, to see if they find any drugs. But the doctor said if it was something that took effect quickly, it might also dissipate quickly."

The doc is quite talkative with a criminal, isn't he? I kept that thought to myself.

"Okay, if you think of anything else." I handed him my card. "I'm sure you remember the number, but..."

I hadn't put my new private line number on the back, just in case Patterson was responsible for having the previous one displayed on the men's room wall at the jail.

We had turned toward the door, but after a couple of steps I turned back—borrowing a maneuver from Columbo, one of my favorite cop-show heroes as a kid. "Oh, one more thing. The first-on-scene officer said there was a witness, who came forward the day after Navarro's murder. He reported a third man running away. But that's not in the case file."

Patterson slowly shook his head. "I don't remember anything about another witness."

"And you didn't take anything out of the file?" I asked, my voice a little sharp. "I won't add any charges if you did, but I need to know."

"No." His voice was stronger, more emphatic. "I handled that case by the book. And I didn't receive any bribe money to do otherwise, in case that's what you're thinking."

He paused, pulled in air again. His face had grown even paler. "But there wasn't much for me to do, since Lewis had already gotten a confession out of those two thugs. I picked up Alvarez and began to interrogate him. He kept saying he didn't know any of those people and hadn't been anywhere near there. Then he lawyered up, and the public defender who showed up told him not to answer any more questions." He was gasping slightly at the end of that speech.

"What about the hairs found on the victim?" I said, in a softer voice. "That info was missing from the file as well."

"What hairs?...Oh, yeah. I remember Bert saying they were a match for Alvarez's under the microscope and he was sending them off to get the DNA tested. But the case was out of my hands by that point. The ASA had already charged him." He paused, took a breath. "I still found it hard to believe Alvarez was guilty though. The whole thing smelled to high heaven."

"Wait, the ASA charged him before you got the report from Bert—*before* the hairs were even analyzed by him?"

Patterson nodded. He grimaced as he pushed himself up some in the bed. His wrists were still bandaged and apparently also still sore.

"Yes," I said, "more than a tad smelly."

Patterson smiled, but his eyelids were fluttering.

Thanks. Sorry to tire you." I turned toward the door.

"Take care, Patterson." Barnes gave him an awkward little wave and followed me out.

In the hallway, she asked, "Do you believe him?"

"Yeah, I think I do."

In the hospital parking lot, my phone pinged. A text from Sam. *Can you get together for lunch? We really need to talk about some things.*

As if in response to the word *lunch,* my stomach rumbled. I glanced at my watch. Twelve-twenty.

I didn't particularly want to have a tense conversation over food. But I did need to eat. Breakfast had been light and quite some time ago.

I'll bring it to you, he texted.

A sudden tightening in my chest. *Guilt.* All too often he'd brought meals to me, accommodating my frequently busier schedule.

I had typed in *Oka–* when I hesitated. My eyes stung and my heart pounded. *Oh my God, I'm going to lose him.*

My next thought was that I couldn't deal with this today.

With a lump in my throat, I backspaced and typed. *Can't, too much going on.*

Maybe later? he responded.

Maybe...

Okay, talk later.

Barnes and I had reached my car. And I had made a decision. "I'm dropping you at your car and then going home. You do the same. There's nothing more we can do on a Sunday, unless somebody comes up with something new."

I needed more sleep. I couldn't deal with all this—the case and Sam—on the few hours I'd caught last night, after essentially being up for almost two full days before that. There was a time I could've done it and been fine, but...

"I'm getting old," I muttered to myself.

"What's that, Chief?" Barnes said, her voice way too cheerful.

I shook my head. "Nothing."

She stopped my car next to her own in the municipal lot and got out.

I slid over, gave her a mock salute, and went home to my cat and my cousin.

But the rest of my Sunday did not go as planned.

I was parking my car in the lot behind my apartment building when Sam called. On my police-issue cell, so there was no ignoring it. He knew I always carried that with me and would always answer.

Also calling that number signaled that he probably wanted to talk shop.

"Hey there," I said, trying for a casual tone.

"Hey yourself." His voice sounded relaxed, pleasant. "I know you're busy, but I wanted to touch base about a couple of things."

"Sure."

"Uh, Joe's a little freaked because the FDLE seems to be poking around in the Patterson assault case."

Joe Hudson, Sam's only true detective besides himself.

"He said some agent," now Sam's voice had a chuckle in it, "named Wellbourne."

I faked a return chuckle. "It's mostly busy work for her. She hasn't been cleared yet for full duty."

"Well, Joe's already found the connection. The CO's younger brother has joined that gang."

"That didn't come out during his background check?" I asked.

"No, because Gerry had already been working at the jail for five years, when little bro signed up with The Pillar."

"Aha. So did his brother ask him for a favor, or did the gang put pressure on him somehow?"

"Don't know that, *yet*," Sam said. "Gerry's still pretending he's innocent, that he was trying to help Patterson, after he found him already bleeding on the floor."

"Yeah, right...Okay, I'll have Wellbourne focus on Hayes."

"Mayor Hayes? I thought you believed he was being set up."

"Well, it's gotten kind of confusing, and a bit harder to sustain that belief." I filled him in on what McAllister had told me yesterday and the mayor's spontaneous camping trip, both of which looked suspicious. Then the burner phones connection, which was supposed to make him look even more suspicious, but he'd turned the one phone into lost-and-found himself. And finally, Bradley's wild theory that Hayes might be intentionally making it seem like a set-up.

"I've always thought Hayes was as straight as an arrow," Sam said.

"Me too, but people can fool you, as we both know..." I trailed off, realizing where that topic could take us.

A part of me knew Sam was trustworthy, that my own issues were the problem, not him. But now I'd been holding him at arm's length for so long, surely he had sensed something was off.

It felt like there was a wedge between us, and I wasn't sure what to do about that. And a couple of unanswered questions were keeping that wedge in place.

My stomach churned.

I decided to take the plunge and clarify one thing, at least. "Um, yesterday...I thought I saw you hovering over Walker, right after the hit-and-run. But I lost you in the crowd."

"No. I didn't come out until a couple of minutes later. I heard the woman scream and the general uproar. I quickly said goodbye to the person I was having coffee with, but by then the crowd had gathered, and it took a minute or two to get through them."

"I know what you mean." Again, I was going for a casual tone, but wasn't sure I'd pulled it off this time. "I was coming through that crowd from the other side."

I paused, took a deep breath. "So, who were you having coffee with?"

"Oh, that was one of the things I was going to tell you about, when you have more time."

"It's okay. I've got a few minutes now."

"It was Caroline's daughter. She was in town to sign some papers related to putting her mother's house up for sale, and I thought it was a good time to tell her about the pregnancy. Turns out she already knew, and this is really sad. The baby was hers."

"Hers? Wait a minute–"

"Caroline was her daughter's surrogate. Deb—that's the daughter—had to have a hysterectomy. So they fertilized one of her eggs and implanted the embryo in Caroline's womb."

"I've heard of cases like that. Must be weird to carry your own grandchild. And that poor girl, Deb. She lost her mom and her baby."

"Yeah. She'd gotten kind of upset as we talked, so I suggested she go out the back of the deli and avoid the crowd out front. I wasn't sure at that point what had happened, but I figured it wasn't good."

"Well, at least that clears up one mystery."

"I'll let you get back to your cases."

"Actually," this time my chuckle wasn't forced, "I've taken to calling it The Case, with capital letters. I think all of it is connected. We laid everything out on our murder board this morning. That helped some to see where to go next. That's why I asked for the Patterson file."

"Mind if I drop by and take a look at it at some point?"

"Not at all. Uh, I better go."

"Sure. See you soon, I hope." The last two words sounded a tad forlorn.

My chest warmed and tightened at the same time. "Yeah, me too."

I disconnected and sighed. Knowing the truth behind Caroline's baby was a relief.

But did it help me to trust Sam again? It should...I mean it *did*, intellectually. But my stomach was still queasy, my whole body a little tense.

Dammit. I wanted things back to the way they'd been between us. And I didn't know how to make that happen.

Maybe it couldn't happen until I knew who or what was behind the strange sightings of "Sam" around town. Until then, my distrustful soul couldn't completely let go of the idea that he might be playing games.

CHAPTER TWENTY-FOUR

As I walked from my car to the back of my building, I texted Well-bourne to focus on Hayes, adding, *CO's brother is in that gang.*

Up in my apartment, Paul was packing. "I've got a place," he said, excitement in his voice.

"That was quick." I reached down to scoop Pipsqueak up, but she struggled in my arms, forcing me to put her down again. If I didn't, I knew from experience I'd end up getting scratched.

She stuck her nose in the air and marched off.

"What's her problem?" Paul asked.

I shrugged. "She gets like that when I have a big case and don't get home much. She has to punish me for a while."

He laughed. "Typical cat. Hey, you wanna see my place?"

"Not today," I blurted out.

His face fell.

"I'm sorry. It's just that I'm exhausted, and I might have to go back in later. I really need to get some sleep."

He nodded. "Okay, I'm about done. I'll be out of your hair soon."

Suddenly feeling hollow inside, I took a step toward him. "It's, um, been good to have some company, even though I haven't been home much."

"Thanks, Cuz." He reached out and chucked me under the chin. "I'll have you over for supper, as soon as I get my furniture out of storage. And I do appreciate you putting me up."

We hugged and said our goodbyes.

I went into my bedroom, and discovered that Paulie, uh, Paul had done my laundry as well as his own.

The beige lounge pajamas from Sam were neatly folded on the end of my bed, along with several blouses. I sat down beside the PJs and fingered the satiny cloth, my eyes stinging.

Anger surged in my chest. I tried to point it at Sam somehow, but I was really angry at myself. Why did I let myself get lured into a relationship? I *knew* that I sucked at them.

Enough of this. I need to sleep.

I shoved the pajamas aside, kicked off my shoes and laid down, fully clothed, on top of the comforter.

A ringing sound dragged me back from oblivion. My police-issue cell rang again on my nightstand.

I picked it up. No name, and I didn't recognize the number.

"Hello," I said, not willing to identify myself in case it was a scammer.

"Chief, it's Mark Hayes."

I sat up, swung my feet off the bed. "Mr. Mayor."

"I'm sorry I ran out on you, but I had to."

"Where are you calling from?"

"One of those disposable phones, with the prepaid minutes."

I'd meant his location.

But before I could ask again, he went on, "I, uh, got a phone call, a muffled voice, telling me to take my kids and leave town, or something bad would happen to one of them..." He choked up some. "Or maybe to all of them, the voice said."

"Mayor Hayes, I really need to talk to you, in person."

"I, um, don't think that's a good idea."

I debated for a second. It was dangerous confronting him over the phone, especially since I didn't know where he was. If he knew he was in deeper trouble than he thought, he might take off for good.

But I still wanted to believe he was one of the good guys, and with all that had been happening lately, his story about a threatening phone call was plausible.

I cleared my throat. "Mr. McAllister has changed his statement. He's saying that you asked him to tell us he'd called you on behalf of the mayor. And that you told him you were in the park meeting a woman, and didn't want your kids to find out. Was the woman a prostitute?"

"What? No...There was *no* woman."

"So why did you ask him to lie?"

"I didn't." His voice rose in pitch, the tone indignant. "He's the one who's lying. I did get a call, from him, asking me to meet the mayor at the park."

"Okay," I said, pretending I believed him. "Bring your kids home. I'll put guards on your house until we get this straightened out."

"No, sorry, Chief. I wish I could. You don't know how much it pains me to break the law...Well, I'm not sure I'm breaking the law. Am I?"

I sighed. "Not at this point."

Only because I don't have enough to arrest you. But actually I did. At least, I would consider it enough for anyone else, despite the discrepancies. However, one does not arrest the mayor—and your own boss, to boot—with a case that has holes in it.

"I'm just thinking your family would be safer under police protection. And more comfortable in their own home."

"I'm not sure about the safe part, Chief. And they're having a good time. We haven't been on a family vacation for I don't know how long."

I tried a different tactic. "Mr. Mayor, I really need your help. I need to interview you in depth about any enemies, anyone who might want to set you up this way." Although honestly, I wasn't totally convinced it was a set-up at this point. Bradley's crazy theory was starting to have some appeal.

No response.

"I can come to you, and I'll make sure I'm not followed. I could meet you somewhere."

Muffled voices in the background. "Sorry, Chief. I really am. But I gotta go."

"Mark, don't–"

But he'd disconnected.

I glanced at my alarm clock. Ten-fifteen.

I'd forgotten to draw the curtains over my bedroom window. The lights of the Starling skyline twinkled on the other side of the glass.

I'd also forgotten to take my personal phone out of my laptop case. I went into the living room and dug it out, toying with the idea of texting Kate, despite the hour. She might still be up.

But I discovered she had texted me earlier.

Sorry. Can't chat tonight after all. Have to help Edie with a science project. Of course, she waited until the last minute to start it. I hope things are going okay with you and Sam.

"Yeah, well, about that..." I muttered and went back to bed.

At 3MB the next morning, one of my aunt's favorite sayings kept running through my mind. The defecation had hit the ventilation system.

Barnes had checked on Bill Walker first thing and found his supply closet empty. A search of the building turned up nothing.

I checked the closet myself. He was normally a neat man—he valued order and cleanliness almost to a fault, which made him a good janitor. He would not have left his bedding in a tousled heap on his cot, but that was where it was.

I went to the watch desk. Sergeant Armstrong had just come on duty. "Sarge, put out a BOLO on Walker, emphasizing that he might be the victim of foul play. And when Lewis comes in this afternoon, I need to talk to him again."

I wanted to go over the Navarro file with him, step by step, and see if he remembered any details that might be helpful.

"He called out sick," Armstrong said.

"When?"

"A few minutes ago. He woke up feeling bad and tested. He has Covid."

"Damn."

Armstrong nodded agreement with that sentiment. "He's calling his doc to get on that new med, Paxlovid. Johnson and I can split his shift, work twelve hours each, if that's okay with you?"

"Sure, that's fine." I tried not to think about the overtime I'd be shelling out. Even with the Paxlovid, Lewis would likely be out for a few days.

I considered calling him but opted to wait. Let him get his meds and some rest.

Bradley popped out of his office as I entered the bullpen. "Florida Highway Patrol called. They might have a lead on our person of interest. A trooper saw a car like his entering a state park near Pensacola this morning. When he turned in, the guy sped up, too fast for him to catch more than a little bit of his license number. Only three letters, but they match our POI's. They lost him in the twists and turns inside the park, but they contacted the park rangers. Both agencies are asking if they should set up a search and flush him out."

I sucked in air, then blew it out again. Shaking my head, I gestured for him and Barnes to follow me to my office, where, behind my closed door, I told them about the call from Hayes last evening.

"Do you believe him?" Bradley asked.

I resisted the urge to throw up my hands. "Honestly, I don't know at this point." I walked behind my desk and sat down. "It doesn't sound like he's trying *that* hard to hide where he's camping, or he would've ditched his car and gotten some other vehicle."

"Or he's totally naïve about how to be a good bad guy," Barnes said with a snicker.

"Sooo," Bradley dragged the word out, "if he's telling the truth about the threat against his kids, we don't really want to draw attention to him."

And I did not relish having him arrested in front of his kids, which would be the only way to force him to come in.

"Ask FHP and the rangers to patrol the park discreetly and if they spot him, not to approach, just let us know. If you or I go get him, he'll probably come in willingly, especially if we tell him that otherwise we'll cuff him in front of the kids."

Bradley nodded. "And I'll warn them to keep an eye out for anyone looking like a gang member."

I frowned. "With this gang, they aren't always obvious. Some clean-cut kid sitting next to you at the lunch counter might be a member of The Pillar."

He nodded again, his expression tight. "One other thing. Collins found an orderly who was taking a smoke break near the side door of the hospital Friday night, at the time the mayor left via that exit. He recognized the mayor, mostly by his loud voice. And as the mayor's car pulled out of its space, he heard another car start up, down the row a ways. It then slowly followed. The guy thought it was intentional and assumed at the time that it was some kind of motorcade."

Excitement bubbled in my chest. I tamped it down.

Good thing, because Bradley's next words were disappointing. "He couldn't identify the car, other than a light-colored sedan. But he did remember a number and a letter from the middle of the plate as it drove past him. J2. He said it stuck with him because his girlfriend's name is Jessica and she was born in 2002. Collins is searching for it now, but it's a bit of a needle in a haystack situation."

"Yeah," I said, "three out of five vehicles in Florida are light-colored sedans."

He gave me his half smile. "And the other two are light-colored pickup trucks."

"Exactly." I paused, thinking. "Well, at least we now know *how* they knew exactly where the mayor's car was en route. Someone was following them, and called the kid to tell him when he should run that stop sign."

"I wasn't followed," Barnes protested.

"They might have team tagged you, one car turning off and another taking over."

"There was hardly any traffic. No cars behind me except maybe three times, for a couple of blocks each. And then..." her face fell, "...they turned off."

"Sometimes lack of traffic," I said, "can make it easier to keep track of a car from a distance."

The muffled sound of Barnes's phone ringing. She popped out of my office to answer it.

Bradley scratched his head. "That would be a lot to set up on the spur of the moment when someone happened to overhear that the mayor was leaving AMA."

"Yes, it would be," I said.

Barnes hung up her phone and came back into my office. "ME's office. Tox screen on the mayor revealed arsenic in his bloodstream. Not a huge amount, but more than would occur naturally."

Skeptical, I said, "How does arsenic occur naturally?"

"They said small amounts are often found in groundwater, but there aren't any high concentrations of it around here. There's enough in his system to suggest that someone had been slowly poisoning him."

"The wife?" Bradley and I said in unison.

Barnes nodded. "The ME suggested asking if he'd been complaining of drowsiness, headaches, diarrhea, vomiting, cramps, or hair loss."

"Wait a minute," Bradley said. "Let me find the report from his doctor." He fiddled on his phone for a few seconds. "Yeah, most of those symptoms they picked up on in the hospital. The mayor said he'd thought it was stress and maybe he was developing an ulcer, but he hadn't had time to go to the doctor about it. He was already slowly going bald, but the hair loss had picked up speed recently. Again, he'd assumed it was from stress."

He shook his head. "And here's something ironic. More extensive blood work had been ordered, to look for specific poisons, to be done on *Saturday* morning."

"Would arsenic explain why he overreacted to the painkillers?" Barnes asked.

"Maybe...probably," I said, "if he was already weakened by it. The wife told us she'd left the hospital before the mayor decided he was checking himself out, and that she would've tried to talk him out of it if she'd still been there." I turned to Barnes. "She did leave first, correct?"

"Yes, a couple of hours before McAllister came and the mayor decided he was going home."

I nodded slowly. "The wife knows her husband well. She may have seen that he was getting antsy."

"Maybe she waited in the parking lot," Bradley said, "figuring he'd eventually leave."

"But how would she know to set up the bogus accident?" I wondered. "She didn't know McAllister was going to say that about the hospital."

"Maybe she did," Barnes said. "Maybe they were in on it together, because they were having an affair?"

"Did you ever see anything suspicious pass between them?" Bradley asked.

She shook her head. "Not really. They seemed almost cool toward each other. But that could've been an act."

I held up a hand. "Okay, let's not get too far into speculation here. Bradley, you go talk to the widow again. Let's see if she tells you a different story. And did she know about that scheduled blood work?"

He nodded, and he and Barnes left my office.

Mid-morning, Sam suddenly appeared in my open doorway.
I jumped a little in my chair.

"Not exactly the reaction I was going for," he said, his mouth quirked up on one end.

I managed a smile.

"Have you had breakfast?" he asked.

My stomach grumbled, making it hard for me to lie. "Does a banana three hours ago count?"

"Apparently not to your stomach." He was flat out grinning now. "Come on, I'll buy you an egg sandwich at the deli."

Damn. I debated if I should make some excuse why I couldn't do that, but I came up empty. *Might as well get this over with,* I thought.

Then, *Great attitude, Anderson.*

As we walked to the deli, I filled Sam in on the morning's developments.

"I took a look at your board," he said when I'd finished. "It's all pretty convoluted, but yeah, I agree, it's one big Case with a capital C."

We ordered egg and cheese sandwiches, bacon on mine, at the deli counter and took seats in a booth.

"Of course," Sam said, "it's still possible that John Black ordered the hit on Patterson, to keep him from testifying. But I'm leaning toward an attempt to shut him up about the Navarro case. The timing is just too coincidental."

"It could be both," I said. "Black may have been taking bribes from this gang to look the other way." My insides relaxed some. Maybe we weren't going to have *the talk* after all.

Sam was nodding. "A distinct possibility."

We talked a bit more about the Case, until Mr. B himself delivered our sandwiches.

"Enjoy," he said with a smile and bustled away.

We ate in silence for a few minutes. My stomach stopped grumbling about halfway through the sandwich. It was sooo good.

Sam put down the remnants of his sandwich and wiped his fingers on a napkin. "So, is it my imagination, or have you withdrawn some from me?"

CHAPTER TWENTY-FIVE

"No," I blurted out as I dropped what was left of my sandwich on my plate.

"No, it isn't me," Sam said, "or no, you haven't withdrawn?"

I considered trying to BS my way through this. But I shook my head slightly. "No, it isn't you."

"Okay...thank you for being honest."

"I always try to be, with you."

He nodded. "So why the withdrawal? Is it because of my doppel-ganger?"

"That's part of it." Dread lay like a brick in my stomach, making me a little queasy. "I mean I don't really think it's you," I said quickly, then blurted out, "Not anymore."

"But you did at first?" he said.

I nodded and dropped my gaze to the tabletop. "And once that idea had slithered into my brain, well..." I trailed off, thinking about the betrayals of my youth. My father promising he wouldn't hit my mother again. Promising her, and later promising me, when I was older. Promises he never kept.

I flashed to my stepmother's note, her admission that she was finally facing the truth about him. That was part of it too. She—and others, including my mother—were always messing with my sense of reality, pretending what was going on wasn't *really* what was going on.

I glanced up. Sam was watching me intently.

I suddenly remembered the photo and sat up straighter. "I got a snapshot of him the other day. With all that's been happening, I forgot all about it." Excitement bubbling, I pulled out my phone and found the pic.

It wasn't a great shot, kind of blurry, and I'd only caught his profile. I handed the phone to Sam.

His nose wrinkled in that cute way it sometimes did, and pain stabbed my heart. My throat closed.

Get a grip, Anderson. Since when do you think of men's noses as cute?

"I guess it could be me," Sam said, skepticism in his voice. He laid the phone down between us.

"It's not only how he looks," I said. The brick of dread was back. "He moves like you do."

He nodded slightly. "You said 'partly.' What's the other part?"

I blew out air. "That, um, has nothing to do with you." I looked around. The booths near us were empty. "It's all this business with Mark Hayes. I thought he was one of the good guys, but... Well, the evidence keeps pointing his way. I want to believe that he's innocent, that he's being set up..." I trailed off.

Sam leaned forward slightly. "Just like you want to believe that this guy you keep seeing, who looks like me, is not me." His voice had a weird edge to it, and his face had gone blank.

I suddenly felt like I was being interrogated by Sheriff Pierson, not having a chat with my lover, Sam. I nodded, not trusting my voice in that moment.

Then I cleared my throat and changed the subject. "What brings you to town, besides a hankering for an egg sandwich?"

He stared at me for a full beat, before picking up the remnants of said sandwich. "Deb, Caroline's daughter, got me to thinking. She was checking land records because there was some kind of glitch with the house's title, maybe because of it sitting on the city/county line like it does. I thought I might check out some other properties' histories, over at the courthouse." He paused to take a bite, chewed and swallowed.

"That CO, Gerald Finch, he comes from an old Clover County family. They have a big farm up near the Georgia border, and they used to have money. But rumor has it that in recent years, they've become land poor. His parents are still alive but not in great health. They aren't really working the farm anymore, only renting out some of the fields."

He popped the last bite of his sandwich into his mouth and leaned back against the booth's bench. "When we checked his bank accounts, there was nothing suspicious. But I'm thinking the records on that farm may tell a different story. His mom has been downright cheerful lately, when I've seen her around."

Talking shop again had given my stomach a chance to settle down. I picked up my sandwich and took a bite.

"I think I'm close to having enough for an arrest," he said. "What do you think?"

I nodded as I swallowed. "Probably, but it would be better if you knew which inmate actually attacked Patterson."

"Oh, I've got a pretty good idea. I just can't prove it. Yet."

I gave him a full-blown smile. "You'll find the evidence. You always do."

I reached out and patted his hand, lying on the table. I wanted to grab it and hold it tight, but no PDAs... And I wasn't sure he wouldn't pull away, so I settled for a pat. "Are we good?" I went for a casual tone, but a lump had formed in my throat.

He looked at me for a long moment, his eyes soft. "I want us to be."

I waited without saying anything, my eyes beginning to sting. *I refuse to cry!*

"Judith, I'm not going anywhere...but I'm disappointed that you don't trust me more by now." He paused, stared at the ceiling for a second, then met my gaze again. "I get it that you have trust issues, and I've tried to be patient with that. But...it hurts that you could think I'd play games like that, walk around town letting you spot me and then duck into the crowd."

Something dawned on me. "Maybe it's part of all this." I waved a hand in the air. "Maybe they're behind the doppelganger, to distract us?"

"The gang, you mean?"

We were both carefully avoiding saying the word *Pillar* in public. "Yeah."

"Maybe." But Sam seemed to lack my enthusiasm for the idea. His eyes were now sad.

He slid along the bench and stood, dropped some bills on the table for the check. "I'd better get started. I'll call you later and tell you what I find." And he was headed for the front door of the deli before I could react.

I jumped up and followed him out.

On the sidewalk, I watched him cross the street to the courthouse. A vise had closed around my chest, making it hard to breathe.

———◆———

Time seemed to have slowed. The morning dragged by.

I tried to focus on reviewing reports, but my mind kept wandering. And I didn't have sleep deprivation as an excuse this time.

I checked in with Barnes. Still no word on the whereabouts of Bill Walker and nothing back from the FDLE lab yet.

I called Bradley for an update. "I've got a call in to the current president of Mayor Daniels's fraternity," he said. "But since UNF doesn't allow the fraternities or sororities to have houses, record-keeping is sketchy. There's no central place to store such records, nor even to have a central office and fraternity-owned computer. In the case of the mayor's fraternity, the officers each year are responsible for keeping track of members."

I scoffed, imagining what kind of records college frat boys would keep.

Bradley chuckled. "Yeah, exactly. I may or may not be able to find out who was in the fraternity around the same time as he was. Oh, and Collins is still trying to track down that car from the hospital parking lot Friday night. Nothing yet."

I thanked him, and we disconnected. Sighing, I went back to the incident reports, which had been sorely neglected the last few days.

At eleven-twenty, Wellbourne appeared in my office doorway. I was inordinately pleased by the interruption, as brief as it turned out to be.

"I'm not finding anything on Hayes," she said. "We should nickname him Mr. Squeaky Clean."

A wave of relief flowed through me, loosening tense muscles. Maybe my instincts weren't as off as I'd feared they were.

Ten minutes later, Pete McAllister called on my police-issue cell. "Chief, I'm so sorry to bother you, but we really need to talk."

"About what?" My tone was sharper than might be politic. I decided I was okay with that, after his abuse of my department in yesterday's paper.

"I'm sorry about the newspaper article," he quickly said. "That reporter, Frost—he took some of what I said out of context. Um, the rest, I'd rather not get into over the phone."

I believed him about Frost, but I still wasn't ready to cut him much slack. I waited.

After a beat, he filled the silence. "Can we meet for an early lunch, or coffee maybe? At the deli?"

I frowned at the phone. I could use a break, but McAllister would not have been my first choice in companions.

However, this would give me an opportunity to ask him about several things, like phone calls he may or may not have made and Mark Hayes's claim that he was lying. And whether or not he was having an affair with Mrs. Daniels.

"Coffee, I guess." I exaggerated a sigh. "Meet you there in ten minutes."

I had a little chat with myself as I went down in the elevator and then walked along the sidewalk. I hadn't particularly disliked Peter McAllister on first sight, but I hadn't particularly liked him either. And my opinion of him had ebbed and flowed ever since.

Now, however, I needed to take him more seriously, since there was a possibility he'd end up being my boss. I realized I was scowling and adjusted my expression as I pulled open the deli's door.

The little bell over it jingled cheerfully, and Mr. Bernstein glanced up. He broke into a big smile. "Chief, I've got just the thing for you. In honor of George Washington, apple pie, fresh from the oven."

I opened my mouth to say *just coffee*, as the scent of warm apples and cinnamon washed over me. My stomach rumbled. "Sounds wonderful, Mr. B," I said instead.

He waved me toward the booths. "And coffee, of course, right?"

"Of course." I smiled at him.

But my smile became a bit forced as I sat down across from McAllister in the farthest back booth. He was already nursing a coffee.

We exchanged greetings, and Mr. B appeared at my shoulder, plate in one hand, coffee mug in the other. "Black, correct?"

"Correct." I flashed him another smile.

With a flourish, he deposited the apple pie in front of me. "I've got chocolate brownies shaped like log cabins, in honor of Abe Lincoln," he said, beaming. "I was nine when my family came to America, old enough to understand when my father told me I was very lucky to grow up in a country where anyone could end up President."

Right, it's Presidents' Day. Thus the red-white-and-blue bunting hanging from the deli's ceiling. It was one of those federal holidays that some institutions honored and others didn't bother with. In Starling, schools, banks, and some businesses were closed, but not the local government nor the courthouse.

McAllister muttered something under his breath as Mr. B turned away. All I caught was "...shouldn't be..." He did that a lot, muttering to himself.

I took a bite of the warm pie. It melted on my tongue.

"Chief," McAllister said, "again, I apologize for yesterday's newspaper article. I did say a few things that were critical of your department's handling of the mayor's death. But those comments were tempered with others supporting you and pointing out that you are new to the job and still learning the ropes."

My body stiffened but I managed to maintain a neutral expression. He made it sound like I was a rookie.

He let out a bark of humorless laughter. "Of course, the media left those statements out of their reports. I wanted you to know that I'm fully committed to seeing that your department has all the resources it needs."

"That's good to hear, but you're sounding like you've already won the mayor's race."

He gave me a weak smile. "Sadly, I may have, by default. I hear that Hayes was a no-show at the mayor's office this morning."

"It was my understanding that he took his kids on a trip, for the long weekend."

McAllister shrugged. "Tell me honestly, Chief, do you believe Hayes killed the mayor?"

"I can't discuss an ongoing investigation with a civilian."

"But what if I were the mayor?" His tone was now wheedling.

"I never discussed specific suspects in a case with Mayor Daniels either, not until I had enough evidence to arrest someone."

His eyebrows rose. "And you feel you don't have enough evidence yet in this case?"

"Again, I can't discuss the case with you." I took another bite of pie. It was cooling off but still good. However, my appetite was fading fast. "What exactly was so urgent, that you called me away from said investigation?"

"I'd like your endorsement for mayor."

"I don't think that would be appropriate," I quickly said.

"Why not? Various sheriffs have endorsed certain candidates for governor in the past." He leaned forward. "And it would show the criminal elements that they'd better not take advantage of the current lack of leadership, that the Chief of Police and the mayor *apparent* are a united front." He paused. "The citizens of this city also need reassurance that *somebody*'s in charge whom they can trust. They know your face and reputation."

I decided to stall. "I'll have to think about it. It still feels like a conflict of interest to me. And as I've said before, I prefer to stay out of the politics."

He smiled. "Preference and reality are not always in sync, Chief."

I took another bite of pie and said nothing.

McAllister put his phone on the table and rested his hand on top of it. "Not that I need your endorsement. As I said, I'm probably going to end up mayor by default. But..."

He slid his hand over and covered my left hand, lying on the table.

I froze. *What the hell?*

"I'd like us to be partners," his voice was syrupy, "maybe in more ways than one."

I tried to tug my hand loose.

He tightened his hold on it. "I think we're going to be a great team, you and me, running the city together."

I fought the urge to jab my fork into his hand. I glared at him instead.

He chuckled and let my hand go. "You're feisty. I like that in a woman."

I opened my mouth, not at all sure what I was going to say. My cell phone rang.

Saved by the proverbial bell.

I pulled the ringing phone out of my jacket pocket, tempted to answer it even if it was a spam call, as an excuse to interrupt the direction of this conversation.

Indeed, the caller ID was just a phone number. I glanced up at McAllister. "Sorry. I need to see who this is." Then into the phone, "Hello?"

"Chief, it's Winters."

It took me a half beat, then I remembered—the officer involved in the Navarro case whom we'd sent out of town with his family. He sounded excited.

"Hang on for a sec." To McAllister, I said, "Um, I need to take this. Excuse me, please." I slid out of the booth.

"Do come back, Chief." That syrupy voice again. "I'll keep your pie company."

I quickly walked out of the deli, my mind racing. What the hell was I going to do? McAllister may very well end up my boss, the most powerful man in the city...and now he was coming on to me, proposing we be partners, quote, "in more ways than one."

Even if I was interested in him—I shuddered—something told me that this man did not share power. I'd always be the underling, never an equal. I couldn't begin to imagine myself in a romantic relationship with him. I wasn't even sure I could work for him now.

"Chief, are you there?" Winters said in my ear.

"Yeah, yeah." I stopped beside a big blue mailbox by the curb. "I wanted to get to a more private spot–"

"It's him!"

"Him who?"

"The witness. He's the guy in the paper."

"Huh?" I was distracted momentarily by the sight of Sam coming out of the courthouse. Had he been researching all this time?

"The one who came forward," Winters said, "the day after the Navarro murder, and said there were three killers. I got tired of Disney tunes and man-sized mice and stayed at the hotel today. I called up yesterday's *Sun* on my laptop to check the basketball scores, and there he was, right on the front page."

My heart rate kicked up a notch. Was he talking about McAllister?

Sam glanced in my direction before turning away. Wait, maybe it wasn't Sam. I couldn't tell for sure from this distance.

"He looked a lot scruffier back then," Winters was saying, "and had that tattoo on his neck. But it's the same guy."

Tattoo...same guy...

Heart full out racing now, my hand tightened around the phone. The officer had my total attention. "The one who just threw his hat in the ring for mayor?" I clarified.

"Yeah, him." A pause. "Is it too soon to bring my family home?" His voice had shifted from excited to a bit forlorn.

I took a deep breath, trying to steady myself. "Yes, I'm afraid it might be, but hopefully we'll get all this sorted out...in another day or two, with any luck. I'll keep you posted. And Winters..."

"Yes, Chief?"

"Good catch. Thanks." I disconnected and stood still on the sidewalk, my head spinning. What did this mean?

Could Winters be mistaken? He said the guy had looked different then.

Was there a reasonable explanation for why McAllister might have come forward after the Navarro homicide, but thought better of it later and made himself scarce? Maybe he was already thinking about running for mayor.

But any reasonable explanation was belied by the tattoo on his neck back then. If Winter's identification was correct, McAllister was or had been a member of The Pillar.

Wait, he and Mayor Daniels had been friends in college. My mind veered back to an earlier, almost nonsensical theory, that Daniels had been a gang member, taken out by a rival gang.

I shook my head. One thing for sure, I definitely needed to ask McAllister some pointed questions. And it dawned on me...somewhere in the last couple of minutes, I'd shifted from a woman worrying about inappropriate advances to police mode.

I marched back inside the deli, debating the best approach to get McAllister over to 3MB, where I wouldn't have to worry about eavesdroppers. *And* where I'd have back-up.

"Sorry about that," I said, as I slid into my seat, preparing myself for an Academy-Award-worthy performance.

McAllister gave me a small smile, but his eyes had turned wary.

My phone, still in my hand, pinged. I glanced down at it.

A text message from Sam. *Wow, just spotted my doppelganger. No wonder you've been distrustful!*

Warmth and relief washed through me. Maybe Sam and I would be okay after all.

"What's going on?" McAllister demanded.

"Oh, nothing important, only some minor developments in the case." I met his gaze and let some of the warm, fuzzy feelings toward Sam soften my face. "Um, the subject we were discussing, I'm thinking we need to continue that conversation in a more private location."

I was hoping he was thinking hotel room. I was thinking my office, or better still, an interview room.

His face relaxed some and his smile widened. "That's an excellent idea. Do you want a box for the rest of your pie?"

I returned his smile and shook my head.

He looked past me, raising his hand to signal for the check. The bell over the door jangled, and his eyes hardened. His mouth flattened into a tight line.

I turned my head toward the front of the deli, spotted Becky coming through the door.

"Ah, the little Jewess has arrived," McAllister sneered from behind me, "coming in for her shift to help out dear old grandpa."

My head jerked around—too quickly—I hadn't completely wiped the horror off my face. Our gazes locked, and something shifted in his eyes.

My blood ran cold. *He knows that I know.*

He reached up with his left hand and touched the side of his neck, a slow grin spreading across his face.

"You had the tattoo removed," I said in a low voice. "That's really why you were at the dermatologist's."

"Yes. Follow-up visit."

I started to slide out of the booth again, my right hand moving toward the Glock at my back. "I need you to come–"

"Stop moving, Chief." His voice was low and urgent. "I have a pistol under the table, aimed at your gut."

I froze.

"One wrong move, and I take the girl hostage."

My heart raced even as time slowed.

I glanced over my shoulder again. The girl was cheerfully greeting customers as she put on her apron. It was adult-sized. She had to wrap it around herself twice. She was so small and young.

My chest aching and my stomach clenched, I returned my gaze to McAllister.

He was pulling his phone toward him with his left hand.

"Hey, it's Gloria the Cop." The granddaughter's voice, already high pitched, rose to a squeal. I grimaced, but not because of the high notes she was hitting.

McAllister looked up and also grimaced. He poked the phone's screen. "It's Mac. We're going with Plan B."

A grunt came from the phone.

"Now," McAllister said to me, "you and I are–"

Rustling beside me. "Everything okay, Chief?" Barnes's voice, neutral. My stomach heaved. Sour-apple bile rose in the back of my throat.

But I dared not glance her way. McAllister and I had locked eyes again, and I wasn't about to look away.

"Why wouldn't it be?" I said in a grouchy voice. "Hey, tell that dumb kid to stop calling you Gloria the Cop. It's unprofessional."

I felt Barnes stiffen beside my shoulder.

"Dismissed, Officer."

Feet shuffling on the floor. "Hey, Becky." Barnes's voice toward the front of the deli. "Shouldn't you be in school?"

"Nope," the girl's voice was cheerful. "School's closed today. Federal holiday."

Barnes's voice again, but lower. I couldn't make out the words, and I dared not look over my shoulder.

"As I was saying," McAllister growled, "before we were so rudely interrupted, we're going out the back. And you've got a couple of choices to consider, while we make our discreet exit."

His voice had shifted to cheerful businessman, which struck me as bizarre.

"You can still join us, which would be extraordinarily lucrative for you, or you can…" He trailed off, giving me a sly smile.

I narrowed my eyes at him. "How lucrative?"

"We'll discuss that, once we're safely out of here. Now nice and easy, and nobody gets hurt."

I glanced over to the door leading to the back storage area of the deli. I'd make my move after we were in there. A stray bullet could still end up in the restaurant, but…

The door suddenly opened. A sandy-haired, broad-shouldered man in khaki stepped into the doorway.

My heart stuttered in my chest.

CHAPTER TWENTY-SIX

Sam met my gaze, and a smile—no, more of an evil grin—spread across his face.

It's not Sam, a voice said firmly inside my head. His nose was too thin. And I'd never seen that expression on *my* Sam's face before.

Plus this guy's eyes were too blue. Probably contacts.

"Let's go," he growled to McAllister.

The latter slid out of the booth and stood up. His hand in his suit jacket pocket made a suspiciously big bulge. I believed him. He had a gun.

"Get up," he said in a harsh, low voice.

My mind was galloping, searching for alternatives, but there really wasn't any choice. I wasn't going to let these men hurt innocents.

I used the action of sliding out of the booth to glance toward the front of the store. The good news was no sign of Barnes or Becky. The bad news, nobody was paying the least bit of attention to us. Or maybe that was good news too.

"Get up," McAllister repeated, his tone impatient.

I did so and meekly followed the Sam clone out the door, with McAllister bringing up the rear.

The second we were in the storage area, the back of my jacket twitched and the weight of my Glock was gone from my waistband. One thing I had to give McAllister, he had a light touch.

I struggled to squash a sense of panic. There was still my back-up piece, my snub-nose .32 tucked in its ankle holster. I told my skittering heart to settle down. I would bide my time.

A white panel truck was parked in the back lot, along with a half dozen other vehicles, including the deli's catering van. A pink and purple bike was propped against the back wall of the building.

The Sam clone slid the side door of the panel truck open.

I slowed my steps. Once in that truck, the odds of my survival went way down.

A hard nudge from behind. "We used to have three of these trucks," McAllister grumbled. "Now, thanks to you, we're down to two."

I looked over my shoulder as I took another step. "Not my fault your people are sloppy."

McAllister snarled and cranked back his fist.

"Cut it out," Not-Sam said in a sharp tone. "Get her in there."

McAllister grabbed my shoulder.

"Police, don't move." A voice from the left.

Bradley!

I dove to the right, toward the bike, landed on one knee and grabbed its seat and handle bars. Bringing it with me, I rose and turned in one fluid motion.

McAllister was bearing down on me, gun raised. I swung the bike toward his face and let it go. Dropping to the ground, I was already rolling as I landed.

Behind a trash can, I pulled out my .32 and peeked out. The Sam clone was climbing into the side of the truck.

I raised my gun and opened my mouth to yell, *Stop, Police.*

But the real Sam dragged him back to the pavement. The two of them stared at each other for half a beat.

Then the real Sam—*my* Sam—twisted his doppelganger around and cuffed him. "You're under ar–"

McAllister jumped up from the ground, his pistol somehow still in his hand. Aimed at Sam.

Nooo! I swung my gun in McAllister's direction. A shot rang out before I could pull the trigger.

My heart stopped. But Sam was still standing.

McAllister screamed. He dropped his pistol and clutched his shoulder, where red blossomed around a hole in his suit jacket.

Bradley tackled him and took him down. Sitting on his back, he cuffed him. McAllister howled the whole time.

Smiling grimly, I rose from behind the trash can—not the best of barriers but fortunately I hadn't needed it to stop a bullet.

I scanned for Barnes. She was leaning over to retrieve McAllister's gun from the pavement.

Suddenly the truck roared backward, swinging around, almost hitting her. She jumped to the side.

Sam fired twice, his gun low. The front tire turned into a blooming onion of shredded rubber.

The truck lurched forward as the driver tried to turn it toward the exit. But the tire wasn't cooperating. What was left of it dragged against the pavement.

Sam raised his pistol toward the driver's door.

The driver gunned it, bouncing off the parked cars. The truck careened into the alley behind the lot. Two shots rang out, the driver's window shattering, and the truck rammed into a telephone pole.

Thuds from the back of the truck.

Sam approached the driver's door, gun raised. Bradley was right behind him. Barnes was standing over the Sam clone and McAllister, both cuffed and sitting on the ground.

I headed for the open side door. The inside was bare, except for black rubber mats. And Bill Walker lying in one corner, tied up and gagged with duct tape.

I glanced toward the seats in the front. The driver was slumped over. He could be faking, but I was pretty sure he was unconscious or dead. An arm dangled down in the gap between the seats, a pistol lying on the floor beneath it.

My own pistol still in hand, I clambered into the truck, reached out and plucked up the gun. Tucking it into my waistband, I scrambled over to Bill.

His eyes lit up at the sight of me. He tried to talk, but from behind the tape it came out as a mumble. His normally blue eyes were a cloudy gray, his skin pale to almost translucent. He mumbled again.

I was tempted to rip the tape off, but knew from painful experience it would take some of his skin with it. His face pinched, Bill looked past me.

I whirled around, pistol raised. But there was no one directly behind me—only Mr. B coming our way across the lot. "Get some cooking oil," I called out.

He stopped, stepped sideways to see past me, then nodded and took off for the deli's back door. He was back in less than thirty seconds. He could really move for an old man.

"Lemme get at that tape." He held up a large plastic bottle and a roll of paper towels.

I hesitated. His presence would contaminate a crime scene, even more than I already had. But I didn't like the way Bill looked. Was he getting enough air with that tape over his mouth?

I glanced again toward the front. The driver's arm hadn't moved.

"Judith." Sam's voice from up there, a strange mix of surprise and dismay, but no alarm.

I signaled for Mr. B to climb in. Then, hunched over, I moved to peek between the seats.

Sam was peering through the open driver's window, tiny shards of bloody glass a macabre frame around his face. "I didn't pull the trigger," he said. "The glass blew outward."

The driver's head had fallen sideways against the deflated and blood-smeared air bag. One sightless eye pointed toward the truck's ceiling, a black hole in that temple.

Of their own volition, my eyes jerked away, toward the passenger's seat. I startled, my heart galloping. I hadn't expected to actually see a passenger.

He was slumped over, his seatbelt holding him up, a gory exit wound in his back. A pistol lay in his lap, his left hand limp around its grip.

Did these two shoot each other?

I didn't recognize the passenger, but when I turned my gaze back to the driver's profile, his identity registered.

It was Sergeant Lewis.

———◆———

"How did you get here so fast?" I asked Bradley. He was still huffing a little from the takedown.

Two uniformed officers had arrived, and Barnes was handing off the prisoners to them.

A paramedic was examining Bill Walker, who was sitting in the open doorway of the white panel truck. He'd crawled over there himself, once

Mr. B had removed the tape from his limbs, insisting he wasn't staying in "that dark and stinky van" for another second.

"Mrs. Daniels called," Bradley finally answered me, when he'd caught his breath. "She was feeling guilty because she hadn't told us something, even though she didn't think it was important, and she'd promised the mayor to keep the secret."

"The mayor had a secret?" I asked, confused.

"No, his friend McAllister did. He and the mayor had been buddies in college, but they'd lost touch when they went off to different law schools. All the mayor had told his wife was that his friend Mac had gotten into some trouble and was looking for a fresh start. So he'd changed his name and had come to Daniels, asking for a job."

"Did she know his old name?"

"No, but she said it also began with M-C, so he could keep the nickname Mac."

"McPherson," we said in unison. One of the missing gang leaders.

Barnes trotted toward us.

"I went to your office to tell you about her call," Bradley said, "but Sis told me you were having coffee with McAllister."

"So we hauled ass over here," Barnes said, as she stopped next to her brother.

I glanced at Sam, who was consulting with the second paramedic over by the driver's door of the truck. The latter wore blue nitrile gloves with blood on the fingers. He shook his head.

Sam gently slapped his shoulder and headed our way.

Bradley nodded in his direction. "The sheriff was in front of the deli, said he'd seen someone suspicious go in the back."

Sam reached us, and immediately wrapped an arm around my shoulders and squeezed.

His touch felt wonderful, warm and soothing.

No PDAs, I thought, then, *hell with it.* I slid an arm around his waist and squeezed him back.

We both let go and acted like nothing had happened. Barnes and Bradley were grinning at us.

"I saw you out front," Sam said to me, "when I came out of the courthouse. I started to wave, but it looked like you were on the phone. That's when I spotted my doppelganger. I jogged over, planning to confront him, but he slipped in the deli's back door. The way he was moving, it somehow set off alarm bells. I came back around to peek in, to see if I could spot you through the front window, and that's when I ran into these two." He gestured at Barnes and Bradley.

I looked toward the ambulance. The paramedics had moved Bill Walker to its back bumper. They now hovered on either side of him, both talking at once. His face was set in a frown, his arms crossed over his chest.

One of them beckoned to me, then met me halfway. "He won't let us take him to the hospital until he's talked to you," he said in a low voice.

"Is he going to be okay?" I whispered back.

The paramedic shrugged. "He's pretty banged up. And unless he wants to walk with a permanent limp, he needs to have a close encounter with an orthopedic surgeon. Soon."

I winced.

"That was his reaction." He gave me a small, humorless smile.

We walked toward the ambulance. "Chief," Bill said.

"How ya doing?" I asked.

He winced. "Not bad, all things considered. These gentlemen are going to take me to the hospital to get some new crutches. Those bastards stole mine."

"How'd they get their hands on you?" I asked.

Bill scowled at the paramedics. They discreetly drifted away.

"I got a call from one of my contacts," Bill said. "He's only been out about two months. He said he had info for me but wasn't willing to say anything over the phone. So I went out to meet him."

"When was this?"

"About four a.m. I had just settled down to get some sleep."

"You didn't try to clean last night?" I demanded. He couldn't be *that* dedicated.

"No, but I'm used to staying up that late. I met the guy, and I'm pretty sure I wasn't followed from the municipal building. But on the way back, two thugs jumped me and dragged me into that panel truck."

"Do you think it was a set-up, to lure you out of the building?"

"I don't know. I hope not, because then what the guy told me will be suspect."

"And what was that?" I asked.

"He said the scuttlebutt in Raiford was that the leader of The Pillar got himself arrested on purpose, along with a couple of his enforcers. He wanted a solid alibi while other things were happening on the outside. Plus, he and his enforcers were working on eliminating the influence of any other gang in the prison." He paused, sucked in air. "Especially the Latino gangs."

Another pause. It dawned on me that Bill's bruised ribs might be downright broken now, after bouncing around inside that truck. "Maybe you should wait to tell me the rest."

He shook his head, sucked in more air, winced slightly. "The Pillar gang members were telling the white convicts that they were creating a haven. That if they joined the gang, they could always seek refuge in a certain city and county, regardless of what crimes they had committed elsewhere."

"Starling," I said.

Bill nodded. "*And* Clover County."

CHAPTER
TWENTY-SEVEN

I lounged in one corner of my old sofa, luxuriating in the feel of the soft leather and the silky sensation of my lounge pajamas against my clean skin. A drop of water dripped from my hair, making a light brown circle on the front of the beige top. It expanded to the size of a nickel.

It reminded me of the red stain growing on McAllister's shoulder. I shook off the memory, not wanting to think about all that right now.

Sam, at the opposite end of the sofa, was massaging my left foot.

I lifted my other foot up onto his lap. "This one's jealous."

A low chuckle and Sam started on that one.

Pipsqueak jumped up onto my stomach. "Ooof," I let out. I glanced down at her as she settled there, purring softly. "I've been forgiven for my absences, huh?"

Another chuckle from Sam. "And Paul's not here to spoil her anymore."

After a pause, he said, "I can't believe the audacity of those guys."

Okay, I guess we're gonna think about it. I really didn't mind, though. Hashing out the events of the day while they were fresh was a good idea.

"It was an ambitious plan," I said.

"I'm figuring they let you see my look-alike because they wanted to break us up. If you stayed as police chief after they made the switch, you would've realized that he wasn't me in a New York minute."

"But if we were no longer dating," I said, "then I wouldn't find your replacement's behavior all that weird. I'd assume that I hadn't known you as well as I thought I had..." I trailed off, thinking about the gang leader, Jared Brandish. No wonder I'd thought his photo from that outdoor café seemed so familiar. Even before any alterations, he'd looked enough like Sam to be his brother.

"Whose idea was it to send Barnes in to do reconnaissance?" I asked.

"Hers."

"Figured as much."

"The plan was to get you out of there, saying you were needed back at 3MB, but she could tell by the way you two were glaring at each other that things had already gone sideways."

"I'm just glad she got the message to get Becky out of harm's way. McAllister was threatening to take the girl hostage."

My insides warmed at the thought of Barnes. She knew me so well. No way was I replacing her with another assistant any time soon. But eventually, when she had more experience under her belt, I'd have to. She deserved to be a detective someday.

"Did Mark Hayes get the word it's safe to come home?" Sam asked, as he kneaded my arch with the heel of his hand.

"Yes," I moaned out, then added, my voice a bit breathless, "A park ranger went out to his campsite."

Sam gave me a salacious grin. "Here's another question. Why were they so blatant about framing Hayes?"

"Yeah. McAllister isn't stupid. He should've realized I wouldn't buy it."

"Maybe he was counting on that. Maybe he didn't want you to arrest him, at least not right away. When he tried to bribe you, if you'd accepted the arrangement, he probably would've tested your loyalty by insisting you arrest Hayes."

His eyes lit up with a new thought, then his mouth narrowed into a grim line. "And maybe even—"

"Order me to make something happen to Hayes while he was in custody."

"And/or," Sam said, "assign you the task of taking me out, so his buddy could take my place."

We shuddered in unison.

"And if you'd refused the bribes," he continued, "he would've used the fact that you hadn't arrested Hayes to make a case for your incompetence and—"

"Tell the press I had slunk away in the middle of the night, knowing he would fire me once he was mayor."

Sam nodded, his face pinched. "They would've packed up your apartment and pretended you'd left town on your own."

He stopped the massage, leaned down and grabbed my fleece-lined slippers. He tucked my still tingling feet into them, giving each a gentle pat.

I sighed. "I could get used to this."

"I wouldn't mind if you did," he replied, with another suggestive grin.

I debated for a second as I lowered my feet to the floor. I hated to break the mood, but I had to know. "When you sent that text, about seeing your double and now understanding, did you mean that all is forgiven?"

His grin softened into a smile as his eyes met mine. He scooted over closer to me. "I'd thought before that you'd seen somebody who kind of looked like me, and you'd let that feed into your old distrust." He paused. "But when I saw that the guy was basically my twin, then I got it. How could you *not* think it was me?"

He put an arm around my shoulders and squeezed.

But my chest had tightened with guilt. He was letting me off too easy.

"Okay, that explains my initial reaction, but I should have..." I trailed off. Should've done what...forced myself to trust him?

You can't force trust.

But I *could* work harder on my "old distrust," as he'd called it. It had been thirty damn years, after all.

Time to let it go. I wasn't sure if that was my mother's voice or my own.

"Well, I owe you an apology, a big one," I said.

"Apology accepted." He nudged my head down onto his shoulder.

I snuggled against him and felt myself relaxing completely. Something that hadn't happened in days, not since this whole roller coaster ride began with that phone call from Juan Alvarez.

Juan was now scheduled for release in the morning. The ASA was dropping all charges against him.

I smiled a little at the memory of that phone call. The kid had thanked me at least a dozen times, choking up twice. The mushy stuff made me antsy, but I was glad I'd called him myself, instead of delegating it to Bradley. I planned to drive to the jail in the morning, so I could shake his hand when he stepped through those doors a free man.

My police-issue cell—lying on my packing box coffee table—pinged. Sam and I groaned in unison.

I struggled upright, picked it up, and shook my head slightly. Had I conjured Bradley up by thinking of him?

Are you still up? His text read. I glanced at Paul's driftwood clock. It was only nine-ten.

I texted back, *Of course. What have you got?*

The phone rang and I was greeted by Bradley's low chuckle. "Just making sure you weren't in the middle of something."

"Watch it, Lieutenant," I said, but I was chuckling myself. "What's up?"

"Um, I got the search warrants for McAllister's and Lewis's apartments," his voice sobered abruptly. "Only one thing useful at McAllister's, otherwise the place looked like a hotel room. But there was a bottle of arsenic, hidden between his mattress and box springs."

"They found arsenic at McAllister's place," I said to Sam, as I put the phone on speaker.

"I looked up the company it came from," Bradley said. "It's marked for research purposes, but they sell it online."

I blew out air. "So, he was poisoning his old friend."

"But he must've gotten impatient," Sam said.

"Yeah," came from the phone as I nodded.

"We're at Lewis's place now," Bradley continued. "Bert found a note. It was in an envelope with Starling PD on it, but part of it is addressed to you, Chief."

I tensed. "What's it say?"

"It's pretty long," Bradley said. "Starts with, 'If someone is reading this, then things did not go well today. I was hoping I could stop them, but apparently I failed. Or maybe I didn't.' Lewis goes on to justify taking bribes from Chief Black because, quote, 'the only people being hurt were whores and junkies.'"

Sam tensed beside me, but neither of us said anything.

"The next part's a little vague," Bradley continued. "It sounds like Thompson and Taft got themselves arrested on purpose, and Lewis was in on that. The gang leadership wanted more muscle in Raiford to intimidate the other gangs."

I flashed to the conversation I'd had with Lewis, where he'd mentioned the "sweet set-up" the gangs had in prison.

"He was okay with that too. But he *wasn't* okay with the gang trying to take over the city, because, quote, 'I believe in law and order.'" Bradley snorted softly. "He tried to back away from the whole mess, but he got a message last night from Chief Black, telling him to call out sick today and show up with the panel truck."

"Wait," Sam said. "Black is in cahoots with this gang?"

"Apparently," Bradley said. "They planned to kidnap the chief, and Lewis figured they were involving him as the driver to make sure there was no way out for him. Then he says, quote, 'But there's always one way out.'"

He cleared his throat. "Here's the part addressed to you, Chief. Quote, 'I know we haven't had the best relationship, but you are the chief now and I couldn't bring myself to go along with what they have planned. I know they won't be able to corrupt you, which means they'll kill you. I can't be a part of that.'"

Bradley paused, cleared his throat again. "'If all else fails, I may have to crash the truck. If so, I won't be coming out of this alive. I have no desire to go to prison.' He goes on to say he hopes he can stop them some other way. He ends with, 'And then you'll never see this letter.'"

A lump had formed in my throat. I hadn't particularly liked Lewis, and I wasn't the least bit surprised he was in on the bribes with John Black. But I never would've wished this fate on him.

"And that explains his meltdown at the crash scene," I said, "the night the mayor was killed."

Sam nodded, and a soft "Yeah," came from the phone.

"Bert said only Lewis's pistol had been fired," Bradley informed us, "not the passenger's."

"So he didn't fail," Sam said in a mournful tone. "He steered toward that pole on purpose, then killed the other guy and shot himself."

"Yeah," Bradley said softly. "Residue around the shot to his temple. It was a through-and-through that then shattered the window. We weren't able to find the bullet."

The three of us were all quiet for a beat.

I swallowed hard. "Did you find anything else in his place?"

"A cash receipt," Bradley said, "for ten prepaid cell phones."

"He was probably supposed to plant it on you at some point," I said.

Sam looked confused.

I turned to him. "I forgot to tell you. We got a call from Foster in Jacksonville late this afternoon. He went out to that phone store where the burners were purchased and caught up with the clerk who'd made the sale. He remembered it because the buyer told him he was a police detective, and he was buying the phones for an undercover operation–"

"Which no real cop would ever disclose," Sam said. "Lemme guess, the buyer was tall, dark-haired and nattily dressed."

"Yes," Bradley said. "They were going to set me up as a co-conspirator in the mayor's death. And thanks for the compliment, Sheriff....I'll keep you posted, Chief, if anything else interesting comes up this evening."

We disconnected, and Sam raised his gaze to the ceiling. "Dear Lord, let Bradley have a boring evening."

I laughed, and we snuggled again into the soft leather of the sofa, his arms around me, and my cheek against the flannel of his shirt.

A soft ping, coming from the floor at the end of the sofa where I'd dropped my laptop case—which also contained my personal cell phone.

I sighed and wiggled for Sam to let me go.

He threw his arms up in the air and groaned.

I retrieved the phone from the laptop case. It was a text from Kate. *Is this a good time to chat?*

"It's my psychologist friend from Maryland. I should talk to her. I've been putting her off for days."

Sam let out another small groan, but then said, "Okay, as long as you put her on speaker so I can meet her."

I called her number.

"Hey, Judith, finally." There was a chuckle in her voice. "So, what's happening with Sam, and your cases?"

My cheeks heated. "Um, Sam's here actually, and you're on speaker."

"Great," Kate exclaimed. "Pleased to meet you, Sam."

"Likewise," he said. "I've heard a lot about you."

Kate's chuckle became full blown. "Same here."

Sam gave me a mock sideways glare and a lopsided grin. He sure was grinning a lot tonight.

"So how are the cases coming along?" Kate asked.

"They're pretty much resolved," I said. "And I was right, they were all interrelated." I told her the long, sorry story, with Sam jumping in at times.

When we had finished, she let out a low whistle. "This gang was going to take over the whole city? That's pretty damned ballsy."

I snorted. "Ballsy? Such language, Kate Huntington."

She snickered. "I've been hanging out with private eyes and cops too much."

A pause. "I'm still not clear on why they were recruiting Black and Latino kids though." Her voice had sobered considerably.

"They used the non-white members for dangerous tasks," I said.

"Like running down the mayor," Sam added. "And they were trying to undermine the power of the non-white gangs, in Starling and at the state prison."

My chest ached at the thought of the kids we'd lost—Christopher Jones and Miguel Navarro, and who knew how many others.

"What are they doing at the state prison to clean up this gang's mess?" Kate asked.

"Good question." I made a mental note to follow up on that tomorrow. This gang could not be allowed to maintain any power there either. They were too dangerous.

"And they were behind Sam's doppelganger," Kate was saying, "but how did they know about Caroline's pregnancy?"

Sam shot me another have-you-been-telling-tales-out-of-school look, then leaned forward toward the phone. "I've discovered one employee, so far, who's linked to the gang, and there may be more. Any of my deputies or civilian staff could have seen the autopsy report in the case file."

"All they had to know was that you had a previous relationship with Caroline," I said quickly, before Kate could blurt it out.

"Which was not a big secret," Sam added.

"But why did they go to such lengths to create a look-alike for you, Sam?" Kate asked. "That's pretty drastic, to get plastic surgery."

"They were going to take over Clover County as well," he said, "by taking me out and replacing me with Brandish, one of their own leaders."

"Would that have worked?" Kate asked from the phone. "Wouldn't your staff have realized it wasn't you?"

"They might've planned on having me out for a while," Sam said, "maybe from some illness or accident. This guy is a little thinner than me—so he comes back, kind of gaunt and acting out of sorts. He probably could've pulled it off."

"Plus," I said, "I would either be out of the picture, or we would've broken up over you gallivanting around town with other women." I gave Sam a small smile.

He answered with a big grin. "Which would offer another explanation for any personality changes in me that people noticed."

"And I'm not sure Brandish had plastic surgery," I said. "He might've just gotten some Botox shots, to fill out his face some. And used shoulder pads and such. He already looked a lot like Sam...Hey, Kate, what were you calling me about? Sorry I had to keep putting you off." I glanced at Sam. "Um, should I take you off speaker?"

Please let me take you off speaker.

"Nah, it's nothing personal. I'm coming down there to visit my parents in St. Augustine during my spring break next month. I wanted to make a plan to get together."

"You and Skip and the kids?" I asked, hoping I'd succeeded in keeping the trepidation out of my voice. Kate's family could be a bit overwhelming, at least to me.

"Nope. Only me. The kids have decided they're too old to go on vacation with their parents, and we're not about to leave them to their own devices at their ages. So Skip and I are taking separate vacations this year, at different times."

"How old are your kids?" Sam asked.

"Fifteen and thirteen," Kate answered. "Going on twenty-five and ten."

"Ten?" Sam said.

"Yes. Thirteen-year-old boys seem to regress some for a while."

Sam laughed and I said, "Thus the close supervision."

"Exactly."

Something else had occurred to me. But I was debating whether to ask Kate about it in front of Sam, not sure how he would react.

No, I chastised myself mentally, *no more assuming Sam is like Dad.* One of the things that had set my father off was another man looking at my mother, and somehow that was her fault.

"Um, Kate, I wanted to ask you...uh, McAllister came on to me, in the diner right before things went sideways." I watched Sam out of the corner of my eye.

He was nodding, his expression normal, curious even. No shifts in his body language, no signs of jealousy.

I stifled a relieved sigh, and my chest filled with warmth. *I really do love this guy.* I didn't even flinch internally at the L word.

"Hmm," Kate said, "and you're wondering what that's about?"

"Yeah. I mean I never really felt any vibes that he was interested."

"Well, don't take offense," she said, "but you know those reports on TV about jailbreaks, and some female jail employee turns out to be in on it? And when you see the pictures of her, she isn't all that attractive."

I laughed. "You could've left out that last part. I'd already figured out where you were going. He thought if he got me to fall for him, that I'd be easier to control."

"Might've been another reason for my double," Sam said, "to get you pissed at me and more susceptible to his advances."

"Could be," came from the phone.

I nodded. "Little did he know, if I felt betrayed by a man, the *last* thing I'd do would be to run into the arms of another one."

"Well, I'll let you two go," Kate said, the chuckle back in her voice, "since you have some celebrating to do."

I looked Sam's way. He was grinning at me, again. I smiled back and bumped his shoulder with mine.

"I'll text you the dates I'll be down there," Kate was saying, "and we'll set something up."

We exchanged goodbyes and disconnected. I turned to Sam.

He had a rueful expression on his face. "Unfortunately, I can't stay tonight. I have a breakfast meeting with the jail superintendent early tomorrow. I wanted to get him away from the jail and my office, to make sure we're not overheard. I'm going to try to root out whoever at the jail is corrupt."

"Do you think he is?"

"I don't, but his responses to my questions should confirm that, or not. Oh, something I forgot to tell you—what I found out at the courthouse. The Finch farm had been mortgaged to the hilt, and his folks were two years behind in taxes. Then when my CO's brother joined The Pillar, the taxes were paid off, in cash." He paused. "And now–"

"The mortgages have mysteriously been paid off as well," I said.

"Yup. The paperwork was filed on Friday, removing all liens. And that's the last piece I needed to get Gerry to confess and flip on the inmate who actually attacked Patterson." He grinned at me.

"You are awfully happy tonight," I teased. "That grin makes a baker's dozen, I believe."

He wrapped an arm around my waist and drew me in against his chest, despite his claim that he had to leave soon. "Why shouldn't I be happy? All our cases are solved, or close enough to it. And we're finishing each other's sentences again."

I looked up at him, grinning myself.

He lowered his lips to mine, giving me one of his wonderful kisses. They start off so slow and tender and then turn *sooo* hot.

When we finally broke for air, he said, "I guess I don't have to go home just yet."

EPILOGUE

Awhile later, I walked Sam to the door, where we lingered over a goodnight kiss.

After he left, I wandered into the kitchen, poured myself a glass of wine and then settled on the old leather sofa. Pipsqueak hopped up and curled into a ball against my thigh.

I stared out the window across from me for a time, enjoying the afterglow and the lit-up skyline of my new city. All was right in my world for a change.

I took a sip of wine, and my eyes fell on the brown wrapping paper and cashmere sweater that I'd tossed—how many days ago now?—onto the pile of my still-packed moving boxes. I leaned forward, plucked up the sweater, and held it against the sleeve of my lounge outfit.

Exactly the same shade. Both Camille and Sam had a good eye for color.

How should I respond to her note? Should I respond at all? I never had before, but...

I glanced at the driftwood clock. Surprisingly, it was only a few minutes after eleven. Kate might still be up, supervising her teenagers.

Should I text, and if she's up, ask her advice about my stepmother?

I fingered the soft fabric again. The sweater was a v-neck, which I preferred.

At least she got that part right.

I recalled the words in her note, *...I know you prefer to wear black and white, but....* So like her to acknowledge my preferences but push her own agenda anyway.

I hadn't felt that way about Sam's gift, though, and he'd also deviated from my standard wardrobe colors. He hadn't even apologized for that, only for the intimacy of the gift.

Although, it certainly didn't feel too intimate now. I smiled, the warm glow still lingering.

Am I being unfair to Camille?

I realized I didn't need to ask Kate about the issue. I knew what her answer would be. But I'd probably tell her about it later, next time we talked.

Is this how friendship works? Sometimes you were each other's sounding boards, and sometimes you just shared the important stuff after the fact. Was I finally getting the hang of this?

I leaned forward again and pulled my laptop out of its leather case on the floor. I booted it up on my lap and started typing.

Dear Camille,

The sweater is beautiful, and you're right, the color is perfect for me.

I stopped, squirmed a little, then backspaced to the end of *color* and typed *does look good on me.*

———————◦◦○◦———————

AUTHOR'S NOTES

If you enjoyed this book, please take a moment to leave a short review on the ebook retailer of your choice. Reviews help with sales and sales keep the stories coming. You can readily find the links to these retailers at the *misterio press* bookstore (https://misteriopress.com/bookstore/).

This is Book 4 in this series; Book 1 is *Lethal Assumptions*, and Book 3 (the one just prior to this one) is a Christmas novelette, *The Twelve Heists of Christmas*. The next installment, Book 5, will hopefully be out in late 2024. It is tentatively titled *Malignant Memory*.

This book was proofread by multiple sets of eyes, but proofreaders are human. If you noticed any errors, please email me at kass@kassan dralamb.com so I can have them corrected.

Heck, email me anyway. I love hearing from readers!

And you may want to sign up for my newsletter at https://kassandr alamb.com to get a heads up about new releases, plus special offers and bonuses for subscribers. You will receive a free novelette, *The Tell-Tale Bark*, the prequel to the Marcia Banks and Buddy cozy series, AND a free novella, *Sweet Sanctuary*, the prequel to my Kate Huntington Mysteries. The C.o.P. on the Scene Mysteries are a spinoff from this series. Judith is a secondary character in that series, first showing up in Book 4, and playing a more extensive role in most of the books after that.

Also, misterio press now has a readers' group on Facebook (https://www.facebook.com/groups/misteriopressmysteries/) where we chat with readers and also offer giveaways, contests and other goodies. Please stop by and check it out!

Bear with me as I spread around some gratitude and then I will share some interesting background information about this book.

First a big thank you to my sister authors at *misterio press*, Shannon Esposito, Kirsten Weiss and Kathy Owen, who helped shape this into a better story with their feedback. Also my unending gratitude to my wonderful editor, Marcy Kennedy, from whom I have learned so much! And to my husband who always does the "final" proofread. I put final in quotes because I have a tendency to mess with things right up until the story goes into production, and sometimes I inadvertently introduce new errors. So any boo-boos you found are my fault, not his.

Readers often ask us writers where we get our story ideas. In this particular case, the idea came from a jury duty experience in the Fall of 2021.

While most people try to avoid or get out of jury duty, I was super excited when I got the summons. What a great way for a mystery writer to witness how the legal system works up close.

Fortunately, I was picked for the first jury panel and got to go through the *voir-dire* experience. I was not picked for the jury however, and had mixed emotions about that (for more on the whole experience, see the blog post, 10 Surprises on Jury Duty, at https://misteriopress.com).

Why mixed emotions? Because the defendant was a young man who had participated in a drug deal gone wrong (i.e., it ended in the death of someone), and he was being tried for felony murder. As the *voir-dire* proceeded, I realized that he probably hadn't actually killed the victim; someone else among his cohorts had done so. I also began to suspect that the someone else had actually gotten a lighter sentence, in exchange for testifying against this young man.

In other words, the real murderer was getting off easier because they were cooperating to convict this chap (who didn't actually commit the murder). I found this rather disturbing. (I later found out that in Florida the only allowable sentences for felony murder are the death penalty or life in prison without parole. I would have been even more disturbed if I'd known that at the time.)

All this started the "what-if" process that generates story ideas. What if someone awaiting trial for felony murder managed to get in touch with Judith, begging her to look into the case because they were innocent? And of course, with the corruption that had been ferreted out in her department in the earlier books, she'd have even more motivation to reopen the case.

One of the reasons I find the felony murder charge a disturbing one is expressed by Judith at one point. I can see how the law's intention is to be a deterrent, but such deterrents rarely work since criminals are not known for carefully weighing consequences.

Thus a drug addict and/or thief could potentially end up facing death or life in prison when a relatively minor crime somehow leads to someone's death. And someone who was just along for the ride could end up in this real-life defendant's situation, facing a felony murder charge for something someone else actually perpetrated.

And then, of course, there is the possibility that the person charged wasn't even there. A felon could say an enemy of theirs was present and offer to turn state's evidence against them, just to get a lighter sentence themselves. When that thought occurred to me, the story was off and running!

On a lighter note, the incident I have attributed to Kate's son, Billy—playing a song full of cuss words in the hallway at school—is similar to one that actually happened with my son when he was in middle school. And the essay explaining why that infringed on others' rights was part of his punishment, although I can't, at this point, recall whether I thought of it or my husband did.

Also, all the phenomena that Kate Huntington advises Judith about are real. Out-group homogeneity is the psychobabble term for the tendency to have trouble telling people apart when they are from a group other than your own. I struggled with this a lot when trying to learn the names of my much-younger students. All the fair-haired boys looked the same to me; all the dark-haired ones, likewise; and the same for the girls. Even at the end of the semester, I was still confusing a few of them in my mind.

Likewise, Kate's explanation for our "instincts" and "gut feelings" is valid. There is indeed an "alert" mechanism in the brain that signals when something seems off in the environment. It's also responsible for the nagging feeling that we've forgotten something. So when it comes to our instincts, we should "trust but verify." There is usually something going on there, although it might be trivial.

It is also valid that one will not remember the last few seconds, maybe even the last few minutes, before one suffers a concussion. There has not been enough time for the information to be processed into long-term memory before the brain is disrupted by the injury.

But the human brain is programmed to "fill in the gaps," so sometimes it will produce a "memory" of those last moments that is probably not all that accurate.

Indeed, human memory is quite fickle. I'll be exploring this theme some more in the next installment in the series, *Malignant Memory*.

In this story, a young woman shows up at the Starling Police Department with one of Judith's business cards in her hand, but with no conscious memory of her own identity or her past. This kind of total amnesia is very rare, but it can happen.

Stay tuned to see how Judith, with Kate Huntington's help, figures out who the woman is and determines whether or not she may have murdered someone.

Oh, did I mention...she has blood on her dress.

ABOUT THE AUTHOR

Kassandra Lamb has never been able to decide which she loves more, psychology or writing. In college, she realized that writers need a day job in order to eat, so she studied psychology. After a career as a psychotherapist and college professor, she is now retired and can pursue her passion for writing.

She spends most of her time in an alternate universe with her characters. The portal to that universe, aka her computer, is located in Florida, where her husband and dog catch occasional glimpses of her.

Kass has completed the ten-book, traditional mystery series, The Kate Huntington Mysteries (set in her native Maryland, about a psychotherapist/amateur sleuth), plus four Kate on Vacation novellas (with the same main characters). She is also the author of the thirteen-book Marcia Banks and Buddy cozy mystery series, about a service dog trainer and her sidekick and mentor dog, Buddy, set in north central Florida.

And she has started a new series of police procedurals, with Lieutenant Judith Anderson from the Kate Huntington series as the main character in the C.o.P. on the Scene Mysteries (four books out with more to come). Judith moves to northern Florida to become the Chief of Police of a small city, and just eight days on the job, she finds herself one step behind a serial killer.

To read and see more about Kassandra and her books, please go to https://kassandralamb.com. Be sure to sign up for the newsletter there to get a heads up about new releases, plus special offers and bonuses for subscribers (and free stories).

Kass's e-mail is kass@kassandralamb.com and she loves hearing from readers! She's also on Facebook (https://www.facebook.com/kassan dralambauthor) and Goodreads (https://www.goodreads.com/autho

r/show/5624939.Kassandra_Lamb) and she blogs about psychological topics and other random things at https://misteriopress.com.

Kassandra also writes romantic suspense under the pen name of Jessica Dale.

~~

Please check out these other great *misterio press* series:

Karma's A Bitch: Pet Psychic Mysteries
by Shannon Esposito

Multiple Motives: Kate Huntington Mysteries
by Kassandra Lamb

The Metaphysical Detective: Riga Hayworth Paranormal Mysteries
by Kirsten Weiss

Dangerous and Unseemly: Concordia Wells Historical Mysteries
by K.B. Owen

Murder, Honey: Carol Sabala Mysteries
by Vinnie Hansen

Payback: Unintended Consequences Romantic Suspense
by Jessica Dale

Full Mortality: Nikki Latrelle Mysteries
by Sasscer Hill

Buried in the Dark: Frankie O'Farrell Mysteries
by Shannon Esposito

Her Little Secret: Detective Mila Harlow Mysteries
by Shannon Esposito

To Kill A Labrador: Marcia Banks and Buddy Cozy Mysteries
by Kassandra Lamb

Lethal Assumptions: C.o.P. on the Scene Mysteries
by Kassandra Lamb

Never Sleep: Chronicles of a Lady Detective Historical Mysteries
by K.B. Owen

Bound: Witches of Doyle Cozy Mysteries
by Kirsten Weiss

At Wits' End Doyle Cozy Mysteries
by Kirsten Weiss

Steeped In Murder: Tea and Tarot Mysteries
by Kirsten Weiss

The Perfectly Proper Paranormal Museum Mysteries

by Kirsten Weiss
Big Shot: The Big Murder Mysteries
by Kirsten Weiss
Steam and Sensibility: Sensibility Grey Steampunk Mysteries
by Kirsten Weiss
ChainLinked: Moccasin Cove Mysteries
by Liz Boeger
Maui Widow Waltz: Islands of Aloha Mysteries
by JoAnn Bassett
Plus even more great mysteries/thrillers in the *misterio press* bookstore (https://misteriopress.com/bookstore/)

www.ingramcontent.com/pod-product-compliance
Lightning Source LLC
Chambersburg PA
CBHW050401260626
47156CB00003B/821